For Fallon

(Chicago Syndicate, #1)

For Fallon

Copyright © 2014 by Soraya Naomi

Published by Soraya Naomi

First edition published by Soraya Naomi.

Book 1 of Chicago Syndicate series.

Top Cover Photo credit: Sandy Manase.
Bottom Cover Photo credit: David Niblack.

For more information about the novel and author:
WEBSITE – www.sorayanaomi.com
FACEBOOK – www.facebook.com/sorayanaomi.author
TWITTER – www.twitter.com/Soraya_Naomi
GOOGLE+ - www.plus.google.com/u/0/+SorayaNaomi/about

Dear Sue,

Always love fiercely.

Soraya Naomi

Table of Contents

Acknowledgements

"Moral wounds have this peculiarity - they may be hidden, but they never close; always painful, always ready to bleed when touched, they remain fresh and open in the heart." ~ Alexandre Dumas, The Count of Monte Cristo.

Prologue

Love. It heals people as much as it can break people. In all its intensity and power, it's one thing we all have in common. It can make you exquisitely happy or tremendously sad. However, without the sad, would we still feel the intensity of the happy?

Everyone fantasizes about it, everyone dreams about it, everyone wants to feel it, everyone cries about it.

Some want to control it, some distrust it, some fear it, some lie for it, but everyone secretly still craves it.

How can such a simple word have so much supremacy over the human mind and heart?

Falling in love causes emotional ecstasy. Falling out of love has the power to provoke unimaginable sorrow and despair.

Love makes our face smile, our eyes light up, our heart glow, and our body fiery.

Love makes our face frown, our eyes cry, our heart blacken, our body ache.

Is there any other word which elicits so many contradictive emotions?

Love is hard work. It requires communication and trust.

Love is one big imperfection. Perfect love does not exist.

Without trust, what is love? Without trust, love is painfully insecure, and it will not endure the obstacles life throws at you.

Love must not suffocate but breathe on its own.

But none of this matters when love is based on a lie. Based on a lie, love will never have a chance to survive. Based on a lie, love dies before it can ever blossom.

CHAPTER 1

Fallon

"I'm staring right back," I comment defiantly while keeping my eyes focused on the tall man across the room. The club lights are flashing around me - purple and soft red - as the loud music engulfs the room in a deep bass. I tap my fingers on my lips and seductively trace the line of my lower lip with the pad of my thumb, not moving my gaze from mystery man.

Teagan looks at me, shaking her head, and hands me a compact from her purse, as she chokes on her laugh.

"What?" I ask, amused and annoyed.

"Fallon, woman, check your mouth."

Snatching the compact out of her hand, I hold it up to my face. *Shit.* I forgot about the red lipstick I'm wearing, which is currently smeared all over my mouth, giving me a crazed clown look. I can't contain my laugh at my own ridiculous attempt at seduction and yank Teagan toward the bathroom in the back of the club. Thankful that there's no line for the ladies room, I duck inside with Teagan on my trail.

She's clutching her stomach in glee. "You're incredibly cute."

8

"Thanks a lot. Because I was going for *cute*," I mutter sarcastically, turning my attention to the floor-length mirror. After removing the remnants of my 'candy apple red' lipstick and adding just some nude lip gloss to my dry lips, I finger the knots out of my long mahogany hair that flows down my lower back and tuck my side-swept bangs behind my ear. I take my black eye pencil out of my purse to line my amber-colored eyes.

It's safer for me to have the focus on my eyes instead of my lips.

My mind wanders back to mystery man. "No! Did he see that, you think? He must've seen my clown lips." I mentally face palm myself while adjusting my bra strap under my champagne short-sleeve cocktail dress.

Teagan, still laughing, tries to calm herself, to no avail.

"Get a grip, will you?" I throw her a mocking stern look and toss my eye pencil back in my purse. "I'm glad my nonexistent seduction skills crack you up. Seriously, did he notice?"

Coming closer behind me, Teagan sprays some perfume behind her ear. "It's dark in the club. I don't think so. Let's go back out and see if he's still there, okay?" She's relentless; still chuckling. "Fallon Michaels, don't be a baby. Come on, don't be shy. It was funny, nothing more." She nudges my shoulder encouragingly and takes my hand in hers. "Let's finish this the correct way."

Not wanting to be petulant, I plaster on my smile and head back out first. While going directly to the purple illuminated bar,

I suggest, "Let's get some drinks because I'm in desperate need to get drunk." But when I turn my head, Teagan's not following behind me. I swiftly scan the room in search of her, but she's lost in the masses of people. Still feeling a bit stupid, I continue on to the bar and order two vodka shots. My phone is in my hand to find out where she's disappeared to. It's midnight - we haven't even been in this bar for an hour, and I've already lost my friend.

Suddenly, I feel a warm hand on my ass. Shocked and angry, I spin around to stare into Teagan's bright grey eyes. Relieved that it's her, I motion to our shots.

She throws her hands in the air, wiggling her fingers in excitement. "Are we getting drunk? I love drunk Fallon!"

In my twenty-five years, I've never known anyone else who can handle liquor better than Teagan. Teagan's the friend who makes me loosen up. The friend who's so brash, fun, and constantly adventurous that she can't help but to rub off on you. I tend to be timid at first, but when I've gotten to know people, I can loosen up quickly – thanks to Teagan. Even though in Teagan's mind I'm still too demure, we've always remained close. She's the kind of woman who makes you want to enjoy the present. Her daily outgoing behavior is very contagious, and she's one of the few people I'm this close and carefree with. I was raised to be somewhat formal, but my friendship with Teagan has opened me up to enjoy everything life has to offer.

Handing her the shot, I toast. "Yes, my friend, start loving me more." And I swallow the alcohol down in one gulp, causing me to grimace. "More shots?"

"More shots?" she yells sarcastically. "Is that a question? *Hell, yes!* Always, and I do mean *always*, more shots."

My friend's already well on her way to Drunkville. Teagan catches my hips with both hands and dances behind me while I order more shots. I take two more shots, and Teagan downs three as she continues dancing provocatively behind me and eyes the room for - I'm sure - a hook-up.

I glimpse around hoping to spot mystery man. Unfortunately, there's no one staring at me anymore. It's the first time I've come to this establishment - the stylish purple décor with brown seating areas gives it a luxurious and cozy feel. Glancing up to the second floor, I observe that we can sing karaoke here.

No, thank you.

I'm appreciating the bar when I spot Nick walking toward Teagan and me. He and I kissed once when I was drunk at one of our office parties. Nick works in the same building as me, different company. It was *not* a memorable kiss, so I tentatively smile at him when he joins us. He's a nice guy, and we used to joke around a lot, but after the kiss our relationship changed, and I've been avoiding him like the plague ever since.

Teagan frantically looks back and forth between the two of us. I know she recognizes him and that unsettles me. I've told her about Nick.

"Nick, this is my friend, Teagan." I know full well I'll regret this little introduction. Normally, Teagan tends to have no mouth filter; drunk Teagan blurts out everything that's on her mind.

Teagan and Nick shake hands, and Teagan makes the monumental mistake of uttering, "Hi, so *you're* the infamous Nick. I've heard a lot about you." No mouth filter. And she has the audacity to wink at me.

"Nice to meet you, Teagan. Well, well. I didn't know I was *infamous*," Nick retorts arrogantly to me, arching his eyebrow and flashing me his white teeth.

Why, oh why would she say that? This is even worse than what I anticipated for her to blurt out. I need to have a chat with this woman about girl code. I *may* have mentioned Nick a few times. This was prior to the kiss, but Teagan knows very well that I've regretted that kiss.

Teagan starts to saunter away, beaming at me, leaving me alone with Nick, and Nick takes Teagan's comment as his cue to make his move. Wanting to get out of this situation immediately, I turn around and hurriedly move away, only to directly collide into another guy. And I do mean collide into - face *and* hand. My face is pressed against a well-toned chest and my left hand is lodged between us, inadvertently touching his balls.

For the love of god!

I've reached the highest level of mortification because I'm definitely copping a feel here. This guy - dressed in an impeccable suit - is either well-endowed or maximally packing.

A fresh, intoxicating citrus scent washes over me and neither of us moves. He's still as a statue except for the brushing of his chest against mine, which I'm too aware of. I have to look up since he towers over me, and I feel his minty breath sweep over my face. Eyes in a deep shade of green rimmed with the blackest eyelashes stare back at me.

People walking past us force us closer, bringing us face to face. This guy is tall, but my nude stilettos have given me some extra height. His light stubble caresses my soft cheek, and we both take a deep breath from the contact. My hand comes around to rest on his taut bicep as his face tilts downward so that he can continue to gaze into my amber irises. A crooked grin tugs at the corner of his lips, but it doesn't reach his eyes. Strands of his wavy, dark auburn hair fall attractively over his forehead. His controlled gaze is questioning, yet surprised. I can still hear the music pumping, but no voices are audible.

His hand shoots out to steady me by my hip. His warm grip heats my body slowly from the point of contact. A hint of recognition, or possibly amazement, flickers across his face. He doesn't push me away nor do I push him away.

Seems like he's waiting for me to speak, but I'm distracted from his touch. In my inebriated state, I belatedly realize that *he* is mystery man and my big round eyes expand more. His clean citrus scent in a club full of people has me absorbed.

Then, just as suddenly as we met, he releases me like I burned him and leaves with a few determined strides.

My head is spinning from all the shots Teagan and I consumed. I look around for my friend as I head back toward the bar to come eye to eye with Nick again. He whispers something incoherently in my ear, and I'm immediately irritated because Nick's smell of liquor and a nauseating cologne is overriding the lingering appealing citrus scent.

When he grabs my waist, I instantly push his hands away. "Yes," I say, distracted, while continuing to search for Teagan. I see her floating on the dance floor and turn back to Nick to say goodbye. He looks amazed by my answer. I need to stop saying 'yes' and 'no' out of habit to people to avoid prolonging conversations and start asking, 'What did you say?' like a normal person.

"Okay!" Nick screams in my ear now.

Confused, I probe, "What, okay?"

He grins broadly. "You can't back out now. You've already agreed to a date."

Why can't this guy read body language? I'm definitely not acting interested, am I? He has me questioning myself now. One too many shots *might* have diminished my assertiveness.

The second Teagan notices me, I wave her back over. She obediently heads my way - probably knowing she has some making up to do after leaving me hanging with Nick - and jumps into my arms.

"I accidentally agreed to a date. You better help me get out of it, or you're going on that date with me," I whisper in her ear quickly with my arms around her neck.

"I…I'll handle it," she slurs but covers her mouth with her hand as her eyes become huge. She holds up her forefinger, signaling for me to wait a second.

Is she going to be sick? "Do we need to go to the bathroom?"

Teagan swallows dramatically.

"That's disgusting, Teagan."

"No, I wasn't sick. I just wanted to mess with you." She throws her arm around me. "I have to use the bathroom now."

As she goes, I grab her upper arm to stop her. "You were going to help me?" I twitch my head toward Nick.

Teagan chews her bottom lip. "Yeah… I got nothing now. When I come back, I'll have a devious plan to get rid of Dicky." She laughs ridiculously hard at her own joke.

I glance back at Nick over my shoulder, checking to see if he overheard. Since he's still flashing me his teeth, odds are he's oblivious. Teagan leaves for the bathroom, and I'm still stuck with Nick. We stand awkwardly together at the bar. Nick constantly touches my arm and hip as he talks to me, and I gently ease his hands off of me every time. When I peer over Nick's shoulder, I'm met with a set of familiar alluring green eyes at the end of the bar. He's transfixed on my every move with Nick, observing it all.

His gaze is piercing through me. He tilts his head and arches one brow in silent question, *Need any help?*

I almost imperceptibly nod my head.

Mystery man speaks to his company, who's leaning with his back against the bar. The other guy whips his head around to look at me and is obviously not agreeing with mystery man's intention to intervene. He disregards his friend's comment and comes over to Nick and me. He walks right up to us to place a secure arm around my waist, tucking me gently into his side and turning slightly so that I'm immersed in his one-arm embrace. His breath strokes over my temple while he speaks. "I'm taking her for a dance." His deep and throaty voice, which exudes sensuality, fits him perfectly. The guy glowers at Nick, daring Nick to defy him. His intimidating stance has Nick backing off instantly, and he leads us both away with his arm firmly holding my middle.

I don't even look back. My eyes are glued to this man, and my mouth quirks up in a smile as he shows me an enthralling sidelong grin.

Just as I'm about to ask his name, he halts. "You're welcome," he whispers the words against my ear. And again, he strolls away.

Everything in my world is currently happening in slow-motion because of the alcohol partying in my system. He strides away again, and I didn't even get his name. He cleverly brought me to Teagan, who's exiting the bathroom and drags me back to the bar. No Nick in sight, luckily.

"I say we need one more shot." Teagan is practically hanging over the bar counter. "Two more vodka shots, bartender." She holds up two fingers, and the guy immediately prepares the shots for her.

"I hope we remember this night tomorrow." I clink my glass with hers, and we toss them back simultaneously. The liquid caresses my insides, making me lose the last of my inhibitions.

Teagan rushes me to the dance floor to show off her moves. After that one dance we both feel nauseous. I look over to my friend, and my nose wrinkles in distaste. "I don't think that last shot was our best idea."

She nods her head slowly in agreement, and we cling to each other as we're trudging to the exit.

"Teagan, we have to get our coats." I blink profusely to regain some normal eyesight.

Teagan just nods because she's too tired and drunk to speak in her state, so I seat her on a stool near the line to retrieve our coats. Her eyes close, and I don't want to leave her. I turn, still holding her up in her seat to prevent her from falling asleep, and I'm taken aback when mystery man stands before me. I strain to focus my vision.

"Can I help you ladies?" He seems genuinely concerned, looking past me to Teagan. He eyes me and the corner of his lip tilts up slightly.

Teagan - suddenly awake - stares at him and slurs rather disgracefully, "Shit, you're hot!" And…she's out again; face falling forward.

I shoot the guy an apologetic look, but he seems amused and repeats, "Help?"

"Uhm…yes, please. Could you retrieve our coats while I stay with my friend?" I request hesitantly.

"Of course." The rich timbre of his voice mesmerizes me.

I hand him my token for our coats. His hand brushing against my hot skin causes an odd, powerful tingling to surge through me.

"I'll be back in a minute." And off he goes.

This is going to take forever - the waiting line is long. But to my surprise, he is actually back within a minute with both our coats.

"Wow, you're fast."

He smirks and holds my coat out for me to put on. Every time he touches the bare skin on my arms or neck, I feel a surge of excitement. We then help Teagan - who's half asleep - into hers.

"I'll help you into a cab," he pronounces, giving me no room to argue, while he helps Teagan up and walks her outside. I follow.

He puts Teagan into the back seat of a random cab and holds the door open for me, motioning for me to get inside.

"Thanks for your help…" I prompt him for his name.

18

"Luca."

"Thank you for your help, Luca."

"You're welcome...?" His warm hand covers mine. I feel comfortable with him. "Fallon."

"Fallon," he echoes and encloses my cold hand within his two warm hands, rubbing it gently. "Where do you need to go, Fallon?"

"I can take it from here," I answer, not wanting to give a stranger my address.

He smiles proudly and nods. I slip into the seat next to a snoring Teagan and close the door while Luca hands the driver a fifty saying, "Take the ladies home safely and wait until they're inside their house to leave."

He gives too much money for the short ten-minute drive from the bar to our condo on West Jackson Boulevard. While I find it endearing that he didn't press for my address and makes sure he gives enough money to the cab driver, I start to object. "No, Luca, that's too much—"

"Fallon." He opens my door again and faces me. "Don't worry. I only want to make sure you get home safely." His attention is focused on my lips. Dark strands of hair fall in his eyes in a slow motion when he bends down to me.

I want to glide my fingers through his thick hair. His sculpted lips and deep green eyes with tiny flecks of gold make me gravitate toward him.

The world around me dwindles away as my mind focuses only on him. I hear nothing but our intensified breathing. I see nothing but his admiring eyes wandering over my face. I smell nothing but his enticing cologne. Lowering my eyes, I clutch my purse on my lap to stop me from pushing my hands into the small V of his dress shirt.

With his hot breath on my ear, Luca whispers, "While I immensely enjoyed your seduction skills, I prefer my women more natural. Your luscious lips don't need fiery red lipstick, Fallon."

My eyes snap up to him and a delightful smile lights up my face.

Luca has already stepped back. Closing the door, he throws me a wink.

CHAPTER 2

Luca

I head back to the club entrance and text Adriano to come out while I round the corner and adjust my handgun from the front to the back of my pants. That was a close call when she crashed straight into me. For the first time in years, I was thrown off guard. Unable to move, I kept her still in front of me so that she wouldn't discover or reveal my handgun. When I caught her sparkling eyes and lush mouth, the ability to look away failed me. Accompanied with smooth legs in a dress that still hid her curves from me, my curiosity prevailed and I let myself feel the flare of her hip.

Fallon.

Her picture doesn't do her justice. In the flesh, she's quite the vixen, yet not. Observing her every move since we spotted her in the club, I saw a calmness in her attitude, an air of innocent mischief in the graceful way she poses herself. A woman intriguing enough to simply watch dance with her loud friend.

I instructed Matteo - one of the cabbies on our payroll - to inform me when he dropped them off. She doesn't give her address to strangers. She's careful in her interactions, which could pose a problem for me. I need to gain her trust.

Adriano comes barging out of the club, and I lift my hand to signal him over.

"What the fuck was that?" he practically yells.

"Tone it down."

He steps closer to me. "What the hell was that for?"

I shrug him off. "I made contact, didn't I?"

Adriano perks a brow. "That was *my* job. Guess she wasn't interested in my ugly face."

"I put her in one of our cabs. She'll take some work, though. But she *has* made this night a lot more fun."

His expression contorts in comical disapproval. "Be careful with that one. You guys were eye fucking the shit out of each other."

"I would like to do more than eye fuck her," I say with a deep groan.

"Do someone tonight at the house. We have enough hot brunettes available for you."

"Not tonight. We have more work. Come on."

Adriano and I move to our second assignment of the night.

"She didn't want to give me her address, so I have to tread carefully. I'm going to the coffee shop where she hangs out tomorrow. I need some intel, quick." The intel isn't a pressing matter, but I'm looking forward to eye fucking Ms. Michaels some more.

A few streets further down from the club, we see our target leaving a café after we've staked out for half an hour. The idiot walks right into the dimly lit alley to snort some coke.

As I approach him, I pull my gun out. "Mr. Brandon."

Adriano stays put at the front of the alley to cover me.

A startled Brandon spins around to me with wide eyes when he hears my voice, white powder smeared all over his nose. "DeMiliano," he spits. The drugs have given him some attitude.

When I slowly crowd him, he starts retreating until his back smashes against the wall. "It's Mr. DeMiliano to you." I hold my gun up between us, uninterestedly eyeing my piece. "I thought we told you - two days ago - to bring in the payment from your boss to us? James and I have been waiting patiently for you."

"I – I didn't know of a payment," he stutters.

"Really? And that is," I ask while pointing my gun to the coke that's fallen on the pavement, "not *our* money you're generously snorting up?"

This guy is pathetic, trembling and sweating too much - giving away all his answers with simply his body language. "Let's call Giacomo Leggia together then? Maybe your boss can explain what happened?"

"No," he implores. "I'll get you the money."

I shake my head and tap the barrel of my gun twice against his temple. "It's too late now. You should've used your head before keeping my money."

"I can have it for you by tomorrow."

How stupid does he think I am? I'm going to let Leggia finish his idiot soldier, so I indulge Brandon. "I'm in a good mood today. You have until tomorrow."

I tuck my gun back into my pants and meet Adriano at the front. "Did you call Leggia and tell him that Brandon is here?"

"Yes, he's on his way. His *Capo* will be here within minutes." Adriano lights a cigarette as we stand watch until Leggia's *Capo* arrives.

The lights of a car round the corner, heading toward us. I nod at the *Capo* as he steps out of his vehicle, and Adriano and I leave.

CHAPTER 3

Fallon

The next morning I wake up feeling unexpectedly well. My bedroom door opens, and Teagan puts a cup of tea on my nightstand.

"Morning," she says cheerily. Her dirty blonde hair looks wildly disheveled, like it's been electrocuted.

"Morning. I see *someone* has not been affected by the amount of alcohol she consumed last night, except for your hair," I tease.

A fond smile crosses her face. I bet she doesn't remember how we got home, and she wants to know what happened last night.

"I'm feeling surprisingly good considering I have no memory of how I ended up in my bed. Since it's only ten, I'm thinking it wasn't a late night for us…" She looks at me expectantly to fill in the blanks.

Sitting up, I sip my tea. "Those last shots killed you. We were home at three. *You* were snoring in the cab."

"That sounds like me." She shrugs. "Want to go out for breakfast?" she asks, trying to untangle her hair.

"Sure. Let's leave in an hour."

"Excellent. And I must warn you, I do remember a guy putting my coat on me. I will be drilling you on who that was." Teagan laughs as she struts into the bathroom.

I shower after Teagan's done with her morning routine and barely have any time to put on light make-up and blow dry my long hair. I rapidly brush on some black mascara, accentuating my already long eyelashes, because I never leave home without mascara and earrings. Opening one of my four jewelry cases filled with earrings, I peruse and decide on my golden triangle-cutout drop earrings for today.

"Fallon, come on. I'm going to die. I'm hungry!" Teagan yells from the kitchen.

"Yes, yes, I'm done." As I run into the living room while fastening the second earring on, she's already at the door putting on her coat. I grab my purse and jacket before we start toward the coffee and pastry shop around the corner of our street.

Sitting at our usual spot at the window, I scan the menu. "I'm going to eat those appetizing English muffins with butter and strawberry jam. It's the weekend, so I can have carbs." I long for a sweet and filling breakfast. During the week, I deny myself carbs because I have such a sweet tooth. I need to control my eating habits somewhat.

"Excellent choice! I'm getting them too," Teagan agrees.

We order the muffins with tea. As both of us are silently enjoying our breakfast, a feeling of serenity settles in my soul. I feel at home here in The Loop, downtown Chicago. While I had a wonderful time growing up in Lake Forest, I always wanted to live in The Loop.

When we came to study at the School of the Art Institute of Chicago, Teagan and I first lived in one of The Institute's residence halls. I finished my master's degree program in Studio and Writing and Teagan her photography degree last year, and we moved to our apartment. She found her dream job as a photographer at a studio close-by our apartment. Teagan realized she wanted to be a photographer when we were in middle school. I, on the other hand, wanted to study something different monthly. I've always been somewhat of a restless soul and didn't know what I wanted to become while growing up. Every week I had a new hobby or interest that couldn't hold my attention. When I saw Swan Lake, I wanted to be a ballerina; I attended one ballet class. Because my father is a brilliant lawyer, and I saw him in court giving his closing argument - passionately defending his client, I was going to law school; never took one law class. When I started guitar lessons at the age of fifteen, I decided I was going to be a musician; that lasted five months until I gave it up. However, when Roald Dahl introduced me to the world of witches disguised as elegant ladies and the chocolate factory that's every kid's dream, books became an integral part of me. Reading is the one hobby that stuck with me. It not only stuck, it's become a full-grown obsession where I'll cancel appointments to stay home, cooped up with a book. My book obsession convinced me to find a path in life that involved the written word. This, thankfully, narrowed down my choices on my education. I attended the broadest writing program I could find - Studio and Writing - and that's how I ended up as a copywriter for Charity Events now.

"Fallon!" Teagan abruptly snaps me out of my reverie. "Where did you go?" she questions.

"Reminiscing." I smile at her. Housing in The Loop can be very expensive. Without Teagan, I couldn't afford the apartment.

"How's everything going for the yearly orphan event? Did you start? Aren't you already working on that project?" Teagan has a habit of firing questions at me.

"We're just in the beginning stages of that event –it's in August, we have almost five months to organize everything - and we're already selling the tables for impressive amounts, so I'm positive we'll raise a huge amount of money. So many sponsors have been attracted to it that we have a surprisingly high budget to work with. Well, in relation to the tight budgets I'm used to, anyway."

"I think your boss himself is one of the biggest sponsors of most of the projects," Teagan utters with a full mouth.

"I think Alex sponsors most of the projects too. I Googled him once. I always thought he was a rich kid, but he doesn't come from a wealthy family. I couldn't find any information on him. I want to know where his fortune comes from. "

Teagan shrugs and eats the rest of her muffin. "Not everybody is on Google," she mockingly declares.

Having no retort, I stick my tongue out.

"Good one. I think there's still some vodka in your system which negatively affects your argumentative side," she jokes softly with a faraway look in her eyes.

"Probably. It does make me feel better when we blame the vodka." Tasting my tea, I notice Teagan starting to slouch forward in her seat slightly.

A sad expression takes over her face. "Fall, I've received an offer to work abroad for a year."

What?

"The studio wants me to work in the European office for a year. One photographer with a long-term contract has left unexpectedly, and they don't want to train a newbie. The Europe office contacted the Chicago studio, and my boss offered me the position. It only came up last Wednesday, and I wanted a few days to consider before I told you. I think this is a once-in-a-lifetime opportunity. But because the photographer left so abruptly, they need a new photographer to start as soon as possible. The current project has been on hold for days, and the delay is costing the studio a fortune."

I'm shocked that she's leaving.

Wrinkles crease her forehead. "Please say something."

"I'm surprised…" I quickly add, "I'm happy for you, of course. I… I'm going to miss you. Where in Europe?"

"London. It's for a year, and then they'll review my contract. The studio arranges everything for me, including housing. You can visit me." Teagan reaches for my hand.

I look at our hands clasped together on the table and instantly my eyes water. "I'm honestly happy for you, but I'm going to miss you. We've done everything together for years. It's the end of an era."

Teagan laughs at my *Friends* reference.

"When do you leave?" Still in a minor state of shock, I stare at my muffin; appetite gone.

"I have to leave in two weeks. But Fallon, I'll take care of everything. You don't have to get another roommate."

I dismiss her comment. "I'm not worried about that. I'm going to be lonely without you at first," I confess my feelings without holding back.

"We'll Skype. I'll come back here. And you *have* to visit me in London. It's not like we won't see each other for a year."

I feel selfish talking about *my* feelings right now. "We should celebrate the exciting offer. I'm so proud of you. How do you feel?"

"I'm scared, but the good kind of scared. You're the first person I've told the news. It's beginning to dawn on me that it's really happening. I'm moving to London, baby!"

"You're moving up in the world. I need another tea; Lady Grey for you too?" I stand up and seat myself again just as rapidly.

Teagan looks confused and turns her head to see what or who caused me to sink back down.

I motion my hands up and down frantically. "No! Don't look yet," I whisper shout before she turns around.

Her brows draw together. "Okay... What's going on?"

"The guy who put your coat on you - the guy I was going to tell you about after the shock of you leaving wore off - is standing at the counter."

"So?" Clearly, she's still confused.

"Well, coat guy *is* mystery man *is* Luca who flirted with me when he put us in a cab home."

Her eyes widen in intrigue. "*Now* it's becoming interesting. Luca flirted with the clown?" she jokes, unceremoniously loud.

Luca - and everybody else in the coffee shop - turns when he hears the turmoil that is Teagan. A lazy grin is directed at me as he holds my eyes, and I dip my chin slightly in greeting before his attention drifts back to the counter.

"Okay, you can look now," I quickly mumble to Teagan.

Teagan's head spins around to check out Luca. "I can't see him very well. Let me get some sugar from the other table." She stands up and discreetly checks out Luca.

Returning to her seat, she announces excitedly, "You definitely had a wet dream about him." She leans in closer and continues conspiratorially. "He's your type; the dark hair and green eyes."

I can't deny that. I give her the down and dirty version of our flirting. "First, I bumped into him, accidentally copped a feel - *dear god,* he's well-endowed - then he helped me evade Nick and saw to us when we left. He paid the driver and told me that he liked his women natural. That I don't need fiery red lipstick." A huge smile lights my being because I think that was a good move.

Teagan claps her hands softly while beaming. "Seems like Luca has a way with the words," she chants. Abruptly, her face scrunches. "Where was I when this happened?"

"You were snoring next to me." I touch her nose affectionately when she frowns.

"How sexy of me. To make it up to you, I'm going to leave you two alone now." She throws a ten on the table and stands up to leave.

My hands shoot forward to grab her. "It's very coincidental that he's here *now.* I practically live in this shop, and this is the first time I've seen him."

Her brows pull together giving me a 'woman, please' look of disdain. "Don't overthink it; maybe you just never noticed him before? He'll come to you. I have to leave *now*, or it'll look suspicious. Make me proud."

"Okay, Sherlock. We'll talk more when I get home, right?"

"Of course. I'll see you in a few." Teagan's out the door immediately.

I continue sipping my tea, and, sure enough, Luca walks over to my table with a coffee in hand.

"Good morning, Fallon," Luca huskily greets.

"Morning, Luca. Isn't this a nice coincidence?" My eyes round and I tilt my head slightly, giving away my doubt of how non-coincidental this might be.

"It is." He ignores my silent distrust and points his forefinger to the chair Teagan's just vacated. "Can I sit?"

"Please do." I beckon to the chair.

Luca sets the coffee on the table, removes his coat to hang over the back of the chair, and takes his seat. He's immaculately dressed on a Sunday morning in his black dress pants and light blue button-up. And he also doesn't look like someone who went clubbing the night before. His wavy dark hair is neatly combed back and a light beard covers his skin. His unshaven look doesn't make him look scruffy, but rather dashing.

"I hope I didn't scare your friend away." He smirks, drinking his coffee while holding my gaze over the rim of his cup. He doesn't wait for me to answer before continuing. "Did you have a good night's sleep? You and your friend were intoxicated."

Quite intoxicated. "Yes, we were actually up early."

He's silent, as if he's waiting for me to continue.

I add, "We woke up and came here for breakfast."

Luca's demeanor slightly relaxes. This guy makes me feel comfortable and uncomfortable simultaneously.

"Did you have a good time at the bar after we left?" All I want to know is if he hooked up with someone.

A crooked smile follows. "I actually left right after you. I'm not a clubber. A friend of mine dragged me there." As he leans forward in a slow and controlled manner, his cologne reaches me, and I recognize the fresh citrus scent, just as divine as last night. "Although I *am* glad I went last night. I was lucky enough to see you five times in one night." He leans back and stretches his long legs. The wooden tables are small and round, so it's impossible to not touch the person sitting across from you. His legs entrap mine, making me heatedly aware of the point of contact.

I shift in my seat to let my legs brush against his, and while my entire body is slowly igniting, he doesn't flinch or recoil. "Five? I think we saw each other four times." I distinctly remember seeing him when I still had on my red lipstick, then bumping into him, then he got me away from Nick, and lastly, at the exit.

"No, no, Fallon." Luca traces his cup with his fingers and changes his posture, trapping me tighter in his legs. "I saw you at the entrance. I saw you with your red lipstick on the first floor; when you flirted with me." He doesn't even attempt to hide his grin. Every movement of his body is presented in such a controlled manner that has me hypnotized.

I try to hide my smile.

He's direct - please don't remind me of that moment.

"I saw you when you couldn't get away from a guy fast enough, and you accidentally copped a feel of me." He raises his eyebrows suggestively. Evidently, he's enjoying mentioning that little fact to me. "I had the pleasure of having you up-close and personal to get you away from that same guy. And I watched you swaying on the dance floor with your friend."

There goes my futile attempt to hide my smile. My phone that has been lying on the table interrupts us, and we both glance at my screen. I'm surprised when I see Danny's name appear. Danny was my first serious boyfriend. We dated when I was seventeen for two years, and we've barely had any contact since we broke up, so I let it ring and shift my attention back to Luca.

"I actually saw you six times," he remarks while brushing his legs ever so lightly against mine. "Let's not forget I put you into a cab."

Blood is rushing to my face from our simple touch. The intimacy isn't registering with him. Either that or he's highly smooth because I can't identify his expression.

I lean in closer just to have our lower bodies touch more and feel his warmth seeping through his clothes. "Lucky you," I tease and notice a guy standing in front of the window stealing glances at us. "Is that a friend of yours?" I indicate toward the guy. I'm not positive if it's the same friend that accompanied him at the club.

Narrowing his eyes slightly, he sighs. "Yes, he's waiting for me. I should go. It was a pleasure seeing you again, Fallon." He brushes a loose strand of hair behind my ear. Again, such an intimate gesture that doesn't make me feel uncomfortable. With his coat back on, he bends and places a feather light kiss on the inside of my hand.

I close my hand, sealing his kiss in my palm. His chivalrous behavior is setting the butterflies loose in my stomach. For the third time, I'm stunned by him.

His friend doesn't seem to be happy with him. Luca keeps his focus on me until they round the corner, and my eyes follow Luca until he's out of sight.

***

At home, I throw my keys and purse on the kitchen table and drop myself onto the couch next to Teagan.

She turns off the television and grabs a magazine from the coffee table. "Someone was shot, found dead, nearby the club we went to last night."

I distantly acknowledge her news as I remove my jacket.

Teagan opens her magazine, and without looking up, she sarcastically states, "And?"

"And what?"

"What did he say?"

"Not much. He had to leave right after you," I inform. We see each other, flirt, and then nothing.

She turns the pages in rapid speed. "That guy I would do. Just saying."

I ignore her comment. "I actually want to continue our conversation. How long until you leave?" Teagan follows me when I go into the kitchen to start the kettle.

She hands me two mugs and my favorite tea: Lady Grey. "I'm going to accept the offer tomorrow. My boss told me that if I do accept, they'll arrange all the documentation quickly and want me on a plane to London asap."

After pouring water and then the teabags into the cups, I stand opposite my friend, pinning her with a look of disbelief. "How long?" I emphasize.

"Within two weeks," she mutters, turning away from me to throw the teabags in the sink.

"Two weeks?" I shriek while I take the bags from the sink and throw them in the trashcan. "That's so soon! Although I'm not going to miss cleaning up after your butt. Just *throw* the bags in the trash when you're finished. It's not that difficult."

"Yes, Mom," Teagan replies, rolling her eyes. "Tomorrow I'll know more, okay? I'll fill you in about everything, I promise. Let's watch movies and order in tonight. I *might* be feeling a little hung over."

As we take our teas back to the couch, Teagan lies down, and I cover her with a blanket. "I was wondering how long it would take for you to admit it." I laugh and get my phone from my purse, and when I see the missed call from Danny, I update Teagan. "Guess who called me today... Danny."

Her body whisks around. "When? What did he want?"

"I don't know. I didn't answer; I was with Luca." I'm hesitant to return his call because I have nothing to say to him. We didn't have a bad break-up, I just rarely think of him. "If it's something important, I'm sure he'll call again. I'm not interested in calling him back."

"Good," she agrees. "That guy was so boring. Most boring first boyfriend award goes to Danny."

"He was not boring," I defend while sliding onto the couch. "Just not memorable." My phone chimes in, and I see my mom's name and number flashing across the screen. "Hi, mom."

Teagan chuckles. "It's the same, you weirdo."

I mouth, "Shut it."

My mom's always happy to hear my voice. "Hi, sweetheart. Your father and I are planning a vacation, but I didn't know when you would come visit us."

"Where are you going?"

"Your father found a six-week round trip from Australia to North Asia. It's a cruise from Sydney to Japan and China."

My parents travel at least twice a year, so I'm not surprised that they're already searching for new trips after just returning from Mexico. "That sounds wonderful. I haven't made any plans to visit. You guys can book the trip. I'll come before or after your vacation."

My father is mumbling in the background. "Okay, sweetie. I'll call you later. We're going to check when the best time to visit Australia is."

"Bye, mom."

Teagan and I enjoy the rest of our lazy Sunday by hanging out on the couch and watching movies.

CHAPTER 4

Fallon

If it was up to Teagan's boss, she would've left within a week, but the legal documentation wasn't ready until a few days ago. Now I'm standing at O'Hare International Airport, reluctant to let my best friend go. I take her hand in mine. "You call me any time you want to talk, day or night. Any time you need positive reinforcements, you call me."

"I will, promise. I'll call you when I land." She pauses to look around. "I'm excited and scared at the same time."

"That's good. It'll keep you sharp the first few days. Don't ever doubt yourself. I've never been more proud of anyone as I am of you today. You're chasing your dreams. You're seizing opportunities, living the life."

"Stop it. You're going to make me cry." She peers around at the hundreds of people all going to different places in the world.

When I notice her teary eyes, I squeeze her hand reassuringly. "You have to stand in line. Get some American treats to eat on the plane."

She winks with a sad, yet hopeful smile. "I'm on it."

We hug it out one more time before Teagan collects her hand luggage and walks through customs. She turns and blows me a kiss. Amused, I catch her kiss and wave. She motions for me to turn and go away. I mock salute her. Then turn to go home. Alone.

I take a cab back to The Loop, and instead of going inside the apartment, I walk to the coffee shop around the corner to treat myself to a pastry. It's probably busy this Saturday afternoon; I hope they still have warm muffins.

To my surprise, the shop isn't crowded and my usual spot by the window's free. After ordering my usual – muffin and Lady Grey tea - at the counter, I happily pace to the table. Sometimes the simple things in life can bring me unimaginable joy. I want to delay going home to my empty apartment as long as possible, so I get my e-reader out of my purse because it's time for my romance novel. Nothing enlightens my life more than reading about fictional love in all its intensity, drama, and beauty.

The waitress comes over with my order, but I'm consumed by my novel already. Without blinking away from my reader, I reach for my tea, and I retreat quickly when I touch a hand and look up into green, powerful eyes that have been popping up in my thoughts for the past two weeks. In the same spot as last time, touching my teacup, is Luca. I palm my chest, "You scared me," I say, expelling my breath loudly.

He looks upset. "What has you so highly oblivious to your surroundings, Fallon?"

I was just kidding when I said he scared me. Well, he did scare me a little, so I should look upset, but I'm also pleased to see him again. I hold up my reader. "My book."

He tilts his head to read the title. "I saw. You've been engrossed by that book for ten minutes. I couldn't get your attention."

Just as I remember, he exudes this raw, intense charm. His hair is slightly in disarray, which only adds to his masculine good looks. He leans his muscular body closer to hand me my tea. I'm aware of his every move; the gentle touch of our hands evoke the tiny hairs along my arms to rise. "Let me greet you properly. Hi, Fallon. I've been hoping to run into you again, and I believe my luck has changed for the positive." He rubs his hand leisurely over his mouth, hiding his smile in a sensual motion. Crossing his long legs in front of him, he looks around and then holds up my phone in his left hand.

Shocked, my eyes roam the table, and I realize he took my phone before I even looked up to notice him. I was so immersed in my novel that I didn't even see it happen. My hands charge forward to grab my phone from him, but he's quicker and pulls back.

He raises his brows. "You need to be more perceptive of your surroundings, Fallon. If I had dishonorable intentions, I could've stolen your phone." He smiles gently and unlocks the screen to type - his number, I presume and hope - into my phone.

"I think you're the only person who has any interest in it." I lean forward to check what he's typing. "What are you doing?" Unless he's typing in his information, I want it back now.

His eyes shoot up to mine for a second, surprised, before he continues handling my phone. "You never know. Since I was stupid enough to forget to ask for your number, I'm now programming my number in here."

"Do add *all* your info. Facebook, Instagram, *birthday...*" I ramble and inquire his age without actually asking. I turn off my e-reader and store it in my purse.

"I don't have Facebook - I have an aversion to social media," he replies without looking up.

"How can you have an aversion to social media?"

"Never bothered to make accounts."

"Wow, there are still people without a social media account. Who would've thought?" I muse.

"I'm twenty-nine, Fallon." Looking back at me confidently, he announces, "I'm calling myself." And he holds my phone up again suggestively.

"By all means." I motion my hand toward him, but he isn't waiting for approval.

I thought he'd be twenty-seven or twenty-eight. Although when he came up to me, clearly displeased, he looked older. I was not met by his deep green eyes - they seemed even darker, giving him a perturbed edge.

Taking a bite of my muffin, a moan escapes me. This food is deliciously buttery. I look up and freeze when I notice that he's sitting eerily still.

Luca speaks quietly. "Please stop moaning."

"You have no idea how good this is." I take another tasty bite.

"I'm getting the idea." And finally his legs entrap mine just like the first time we met here. I've been secretly waiting for him to touch me.

"Here, take a bite and tell me that's not scrumptiously good," I dare him, holding out my muffin.

To my surprise he leans forward, grabs my wrist, and takes a bite. Keeping his long fingers secure around my wrist while he chews unhurriedly, his eyes hold mine. I was expecting him to take the muffin out of my hand before having a bite. Now it's his turn to moan.

I beam. "Good, right?" And wait expectantly for his answer.

"You do know good food," he concedes. This time the intimacy of our interaction *did* register to him. Slowly, he releases my wrist from his hold. He's quiet and looks outside for a moment, lost in his thoughts.

I finish the last bites of my muffin and drink my tea. The lack of conversation feels remarkably relaxed, and we're both obviously not searching to fill the silence with meaningless talk.

When I finish my tea, he asks, "Another tea?"

"No, thanks. I should go home."

"I do believe we have established to have an unconventional relationship," he mentions suddenly.

He uses the word relationship fleetingly and without flinching. This guy is constantly in control of his movements. It's

44

challenging to ascertain whether he's pleased or not about our 'relationship.'

"Unconventional?"

"Yes," he replies. "You went to third base the first time we met, before we ever had a date. We're doing things backward." Now he's obviously pleased, with that grin being directed at me.

"Is this a date?"

"Yes," he answers resolutely. Luca leans toward me. "But I will take you out on a proper date, Fallon."

I wait for him to continue, but the actual asking me out on a date doesn't follow. "I need to go home." Before I have time to open my wallet, Luca has already settled the check.

He holds out my coat for me to wear. "Are you here often, Fallon?"

"I am." Turning around to move my arms into my coat, I don't elaborate. Let him call me for a date. "Bye, Luca." I offer him my sweetest sidelong smile and leave.

He halts me with both hands on my shoulders, pulling me back to his honed chest, and I get a smirk in return. Bending his head, his lips graze the shell of my ear. "I'll see you soon, Fallon." And he slides his hands down my arms before releasing me.

A warm, agreeable shudder ripples through my frame. I take the two-minute walk home with a smile plastered on my face.

Faced with a lonely apartment, I sigh, looking around the house and missing Teagan's presence. I look at my phone to check the time. In a couple of hours, Teagan will be landing.

CHAPTER 5

Luca

I watch Fallon leave the coffee shop confidently. It's refreshing to be around a woman who doesn't throw herself at me. This woman is fucking sexy without even knowing. She's becoming impossible to resist, and the throbbing below is pushing me to have her.

Last time, Adriano ominously waiting in front of the coffee shop blew my game. I needed to talk to her alone, so I left. Adriano's unease is growing. He's sensing that my interest in her is more than professional. But my *Capo* is in Crystal Lake today, which gave me time to visit Fallon while he's not around.

I came in with one goal: get to her phone. Mission accomplished. I didn't even need to talk to her because she made it too easy for me to access it. As I stared at her reading her book, she was unaware of me, so I snatched the phone off of the table and looked for information on it. I found one thing of importance that confirmed my suspicion.

I could've discreetly put the phone back in its original place because Fallon was lost in that e-reader. Yet that's not what I did. I sat there for ten minutes, observing her. How she constantly brushes back her hair behind her ear. How she refuses to stop reading for even a second. How the side of her sexy mouth turns up just a little when she reads something comical. How her face flushes as she - I assume - reads something sensual.

One guy passed her and gawked at her beautiful downturned face while she was unmindful. He was walking up to Fallon when I cut him off and decided to make my presence known to her. I shot the guy a look to fuck off - he scurried away.

One of my phones vibrates in my pocket. "Yes."

"I need you here. They want to talk to the underboss or the boss. James won't come," Adriano informs me.

"What happened?" I head out the door.

"They want to renegotiate territory borders. Since we've been discussing cutting Crystal Lake, I thought it might be wise."

"It could be a good move. Too many loose cannons are in that territory. I'll discuss it with Salvatore." In accordance with our *Cosa Nostra* rules, our lawyer must be up to date on all business decisions.

"*Consigliere* has been informed by James. Salvatore will contact you."

"I'm going to make them wait a few days. I'll be there Tuesday. Set up the meet. I need to check to make sure we didn't overlook anything as to why they might want the territory, although I'm pretty sure I won't find anything newsworthy. Then we'll hand Crystal Lake over to Leggia." I end the call.

Stepping into my black Maserati Quattroporte that I've parked a block away, I plan how far I can take this with Fallon. Only James and Adriano know about me tracking her every move. As long as I haven't gained the information I need, I could see her without raising suspicion with James. Adriano is my *Capo* and my friend. I'm not worried about him because he's only looking out for me. But James, my *Capo crimine*, I answer to.

CHAPTER 6

Fallon

I call Teagan the next day.

"Hi, babe," she answers on the second ring and yawns loudly into the receiver.

"How was your first night?" I sit on the couch with a cup of tea in my other hand.

"Urgh, there were children screaming on the plane, so I couldn't sleep." Teagan is not a mommy-type. "I was freaking tired," she says, grunting. "I have a major jetlag. I'm lying in bed. It's almost noon here. How is it without me?"

I snort. "The apartment is too quiet without you."

"I *am* a loud bitch."

"True that," I acknowledge her statement. "But you will never guess who I ran into yesterday at the coffee shop?"

"A guy?"

"Yep."

"Luca? Right?"

"Yep."

"Why didn't you text me the minute you saw him? Never mind. Tell me," she demands.

"We talked, but I wasn't in the best mood because I was dreading coming to the condo. You have no idea how lonely it is without you."

"Aw, babe."

"I was reading at the coffee shop, and he took my phone and added his number. We talked... He's ...interesting." There's something pulling me to him. An attraction I can't seem to shake. An attraction I don't want to shake. "I flirted with him."

"You flirted?" she blurts.

"Don't act so surprised. I *can* flirt."

"I know that. And? He asked you out?"

"Uhm no." I hesitate. "He did mention he was going to take me out on a proper date, but he didn't specifically ask me out. He was ever the gentleman."

"I bet he's jerking off to the thought of you as we speak." She laughs loudly.

I hold the phone away from my ear and scrunch my nose. "Shut up! Go sleep some more. I'll talk to you later. Go rest."

"I bet you can't get that mental image out of your head now?"

I smile because she knows me too well. "Go back to bed, woman." I click end before she can respond.

***

Unfortunately, Luca didn't call all week.

The next weekend, I yearn for carbs. I enter the shop and slide into my regular spot. As I turn on my book and glance at the door, I see Luca strolling in.

He closes the distance between us surprisingly fast. "Hi, Fallon."

Has he suddenly become a regular here? "Hi. You came back for the delicious muffins?" I tease.

Luca resumes his usual seat and squeezes my knee gently and caresses my thigh, the heat of his hand leaving a trail of desire, but the waitress interrupts us.

Luca sits back in his seat without breaking eye contact with me. "Fallon. Lady Grey?"

I nod and *do* take a look at the waitress who's doing her best to get Luca's attention. Even with our intimate pose, she still tries to flirt with him. I inspect him to see how he'll handle this.

He glances at her. "Lady Grey and an espresso, please." His attention is instantly focused back on me.

He's been in this situation before. He knows to give his undivided focus to his present company.

His eyes rove over my face. "I've been thinking of you all week. It wasn't easy to refrain from calling you. So Fallon, who likes good food and books, I want to know more about you," he states in demanding, yet gentle, tone.

The waitress leaves, but not before sending me an indignant look, and I inwardly laugh at her. "I'm actually from around here. Born and raised in Chicago, at Lake Forest. I moved to The Loop with my best friend, Teagan. I live near here."

"Would that be the lovely lady who was snoring in the cab when we met?" His lips curve in a restrained grin.

I laugh while taking in his customary handsome attire. "Yes, that would be her. Not her finest moment." Our drinks are delivered, and we both palm our cups while Luca's legs are contentedly hugging mine. "I came here with Teagan to study Studio and Writing at the School of the Art Institute of Chicago, and I never left. After graduation, I worked several jobs and am currently a copywriter at Charity Events."

"What does a copywriter at Charity Events do?"

"Charity Events hosts parties for different charities to raise money and attract sponsors. The company has relations with several wealthy benefactors, which allows us to host these events without any costs to the charities. They hire us. We have a small team of seven people who arrange everything surrounding an event. We have fixed contracts with caterers and several locations to keep the budget low. We organize costume balls, high teas, and club parties. The invites to the events are highly coveted and expensive; we usually make a profit solely on the sold invites. With the profit of each event, we pay the costs of organizing, and the rest goes to the charity. Our team is being paid by the owner, and ten percent of our income is also invested into every event." I catch his eyes thinning briefly. "I, as the copywriter, am responsible for all the written communication:

letters to our benefactors and charities, invites, publicity ads for the events. Have you heard of us?"

"I can tell that you enjoy your job."

"I do. I tend to get distracted quickly, but - for now - I'm content with this job. I'm elated to work for these charities, to raise money without charging them any money for our work."

"That does sound admirable," he murmurs as his phone rings. He takes it out of his pocket and puts it on silent.

"Luca, tell me about you."

He ponders for a while before starting. "I've also lived in Chicago my entire life. My father was Italian, my mother American. No siblings. You?"

I shake my head. "No siblings either. You speak Italian?"

"A little." His relaxed demeanor has slightly changed. "Grew up on the streets of The Loop. I'm a software developer; security software." He shifts in his seat when his phone vibrates continuously.

"Where do you live? Work?" I ask.

Luca gives me a curious stare, and I can't tell what he's thinking. "The Blackhall, by the Museum of Contemporary Art Store. I work for myself, with a partner."

"Is your partner your friend who was waiting for you last time we met here?"

"Yes," he counters firmly. "I assume it's Teagan who left the country for work?"

54

"Yes. She's a photographer. She's in London now. We've known each other since we started high school."

"How are you coping since she left?" He runs his hand through his hair that's falling over his forehead, giving him an appealingly disheveled look.

I show him my reader. "I have my books to keep me company. Do not ask me if I like reading," I warn, smiling warmly at him. My interest in reading goes far beyond 'liking' it. "Reading is my addiction. I usually have the e-book and paperback of the book I'm currently reading. From my favorite books, I try to purchase a copy of every paperback with a different cover. I get aggravated if I haven't read at all during the day. Romance novels are my first love. Teagan and my parents always good-naturedly complain that I'm continually lost in books."

His response makes my heart skip a beat. "When you compare the sorrows of real life to the pleasures of the imaginary one, you will never want to live again, only to dream forever."

This is the moment I know I could fall for this guy. Of all the books in the world he could've chosen to quote, Luca quotes one of my all-time favorite classics: Alexandre Dumas' *The Count of Monte Cristo*.

I stare at him in silence after he quotes Dumas, amazed that he chose to iterate that specific one.

Luca leans toward me. "I'm good, right?" Amusement twinkles all over his face.

I can't hold in my wide grin. "You were until you added *that*." Referring to his last arrogant sentence. "You did happen to relay a quote from one of my favorites."

"Dumas," we both breathe.

Drinking my Lady Grey, I sigh in contentment of my warm tea. "Tell me more about you? You talked about your parents in past tense?"

For a moment, he's lost in melancholy. "I lost my parents in a car accident when I was ten. Raised by my uncle - *mio zio* Joseph," he huskily says it in Italian. "*Mio zio* resides in Venice now, but he raised me."

I trace my fingertips over his hand as he tells me about his parents. I do it automatically and cease instantly when I notice my action. Peeking at my fingers and up at him, I see him smile at me reassuringly, so I carry on tracing. I don't comment, only listen and smile as my heart aches for a little boy that lost his parents.

"No other family?"

He pauses. "No." And he turns his hand quickly to catch mine. His thumb leisurely circles the inside of my hand while holding on to it. Luca's fingers work their way up my wrist, under my sleeve.

I hold in a moan as his simple touch causes my breathing to increase. "Are you close to your uncle?"

His eyes brighten with love. "Very. He was the one who helped me when my parents passed. If it wasn't for him, I would've been put in the foster care system. I miss him when he's so far away. His happiness - and he's much happier in Italy than he ever was here - is important to me. I visit him often."

"How often?"

"I try to visit him yearly." His hand absently caresses my wrist. Every touch sends me spiraling down the path of desire. We talk. We flirt. We touch. We laugh. We seduce.

He vocalizes his thoughts elegantly and accompanied with a passionate intensity.

It's getting darker outside. The sky has turned from clear blue into a dark reddish hue, announcing the evening. After I finish my tea, I say, "I think it's time for me to get home." I grab my coat from the back of my seat.

Already standing, Luca states, not asks, "I'll walk you home, Fallon." He walks up behind me to help me slide out of my seat.

Not in the least bothered by his lack of questioning tone, I reply, "I would like that."

Luca pays the bill at the counter, refusing to take any money from me, and we walk out together - serenely silent - to my apartment around the corner.

Standing before the entrance of my condo, I search for my keys in my purse. I'm forever searching for my keys, and I frustrate myself because I don't know why I can't leave them in the compartment designed for keys. Since he's patiently waiting beside me, I invite him in. "Would you like to come in for a drink, maybe?"

He considers my offer and moves closer, aligned to touch. Our body heat mingles. He can enclose my entire body with his. I look up through my lashes into his eyes which are darkening with lust. The deep green of his irises have been overtaken by his black pupils. His hooded gaze is fixated on my lips.

Luca's nose traces my jaw as he takes in a shaky breath. "You smell so sweet." His hands come around my waist, pulling me to him tightly. His lips graze over my mouth, back and forth ever so lightly, while one hand pulls my head back to expose my throat. His lips start a tingling path beneath my left ear, his tongue flicking over the sensitive skin where my neck meets my shoulder. And then he finally lifts me up to him and kisses me.

Our lips touch gently at first, but the moment our mouths open, we both lose control. Our tongues entwine feverishly. His kiss tastes full of promised desire. He pulls back a fraction, and I immediately close the distance between us. Luca smiles against my mouth, because I think he likes this push and pull game we're playing. The kiss is gentle, fiery, and sensuous. It sends tingles straight to my lower stomach. He kisses me on my lips, but I feel him all over my skin.

Our bodies melt together while our tongues passionately taste each other. The traffic around us fades away until there is only him and me. Luca pulls my lower lip between his teeth and lets go gradually. He traces my lips with his tongue.

Our kiss deepens when he palms my head. I feel myself drifting away in the high of his taste. My breath intensifies. I suck on his tongue and am rewarded with a deep growl from him. My face is hot from our seduction and mingled breaths. Our chests are rising and falling rapidly.

"I want to, but I have an appointment," he grumbles, disappointed.

The world invades our private embrace. He's still holding me, but I notice the traffic and people again as I try to step away to clear my focus. That kiss has left me spinning. We're silent as our breathing calms down. Not touching, only looking.

I don't speak and turn to open the door, glancing back at Luca whose eyes are still overtaken by the black of his pupils.

"I'll call you, Fallon. That's a promise." It comes out in an enticing threatening tone that makes me yearn for him. Luca's tracing the pad of his thumb on his lower lip while he waits for me to disappear into the building.

When I enter my apartment, I let myself fall onto the couch with my coat still on, tossing my keys and purse on the coffee table. I touch my lips with my fingertips and bite my lower lip, lost in thought. My grin widens as I feel my heated cheek with the back of my hand.

Heading to the kitchen, I open my fridge to see what I can make for dinner. I should eat a chicken salad tonight after devouring too many muffins these last weeks.

I decide all I need are my friends and my books. By friends, I mean my book friends. I power on my laptop on my desk in the living room and pull my hair up into a messy bun. First thing I do is sign in to Goodreads - my online book club - to check what all my book friends are currently reading. Usually, I love my user profile, but today it tells me I'm two books behind on my yearly book challenge. I wanted to read one hundred fifty books this year, and I'm already behind schedule in the spring. Not good. Seriously, that can give a girl stress. Need. To. Read. Faster. I close my laptop.

Taking my phone off the table and the paperback version of the e-book I'm reading from my bookshelf, I lie back on the couch. I unfold the blue fleece blanket that's hanging off the back of the couch and open my paperback to chapter nine and become quickly immersed in my novel again.

After I don't know how long, I receive an incoming message.

Fallon, I bet you're lost in a fictional couple? I want to take you to dinner tomorrow at 7?

His message makes my lips curve into a broad smile. I've never wanted someone the way I'm starting to desire him.

Busted! I'm preoccupied with a hot Russian soldier currently. It's a date.

CHAPTER 7

Luca

Why didn't my information file state she works for Alex? This woman is indirectly tied to the Syndicate on so many levels.

I shouldn't have kissed her. I couldn't *not* kiss her. Her soft little moans excited me even more. Earlier today, it took everything in me not to carry her across the threshold of her apartment. I keep telling myself that I only keep meeting her to obtain essential info. My gut is telling me she'll be of no help and I'm deluding myself. This is becoming much more than gathering information. Fallon's starting to consume my thoughts. She's seeping into my psyche. After I left, I instantly regretted not taking her up on her offer. I was fighting not calling her and caved in. I shouldn't have asked her out on a date, and I sure as hell amazed myself when I told her my actual address and about our company. The company Adriano and I built that is also used as a front to launder money.

Turning into the parking lot of the restaurant where I'm meeting Adriano, I cut off the engine and rake my hands through my hair. I've stopped listening to my rational side when it comes to her. As the underboss, I'm treading on dangerous ground if I become attached to Fallon.

Opening the door of the Italian restaurant, I see Adriano's already seated in the back booth. "Luca," he welcomes.

I nod my head. "Did you finish everything in Crystal Lake?" Adriano stayed behind to relay the rules of the territory to Leggia's men. They can pretend to regulate the drug traffic there. Additional investigation surrounding the Crystal Lake territory came up empty. Leggia wants it for no apparent reason; he can have it.

"Yes. It's all done. They weren't—"

The waitress, a tall redhead, hands us menus.

Adriano flirts with her and the shy little thing doesn't know how to react to him. "I'll be back to take your order, sir."

He continues after red is out of hearing distance. "They weren't receptive. Where Leggia finds his arrogant soldiers, I'll never know."

"I don't get why Leggia wanted it in the first place. Salvatore didn't find anything interesting we might've overlooked. They're now solely responsible for any drug activity on Crystal Lake ground, and that place is abhorrent to rule."

"Good riddance," Adriano agrees. "I'm getting the *Arrabbiata* pasta." He waves over the redhead. "And I'm thinking of getting her too. A fiery redhead will do me some good tonight."

"I'll have the same." I take another good look at red. "Good luck. She's seems pretty timid to me."

She hurries toward us. "Did you make a choice, sir?"

I indicate with a swift nod to Adriano to play his game with her. "Two *Arriabbiata*, with extra *Parmigiano*."

I hand her my menu. When she takes Adriano's, he holds on to it to get her attention. He winks at her and her cheeks redden before she turns away.

"If I can't have *her* tonight, I'm going to the house."

James uses a house alongside the North Shore of Chicago's suburbs as our center of operations. It's located in a secluded area without neighbors in sight, and the deed is in Alessa's maiden name. Alessa is James' wife, but they never legally married. We - the highest ranking members of the Chicago Calderone Syndicate - all know her as Alessa Calderone, but legally and officially, she isn't connected to James whatsoever.

"Haven't you been through all the women at the house?" I joke, although there could be some truth in that statement.

"Probably, but I want to fuck tonight." Adriano sits back and is cautious to ask me his next question. "What did you do today?"

I sigh, realizing he wants to know if I was with her. "Fallon."

He's not even surprised. "You talked to her again? Did you get any resourceful info for us? We need Danny," he reminds me.

Danny Mancuso is number one on our wanted list. Danny worked for James behind the scenes for years. Even the Mafia needs IT men. We need them to hack into every government system that could have important information for us and to make the people we finish off disappear from every system as if they never existed. Danny's one of the best hackers in town.

After five years, Salvatore found out that Danny also became avaricious. He was programming and leaving behind viruses so that we had to pay him more to eliminate those viruses before the hacked system detected that we had access to it.

Being a hacker for our crime syndicate is a covetous job. The reward is high but so is the risk. The hacker has inside information on what we do; therefore the hacker will never get out alive, he'll always be associated with us. You can only leave this job if you're dead.

For Danny, apparently the monetary compensation wasn't enough. He's a man looking for prestige, acknowledgement, wanting to move up in rank. A hacker is not considered a true member and can never be ranked in our Syndicate. Danny sensed the net closing in on him and disappeared abruptly. He's a liability we can't afford, and James wants him finished off. He was spotted in The Loop, and I found out that the only person of interest he has in that area is Fallon Michaels, his ex-girlfriend.

"I talked to her this afternoon. I checked her phone and phone records. She didn't return his call. They haven't had any contact in years. He's desperate if he calls an ex who he hasn't spoken to in a long time. So far, it seems like she's not helping him hide in any way." I pause, hesitant to tell him everything. "I'm going out with her tomorrow."

Now amazement is thrown my way. "On a date?"

"Yes," I coolly say. "I'm drawn to her. I can't explain it, Adriano. She's ruling my thoughts."

"Fuck, Luca. Be careful. Attachments are dangerous. Especially with her, *now*. I think you need to come to the house with me tonight."

I rub my palm over mouth. "Maybe I should."

Our food arrives and by this time, Adriano is bored with the timid waitress. "Red's no fun. Eat up." He points his fork to my pasta dish. "We're going to the house."

Driving separately to our destination, I park in the circular driveway. The mundane but fairly large three-story, white brick house is our main quarters. As usual, a prospect is guarding the front entrance. The front doors open into a foyer covered in grey marble tiles. We ascend the stairwell in the quiet house and move to the right, toward the largest room on the second floor, which - in essence - is just an in-house strip club. Adriano cracks his knuckles for emphasis before he places his hands on the doorknobs of the double doors.

Soft music is filling the burgundy-decked-out room. Two men, Adriano's soldiers, are slouching on the massive half-round couch in the middle of the room, each with a girl on his lap. Both stand abruptly as we enter. "*Padrino*," they greet simultaneously. Inferiors address their superiors as *Padrino* in our Syndicate.

We nod and allow them to carry on while the scantily clad women eye me.

65

"Have some fun, Luca. I'm going to enjoy Camilla," Adriano announces and wanders to the bar to our left where she's sitting on a stool.

Camilla is Adriano's favorite girl. She's an exotic Italian with long legs and unblemished olive skin that she doesn't cover in make-up. Adriano and I share a preference for natural looking women. She's clever and pensive. The only woman here I converse with on a friendly level. Most of these girls will do anything if we throw them enough money. Not Camilla, who's frankly reserved for our little strip club. She tends the small bar set up on the left side of the room. Adriano saw her the first night and forbade any of the soldiers to touch her. The *Capi* respect each other and wouldn't dare defy Adriano either. She's been here for over a year and Adriano is infatuated with her, so he keeps her all to himself. She's in love with him. I've seen her hurt expression when the men talk about Adriano's whorish ways. He's not ignorant - he knows she's in love with him. He's adamant about not wanting any attachments, but unfortunately for him, he can't stay away from her.

Behind the bar, I grab a water bottle instead of an alcohol-infused drink. Rarely do I drink, only when I'm extremely wound up and I need to calm down. Taking big gulps of water, I spot a brunette, Skye, walking up to me.

The first few years, I used to be on this side of the house often, enjoying myself with different women. But meaningless, nameless sex lost my interest as the years went by. I would still indulge myself once in a while, but I couldn't find satisfaction in any of this anymore. This life, Adriano and I would never have gotten involved in if it wasn't for James' nephew.

Uncle Joseph - *mio zio* - raised me after my parents died when I was ten. He always tried to make up for the loss of both my parents. Even though we didn't have a lot of means and money, parental affection was in abundance from *mio zio* Joseph. When his heart failure forced him to cease working, I was just a boy coming into the way of the world. A boy of seventeen wanting to take care of his second father.

One choice changed the course of my life from carefree teenager to a young man groomed to be in the Mafia. I landed a job at a bakery in the city to help support my family of two. An American-Italian bakery run by Alessa Calderone. Every day after school, I worked and I didn't have any plans to attend college. I lived day by day, praying daily that my uncle's health wouldn't deteriorate. But *zio* Joseph was slowly dying, living here in Chicago, cooped up inside the house. I knew that if it wasn't for me, he would be moving back to his beloved Italy.

The first day at the bakery, I met Adriano. He was one year my junior, and we shared common teenage boys interests like roughhousing, football, biking, and, of course, our responsiveness to pretty girls bonded us most. Adriano also worked daily after school, and we became close friends.

After working at the bakery for a month, we both noticed there were regular customers coming in. Alessa catered to a menacing-looking crowd of men in fitted suits and angry expressions covering their faces. Apart from the regulars, the bakery wasn't busy often, but it was still open daily until eleven p.m. We actually never questioned that back then.

One night, an Italian boy came running into the bakery when Alessa was gone and only Adriano and I were present. Out of breath, he closed the door and looked around, scared. He begged us for help because some men were after him. Adriano and I shrugged and were looking forward to some action on an otherwise dull Tuesday night. We told the boy to hide behind the counter as Adriano and I put on our invincible façade. Three men in wrinkled suits – men that we had seen before - were checking the bakery and the area outside before they dared stepping in and drilling us. Neither Adriano nor I recoiled. I didn't think they would dare touch us since Alessa adored both Adriano and me, and all men feared Alessa. I told them to fuck off and one of them drew his fist into my face, ordering me to surrender the boy or they would light the place on fire. Adriano and I both laughed, standing our ground. I laughed even though I was scared, but one thing I learned from my uncle was to never show fear. Intimidation preys on fear. I remembered Alessa telling me on my first day that if the shop was ever robbed, I was to mention the name James Calderone, so I told the three men that James was already on his way. This made them back off and they scampered away.

I should've never mingled in this situation if I wanted to stay off the radar of James Calderone. The boy was Alessa's nephew, and he told Alessa how I saved him. Alessa - in turn - told James, and the truth always gets contorted with each passing person, making it more heroic than it was in reality. James came in the next day and promised two impressionable young boys money, power, and women. Money for me to send *zio* Joseph back to live a peaceful and healthy life in Italy.

Adriano and I fell for his story and became his prospects. We were prospective Mafiosi without knowing. James had a mandatory stipulation that we attend business college, always reminding us how valuable business skills are in the *Cosa Nostra,* or Syndicate, as James likes to call it. Money and women ruled our life for four years of college. Adriano and I had inquisitive young minds and breezed through college living as young princes. James ensured membership for both Adriano and me after graduation when we were twenty-two.

As with all prospective Mafiosi, we were bound into silence – *omertà*, the code of silence and secrecy that prohibits us from disclosing information about the activities of our criminal organization - by being required to commit murder to prove our loyalty.

Adriano and I shared everything from prospects to made men. I witnessed his first kill and he mine. I pulled my trigger the first time on a young associate, who was an informant for the FBI, in an abandoned warehouse on the north side of Chicago that's used to torture captives. It was a clean, quick, and simple kill. An associate works for or aids the clan but isn't considered a true member. Non-true members may be killed without permission of the *Capo crimine* or underboss; therefore those kills are simple. This profoundly changed us. Killing a person, ending a life haunts you forever. The crazy thing is that your mind adapts. It now justifies the taking of lives because they're not innocents. As time passes and you live in a world where every human life is expendable, 'normal' emotions get phased out and you become detached to the viciousness. We made the conscious choice to never get attached to an outside woman; sustaining a relationship with a regular citizen is impossible.

James was the underboss back then. When James became the *Capo crimine* – boss - of our Syndicate, I was promoted from *Capo* to underboss at the age of twenty-six. Adriano was promoted from soldier to *Capo*. Everybody started calling me *Padrino*.

The power didn't excite me, the world didn't excite me, and the women didn't excite me anymore. The constant worrying, arranging, and scheming tires me. Never can I just *be*. I will forever be on guard with everything I do. Once in, you can never *ever* leave alive.

Skye places her hands on my chest. "Want me to take your mind of things, Luca?" She takes hold of my hand and leads me to one of the three private rooms in the back. When she holds the door open for me, I step inside the grey-white room with a four-poster bed in the center and sit on the bed while I undo the button of my suit jacket. Skye slides it off my shoulders, and I close my eyes.

Fallon.

Remembering how it felt to finally caress her smooth skin with my lips, I feel an undeniable passion threatening to boil inside me. I try my best to stay in this moment while Skye attempts to push back my hair that's clinging to my forehead, but I still her movement with my fingers wrapped forcefully around her arm. "Get out," I order in a low voice and release her arm, shoving her away from me.

Confusion is setting in. Fallon is starting to creep under my skin. She's igniting a sensation I'm unfamiliar with, beyond any sensation I've experienced before, and I am going to pursue her.

CHAPTER 8

Fallon

Sundays have always been a lazy day for me. This Sunday, as usual, I read and lounge around the apartment, but I did go running this morning. I paint my nails, toes and fingers, in a vivid red color. I start my grooming around five: shave my legs, scrub my skin until it feels like satin, blow dry my hair and curl the ends, which are now flowing in light waves over one shoulder. My bangs are swept to the side, and I decide on light *au naturel* makeup: some mascara, blush, and nude lipstick.

Standing before my closet in my black lace underwear, I look through my dresses that are hanging in the closet and stop at my dark blue dress to remove it from the hook. I also decide on my strappy black sandals. Since spring just started – and winter recently ended - I wear my black thigh high stockings. My dress has a silver beaded halter top that ties around my neck in a big bow and a knee length A-line skirt. The soft fabric complements my silky soft skin, and I finish my look with white gold diamond studs that I only wear on special occasions. I'm tying the straps on my sandals when my phone rings, and I grab it off of the bed.

Before I get the chance to speak, Teagan yells, "Hey, babe!"

"Hey, babe. What did you do today?"

"I went shopping at *Harrods*."

"I'm getting ready for my date with Luca." I sit back up without tying my left sandal.

"I told you he'd call."

"He didn't call. Well, not to ask me out. I saw him again at the shop yesterday."

"I was kind of right," Teagan persists.

Wanting her opinion on my dress, I tell her, "I'm wearing the blue dress with the beaded halter."

"The silver beading?"

"Yes," I confirm.

"Fabulous choice. Is he still cute? You usually lose interest once you've had a conversation with a guy."

"He actually quoted Alexandre Dumas," I boast.

"Well, then you have *got* to marry him," she mocks. "Are you having dinner or what?"

"Yes, dinner. He's picking me up in a few."

"Did you shave your legs?" she probes softly.

"I did but not for reasons you think," I retort quickly to stop her.

"My girl is going to get laid. *Now* I'm proud."

"I have to finish. I was putting on my black sandals when you called."

"Another sexy choice. I approve."

"I'm glad," I reply dryly.

"You do realize I will be texting you throughout the night," she says in a matter-of-fact tone.

I groan through my smile. "I know. Just don't expect me to answer you right away."

"You better. Or on second thought, only answer when the steamy stuff happens."

"Yeah, that won't happen. I won't be thinking of you then." I add, "I hope." And we both laugh.

"He's not doing a good job if you're thinking of me then. Go have fun. We'll talk, or text, or e-mail. Do things I would I do." Teagan makes a kissing noise.

"We'll text later. Bye bye."

I toss my phone on the bed and finish putting on my shoes. Standing in front of the mirror, I approve of my look. The doorbell rings right on time, and I buzz Luca in. Pitching my phone in my purse, I check myself one final time as Luca knocks softly. When I open the door, my mouth almost hits the ground taking in the sight of him. Funnily enough, we match in dark blue. He's wearing a midnight navy pinstripe suit with a white dress shirt - no tie - that shows off his muscular physique. I shamelessly check him out from top to bottom. His top button is undone. As I gaze back up, our eyes meet - he was also checking me out. His hair is neatly combed back, but some strands won't stay in place, and I'm ecstatic that he didn't shave but only trimmed. He stares at me for a moment longer while I timidly stand there for a second before stepping aside, inviting him in.

Luca steps closer to me and bends his head to give me a kiss on my cheek, and the corner of our mouths touch. He lingers there. "You look exquisite, Fallon." His lips are touching mine but not kissing me. This is more intimate than an actual kiss on the mouth. The heat of his lips ignites my cheeks.

As usual, his scent awakens my senses - citrus and clean air and all Luca. "Thank you." I move my head slightly toward him, our lips brushing. I feel Luca smile against my mouth before stepping back and walking in. It takes me a moment to gather my thoughts and close the door.

He stands confidently in the living room. "Are you ready to go?" he asks when I turn around to face him.

"Yes." My skin is flushed from the thoughts roaring through my mind. Luca takes my coat off the back of the kitchen chair and holds it out for me, so I tuck my arms in and close the buttons.

He tenderly releases my trapped hair from under my coat and caresses a few strands before letting it fall back over one shoulder. "Shall we go?" He opens the door for me.

"Let's go."

I'm stunned by the sight of his car when Luca clicks the device that unlocks the doors of his black Maserati as we walk toward it, and we step into the immaculate and sleek car.

"Where are you taking me, Luca?" I watch him easily maneuver his car through traffic.

A smile tugs at his lips. "It's a surprise."

"As long as there's food, I'll be happy."

His eyes stay focused on the road. "So easy to please, Fallon."

"Isn't that a good thing?"

"Depends on the situation," he counters suggestively.

I raise my brow and shake my head, and then I watch the city go by while we drive in peaceful silence until arriving at a high rise.

Luca hands his keys to the valet and comes over to open my door. We head toward the elevator, through a lobby with an old French, burlesque-style décor. My eyes are darting around, taking in the superb sight. I greet a man that has disrupted my line of vision, and Luca places his hand possessively on the small of my back at that moment. I tilt my head and smirk.

He returns a guiltless smile and Luca leans in to say, "When we return from dinner, we'll enjoy the art in the lobby."

My eyes twinkle because he's in tune with my thoughts constantly.

The elevator takes us to the eightieth floor, to a restaurant with the most spectacular view of Chicago. I frown when I realize I've never heard of this restaurant. Not that I know all the restaurants around here, but I would think that a high-class restaurant with this view would be more popular. There are only a few tables, maybe ten.

The hostess, an Italian beauty, greets us, "Mr. DeMiliano, your table is ready."

She takes my coat, and I follow her through the entirely-carpeted restaurant. The floor and walls are adorned in deep red and gold velvet carpet, providing it a distinguished look. As Luca treads behind me, I mouth melodramatically *Mr. DeMiliano* over my shoulder and send him a charmed smile.

He motions with his forefinger for me to turn around and keep walking while he's restraining his amused expression.

She seats us at the floor-to-ceiling window. The moment I sit down, the city lights are powering on through Chicago. From left to right the golden yellow lights illuminate a darkening purple city and sky.

Luca holds my chair out for me to sit and discusses something with the hostess before taking his seat. "Can I surprise you with excellent Italian wine?"

"Yes, please." I take in the man seated across from me. The subtle lighting in the restaurant makes his eyes look darker. He exudes confidence and strength in every pose. My focus shifts to the amazing view. The entire city is lighted as the sky is blackening. A waitress hands me a menu while she explains that it's fusion cuisine, French and Italian, then she leaves.

Luca's looking at me expectantly. "Do you want to order from the menu, or I can ask the chef to make us small samples?"

I beam a dazzling smile at him. "You had me at small samples."

An appreciative gaze takes over his eyes. He momentarily looks at the bar, and I'm amazed by the waitress, who is at our table within seconds with our drinks, and Luca gives our order.

I scrutinize my surroundings. There are actually only twelve tables here. Four are occupied by other couples. Two men, who quickly look away when I turn around, are seated at one table. The man who sits facing me continues talking to his company, but there's a slight shift in their posture. They have a threatening appearance.

"Fallon.... Fallon."

I turn back to Luca.

"What's wrong?" Luca looks beyond me and then immediately back to me.

"You know those men?"

"I've seen them here before. They're also regulars."

I relax. "Okay, I think they recognized you too."

"I do come here often."

"It's a beautiful restaurant. I've never heard of it."

"It caters to just a few clients."

"Really? And Mr. DeMiliano is one of those clients."

"Fallon." He shakes his head amusingly. "Stop saying my name constantly. You have no idea what it does to me." His lips curve in a sexy grin.

I can guess what it does. "It's a sexy last name." I raise my brows a few times in quick succession.

He laughs as we both raise our glasses. "To a wonderful evening, Fallon."

"To a wonderful evening, Mr.— Luca."

Throughout dinner we laugh and tease. I've eaten the most delectable hors d'oeuvres: prosciutto with olive and oranges, mushroom tuna, lobster salad on endive spears. He feeds me some of his favorite foods, and I have to admit: he has excellent taste in food. We eat our dessert – a dark chocolate cake - in silence. Best. Dessert. Ever.

When we leave the restaurant, Luca shows me the artwork in the lobby, but my mind is somewhere else. During the car ride home, I check my phone; two messages from Teagan asking me if I've already gotten laid.

Luca's lost in thought when his phone rings, and he silences it without checking the caller ID. He takes my hand and places it on his thigh, absentmindedly stroking my fingers while he drives me home. He parks in front of the condominium and walks me up to the entrance.

"Coming up with me?" I ask reservedly. I'm a little hurt when he seems to consider my offer instead of answering right away.

Luca takes my keys out of my hands. "Yes." He opens the door and we take the stairs to the first floor.

After we enter my apartment, he instantly takes my coat and his jacket to hang them on the solid wood coat rack. Luca walks over to the window and looks at the street. "In the middle of all the action," he speaks dreamily.

"Do you want wine or something else to drink?" I casually lean against the wall connecting to the open kitchen and try to act nonchalant. He turns to gaze at me in full force, and I feel heated under his scrutiny as the air thickens.

"No." He saunters over to me gradually, licking his lips while his look is full of lust and fire.

I push off the wall, drawn to him, and he catches me when I fall into his arms and his lips search for mine. His hands palm my neck and hip aggressively while his lips capture mine. Our mouths open instantaneously and our tongues push against one another. Luca's taste of wine and mint has me moaning in his mouth, and passion flares wildly in my lower stomach from his rough kisses. He groans as his hands dig into my hip and my ass, lifting me to him. I stand on my toes when he molds me against his body. Every part of our bodies is tightly pressed together as we hungrily devour each other, and the tips of his fingers stroke the bare skin under my dress. I feel his arousal growing against the soft flesh of my stomach and let my fingers sink into his silky, dark strands of hair.

What I've wanted to do since that first night we met. He sighs in appreciation and bites my lower lip, then traces his tongue smoothly over his bite mark. He never breaks eye contact. Luca's sensuous and skillful kisses are tender yet rough.

We're both panting as he forces me backward, and we fall on the couch without breaking our kiss. Every time I think Luca will end the kiss, he explores me more deeply. I grind my hips against his arousal and hurriedly tug his shirt out of his pants as he lifts himself slightly off me to help. Our movements are equally frantic, and I bury my hands under his shirt to trace his abs, sides, and back. His hot skin is smooth to the touch. I feel him shudder under my caress when I dig my nails gently into his back, and he moans while pushing his hardening arousal between my legs.

He breaks our kiss to untie the knot of my halter at my neck. Luca helps me to sit up as he kneels on the floor, between my thighs, and sweeps my hair tenderly over one shoulder while he grazes his teeth over my flushed skin. His hands roam over my lower body, bunching my dress in his palms, bringing it over my head as I lift my arms, and throwing it behind me. I'm greeted by a boyish grin when he notices that I'm not wearing a bra. He cups my breasts forcefully while kissing the tender spot where my shoulder and neck meet. Then he yanks off my panties in one fluid motion. I smile up at him sweetly as the air hits my naked skin, sitting before him in only black stockings with embroidered lace at the top and my sandals.

He stills and just stares at me for a moment. Luca shakes his head as if he's clearing his mind of an unpleasant thought, and his eyes darken even more, the green entirely invisible. *"Sei da mozzare il fiato."* You're breathtaking. His hands sweep over my body, from my legs up to my narrow hips, over my stomach to palm my breasts.

All I hear is our heavy breathing. All I feel is his touch on my soft skin. My whole body is on fire from his touch everywhere, and my skin revels in the quiet of his caress.

Luca twists his hand in my hair and leans me toward him to taste my lips again. I pull back from his kiss to undo the upper buttons of his shirt because I'm naked and he's still fully clothed. He smirks and watches me work his buttons while his fingers gently brush my bangs out of my face. The manner in which he's constantly touching and caressing me overwhelms me. I push back his shirt over his shoulders and let it flutter to the ground. Luca watches me tracing the outline of his well-defined muscles and hisses when I unbuckle his belt and palm his hardening length through his boxers. I stroke him a few times before he grabs both my legs and pulls me forward. He's on his knees between my legs, so we're at eye level. Luca forces me to the edge of the couch by grabbing my behind and pulling me toward him.

Molding my soft flesh, he says between kisses, "I've been wanting to taste you for a while." And he coaxes me to lie back against the couch with his hand on my cleavage.

I lean back, exposed to him. The coldness of the couch on my back and the warmth of his hands on my body are a titillating contradiction. Luca's head lowers to lick my nipple. My head falls back, and I twist my hands into his hair, pushing my breast into his mouth. He sucks hard on my nipple and groans against my breast while his right hand trails down leisurely over my stomach and between my legs. His fingers caress me, then he pushes his middle finger inside me once, twice before stopping. I writhe underneath his passionate touch when Luca licks and bites his way down my body and grabs me behind my knees to urge them apart. As he breathes in deeply, I feel the cold rush of his breath against my inner thighs, making me hyperaware of every moment of his passionate seduction. My back bows in anticipation of his mouth on me.

"Pull your legs up, Fallon," he directs me in a lustful tone.

I pull my knees up to my chest and Luca secures his fingers around my ankles, holding them firmly in place. He hisses in satisfaction as his eyes are fixated on me before he lowers his mouth on me. Moaning loudly, I push back against his face. Our slow seduction has fueled our unbridled craving for each other. I open my eyes to watch him taste me and am met with his lust-filled stare. He's been constantly watching my reaction to his seduction. Chills run through my body when he plunges his tongue inside me. The pad of his thumb rubs me carefully, yet fiercely, as the tingles start to form in my lower stomach. I'm on the precipice of exploding as he relentlessly pleasures me with his tongue. The powerful circulating motion on my most sensitive part and his silky tongue make it impossible for me to keep my eyes open, so they roll back, and my other senses intensify again now that I've shut out the world.

I scream and moan his name before reaching my peak. "Luca! Luca!" I shudder when ecstasy reaches me, and my body pulsates with the pleasure he's given me. I ride out my orgasm, only aware of my breathing and Luca's continuous groans. He continues to lick me leisurely and confidently, until he feels my orgasm subsiding.

He's about to say something - standing between my legs with his hands trailing up and down my thigh - when we're interrupted by his ringing phone.

Didn't he put it on vibrate earlier? And doesn't he have voicemail?

It keeps on ringing and ringing, so I raise my brows, hoping to prompt him to speak.

He sighs and gets up to answer his phone.

I dress in my panties, pick up my bra and dress, and head to my bedroom. Grabbing my silk robe in the bathroom, I put it on and meet Luca back in the living room. He's standing by the coat rack with his phone in hand, swiftly typing away. His shirt has been buttoned and tucked back into his pants. One hand tangles through his hair, and his demeanor reminds me of the night we met in the club. There's a hard edge to him, a contradiction in his actions and emotions that make him equally desirable and unsettling. I take this moment to slowly walk up to him.

Without looking up, he informs me, "I have to go."

I glance at the screen and notice he has many missed calls and messages. He's obviously troubled about something. "Okay, you can wash up in the bathroom, if you want?"

His phone disappears in his pocket. "No, I want to smell you on me."

I scrunch up my nose, but I can't prevent the corner of my lip from tilting up at his dirty confession.

He laughs at me.

"I'm glad you can still laugh. Is something wrong that you have to leave so suddenly?" I ask him tentatively.

A rueful smile shows on his face before he masks it. "Yes, a situation with a friend of mine." He cups my chin. "I'll call you."

I have no idea what just happened, so I only stare at him with a blank expression.

Luca takes his suit jacket - which seems oddly heavy - and opens the door. A gentle kiss is placed on my lips, and he immediately stills for a second, making me think that he has surprised himself by initiating this kiss.

I close the door immediately and lean back against it. He had a lot of missed calls. I'm a little confused about why he left so abruptly. I still feel his hands all over my body, and glancing at the couch, I can't hold the upward curve of my lips. Teagan would be proud of me.

I grab my purse and head back to my bedroom to take a shower, but I stop to look at myself in my mirror. My lips are swollen, my hair is all over the place, and I have bite marks on my neck. I trace the marks with my fingers, a tangible memory. My phone alerts me of a message.

```
Fallon, I'll call you later. I had a
wonderful evening with you.
```

Then why leave so abruptly? I can never tell what's next with Luca. During my shower, I remember I have a busy week ahead, so I text him back when I'm lying in bed.

```
Luca, I'm actually very tired and
decided to head to bed early. I'll talk to
you this week. Night
```

Silencing my phone, I leave it on my nightstand beside my bed.

CHAPTER 9

Luca

Luca, I'm actually very tired and decided to head to bed early. I'll talk to you this week. Night

I read her text and realize that I need to handle this more delicately because I can't believe I feel remorse over leaving her. And I actually give a shit that she could be mad. Instead of pacifying my desire for her, this date has accomplished the exact opposite.

I connect my phone to the car charger while I'm speeding through the streets to aid Adriano at the warehouse up north. The last money drop-off to our Syndicate regarding Crystal Lake was compromised, and Adriano and I need to find out why.

I'm calling her now. It rings and rings. And voicemail.

My agitated state disperses when I smell a hint of her on me. A small smile tugs at my lips as I think about how her presence calmed me during dinner. For a guy who can never put his guard down, she made me feel peaceful and relaxed to live in the moment. I lick my lips and adjust my pants thinking about how badly I want to drive myself into her. Watching her climb toward release with my lips on her had me rock hard and begging for relief.

Her soft skin that feels like satin and her breasts that fit perfectly in my palms.

Focusing on the street, I reach the old, brown-brick warehouse quicker than expected. I'll handle Fallon tomorrow.

Adriano's sapphire black M3 is parked to the side. Before exiting my car, I call Adriano to let him know that I'm here and take my compact semi-automatic Smith & Wesson .45 ACP out of my jacket. The door unlocks before I reach it.

"Damian," I greet. One of our soldiers on Adriano's team lets me in.

Adriano's voice is rising in the warehouse. "I'm losing patience with you, *idiota.*"

The scene is set up in the left corner. The warehouse has four rooms on the right for private handlings, but Adriano likes the effect of the big warehouse where his voice can resonate off the walls.

One man, face dripping in blood, is strapped to a wooden chair with his hands tied to the back and feet tied together. The chair has plastic underneath for quicker clean-up, a job handled by the prospects and soldiers.

Adriano's wearing his white latex gloves to prevent from leaving fingerprints and grips the guy's hair, yanking his head back in one quick move. An agonizing whine comes from our captive. "Look who's here," Adriano says to Jack.

The guy's eye is almost swollen shut and is turning purple. He looks at me through the slit of his eyelid.

"Luca." Adriano gives me an exasperating look. "He's lying and covering for someone." Adriano forces the guy's head back more, stretching his throat as Adriano stands over him. "I brought in the big guns now. Pun intended." My *Capo's* mouth twists in a satanic smile. "You'll be sorry you didn't confess when it was just me."

Adriano joins me in front of the guy and hands me a pair of gloves.

"Name?" I ask Adriano while I put them on.

"Jack." Adriano removes his knife from his pocket.

My gun is stashed in my back pocket, concealing it from Jack. I move closer to him.

"Help me," Jack begs.

I crouch down in front him to be less intimidating. "Jack, I can only help you if you give me straight answers. Do you have a family?"

He stammers, "Y-Yes, a daughter. You can have her; she's young and a virgin."

Fucker. It's sickening how quickly men cave under torture. He could've extended his life if he wanted to protect his family; I might have some sympathy then, but this man only thinks of himself. "I don't want your daughter," I keep speaking evenly. "You can choose, Jack. I will ask you one question. If you do not answer truthfully, Adriano will torture you for hours with a blunt knife." I stand up and resume Adriano's former position behind Jack. "Or talk now and I'll let you go."

Jack doesn't make a sound.

Adriano drops to his haunches and cuts open Jack's right pant leg up to his thigh. Without warning, he drives his knife into Jack's knee and - ever so slowly - slices open the skin to the middle of his shin.

I muffle Jack's tormented screams by roughly covering his mouth with a white cloth. His head's frenziedly swaying from side to side. Red covers his leg and blood pools on the floor beneath Jack's right foot.

I signal for Adriano to stop. "Ready to talk, Jack?" I remove the cloth, and Jack hyperventilates through his cries yet stays silent.

Adriano moves his knife lower, slicing open more skin, and I smother Jack's cries again.

"Ready now?" I taunt.

Jack nods his head slowly. "You'll kill me anyway after I've given answers."

"I might, or not. Do you want to take that chance? Adriano can keep going if you want."

"NO. Stop. I can't take it anymore." Jack coughs up spit mingled with blood.

Adriano steps back just in time so the blood doesn't splash on him. Revolted, he wordlessly begs me to finish this quickly.

"Talk. Why were you interfering with the last money drop-off at Crystal Lake? You only get one shot," I warn him.

"Leggia paid me to botch it up." Jack's voice is growing weaker. Blood is leaving his body, fast. "That's all I know. He gave me ten thousand to make sure you wouldn't receive your last payment for Crystal Lake."

This is interesting.

I release Jack's head, letting it slouch forward, and go to Adriano. "Did you find money on him?"

"I found ten in the trunk of his car. This could be true. We still don't know why Leggia wanted Crystal Lake."

I reach for my gun. *Shit.* I left the silencer in my glove compartment. "Have a silencer on you?" I ask Adriano.

"You forgot?" he answers in disbelief.

I was distracted by Fallon. I never come unprepared to the warehouse, except for today. I raise my brow impatiently. "Yes or no."

"No, not for that one." He signals to my Smith & Wesson.

"Give me yours."

Adriano hands me his gun and reaches for the silencer from his back pocket.

I attach it to the barrel of the weapon and stand beside Jack, aiming the gun at his temple. The infinitely small part of my conscience that's left feels sorry for ending this man's life. Who am I to be judge and executioner? I have no answer for that question. All I know is that in this Syndicate, it always comes down to *you* or *him*. And I'm selfish enough to choose myself repeatedly. Every time I kill, the face of that first associate I finished off pops up in my head. As I pull the trigger, the thwack resounds through the warehouse, ending Jack's agony with one bullet.

Adriano removes his gloves and takes two shirts from a garbage bag he brought with him. My collared shirt has blood spatters, but my pants and shoes are still clean. We change our shirts and ditch the bloodied ones in the bag, along with the gloves.

I instruct Damian when he comes up to us. "Burn the garbage bag. Dispose of the body on Crystal Lake ground."

"Yes, *Padrino*." Damian begins cleaning the evidence.

Adriano and I leave the warehouse.

At our cars, Adriano expresses his concern. "How do we know it was Leggia for sure? We don't have anything to back Jack's story and you've already killed him."

We lean against his car, and Adriano reaches for his pack of cigarettes in his pocket.

"I went to *Francitalia* for dinner with Fallon. Guess who was there, out in the open, following me? One of Leggia's men. I've only seen him once before, at Leggia's house months ago. I never forget faces. He's up to something."

"But disposing of the body on his turf will start an all-out war."

I pinch the bridge of my nose and tiredly say, "I think he already started the war."

"So he saw you with Fallon?"

My lips thin and I say with bite, "Yes. He clearly saw her too and is most likely doing a background check on her as we speak."

"Luca, this is bringing her deeper into our messy world. What does she think you do for a living?"

"I told her about our company, of course. You almost blew my cover, by the way. I took both phones with me to her apartment and forgot to silence the disposable one."

"You seem agitated, yet not. Tell me you didn't…"

"I was interrupted."

Adriano grins. "What is it with her?" He inhales another deep puff of his cigarette. "Tell me this. Was it good or not as good as you thought it would be?"

I slowly nod my head. Never have I waited this long before becoming intimate with a woman. But this night has already made the wait worth it. "It was fucking better. I didn't want to leave. Your timing sucked."

Adriano doesn't know how to respond.

I'm breaking my rule to not get attached, but at this moment, I don't care. "I need to be careful - Fallon's smart. She was visibly unhappy when I left."

"That's women for you." Adriano lets out a half-hearted laugh, followed by a puckered brow. "Is she suspicious?"

"I don't think she's consciously suspicious yet. She did clearly see me silence my smartphone in the car, and then the disposable one rang when we were inside. She also eyed my suit jacket which was holding my gun."

Adriano flicks his cigarette butt away. "I'm just going to repeat myself - be cautious."

CHAPTER 10

Fallon

I squint my eyes open the next morning and jump out of bed when I see it's almost nine and quickly check my messages: Teagan and Luca. Luca called right after he received my text. Around six in the morning, he sent a text.

Good morning, Fallon. Be not afraid of greatness. Some are born great, some achieve greatness, and others have greatness thrust upon them. - Shakespeare

I smile to myself while reading the quote from *Twelfth Night*. Luca knows I collect book quotes and write them down everywhere. A lazy grin pulls at my mouth as I sit on my bed thinking about last night, first thing in the morning; that's what he wanted and why he sent the message at six. He's up early.

Reminded of the fact that I'm already running late for work, I decide to text him back later and shower in record time.

The entire day is busy, and I'm home late that night. All I want to do when I arrive home is eat dinner, shower, and visit my bed. After ordering a deep dish pizza – screw the no-carb

policy - I skip the shower because I'm too tired and climb into
my bed.

***

After discussing some more changes to be made on the texts
and font of several invites with Alex on Tuesday, he offers for us
to have lunch together. We visit the deli across the street. He has
a sandwich, and I order a shrimp salad. I've never felt
completely relaxed with Alex, partly because he's my boss, and
also because he's a distant man. During lunch, we discuss
several charities and other events he's working on. I notice that
he's been acting agitated, and he appears stressed while he eats
hurriedly. Apparently, he has a lot of work waiting for him at the
office.

I'm not even halfway through my salad when Alex checks
his phone and rises out of his seat. "Fallon, I have to take care of
an urgent e-mail."

I want to finish my lunch. "Okay. Go. I'll finish and then
return too."

His mouth quirks up uncertainly. "See you in a few."

I don't even get to say goodbye before he hurries out of the
deli. I'm pleased he left because his distressed mood was
annoying me. This gives me time to read a few pages, so I get
my e-reader out of my bag and am engrossed in an astonishingly
emotional historical romance that I've already added to my

'favorite' shelf on Goodreads, before I've finished the trilogy. "Oh Shura, don't you dare go in there!" Every so often, I talk to my book characters. It helps me cope with my feelings, and at the moment, I'm pissed off at the male lead. I'm dangerously close to throwing my e-reader across the room.

I finish my salad and order another tea. My tea arrives. "Thank you." I don't want to stop reading for a second, so I don't even look up to the waitress. The shadow that falls over me - I thought it was the waitress - doesn't move. My head snaps up to a tall, striking Italian.

"Fallon, always with your face in the books. Do you even realize how sexy that is?" he says in a throaty voice and bends down to place a feather light kiss on my lips.

"Luca. Hi…." It takes a minute for me to compose myself. I was going to text or call him back tonight because I was too tired last night. "What are you doing here?"

"Lunch." He looks at his watch, and his lip twitches for a second. "Are you on your lunch break?"

"I am." He knows I work across the street, and I think he scheduled his lunch here hoping to run into me. "I was here with my boss, but he had to get back. Some emergency he had to handle immediately. Sit."

His brows furrow while he looks around the place. "Thank you." Luca smiles tenderly at me as he decides to sit down next to me. "I was hoping you would text me back." His tone is serious now.

I tilt my head. "It's been two days. Don't tell me you're missing me?" I ask with a hint of disbelief just to goad him.

Luca braces his hand on my neck to bring me closer to him and runs his fingers over my collarbone. "Maybe I did. Your taste is addictive. I. Want. More." He pulls me further into him by my small waist.

I turn my head, and our noses touch as his breath fans over my cheek. "Maybe more can be arranged," I huskily counter and almost press my lips to his before retreating. "I have to get back to work now." Next time will happen on my terms.

I attempt to rise and Luca's hand grabs my wrist to stop me. With an enormous smirk, he lifts his eyes to me. "I'm calling you tonight."

CHAPTER 11

Luca

I needed to keep my distance from her for a few days after our first official date, which is why I didn't mind her withdrawn behavior. However, after two days of following her to guarantee she was safe from Leggia's men, I couldn't refrain and sought to touch her when she was reading alone in the deli. I would've planned to see her tonight, but James wants to discuss new businesses with me and Salvatore alone. I have to be at the house for the next two days, but Friday I'm coming straight back to The Loop.

Our Syndicate is scattered all over the city. None of us actually live at the house or even close-by. Adriano and I are the only two members of the Calderone Syndicate to live in The Loop, and no one except James, Salvatore, and Adriano knows my home address. Only Adriano's welcome in my home, and a few non-Syndicate-related women have been here for a couple of hours.

While I'm packing, I call Fallon.

"Hi." She clears her throat.

"Hi, did I wake you?"

She clears her throat again, her voice is still coarse. "I fell asleep on the couch."

"Shall I call you tomorrow then?" My tone is soft.

"I can talk now. What time is it?"

I glance at my phone for the time. "Midnight," I answer. "It's late. You should go back to sleep, so I'll keep it short. I want to have you all to myself Friday night."

A door closes on her end. "Are you home?"

"Yes, I just got here."

"Oh okay, we can talk tomorrow then." She sounds disappointed.

"That's not what I meant. I'm happy to talk to you." And I truly am. Even if it's for a few seconds; I'm already starting to crave her daily.

"I'm in bed now."

I growl, thinking of her in bed. "I'm looking forward to tasting you again, Fallon," I admit in a low voice.

I hear her moving around in the background; she's undressing. "Sweet talk will get you everywhere," she replies, followed by a yawn.

"You should sleep. Good night, Fallon."

"Friday night," she confirms. "Night, Luca."

I finish packing and drive to the headquarters. The house is busy. All three *Capi* are present with most of their soldiers in the living room, and Adriano's talking to his equals. I greet Alesandro and Robert and start toward the third floor to my private room. Only James and I have a private room on the third floor and an office on the second floor in this house. The *Capi* are allowed to occupy rooms adjacent to the 'strip club,' but the third floor is off limits unless they're invited by either James or me. After dumping my belongings, I meet James in his office.

"Luca." He motions for me to enter from behind his desk when I darken his doorway.

I close the door and make my way across the room, greeting James with a firm handshake and my left arm wrapped around his shoulder.

James has a commanding personality that has also been instilled in me. He's fatherly and intimidating. Always calm and controlled, thinking deeply before he speaks his mind.

I revel in always being calm and controlled too. Lately I can think of several occasions where I've been confronted with unknown emotions, where I debate letting go of my controlled reaction - with Fallon.

"Sit, son." James' fifty-five years aren't apparent in his outer appearance because he's fit and always polished in his Italian suits. Only his grey hairs reveal his age.

I sit across from him as he resumes his seat. "Thanks, James."

"Giacomo Leggia contacted me. He wanted to know what finding Jack's body meant." James' tone, of course, is bland.

"It was a message that I know he's after us," I disclose.

"Good thinking, son. Leggia is always running behind on all the facts. He was so dead set on taking over Calderone territory that he didn't even think twice about why we would hand it over.

He's power hungry and jealous. Too volatile. Alessandro's spy in the Leggia Syndicate discovered that Leggia was on a rampage after he found out that most dealers in Crystal Lake weren't pledged to a Syndicate. They answer to no one, which will make it impossible for him to manage the money, and he'll encounter the same problems we did."

"He must be driven by his jealousy to take over our territory so carelessly. I want him to know that we're always one step ahead of him."

"He knows. I was amicable to him. He surrounds himself with incapable *Capi*. Let's wait and see what he does next."

I lean forward and pour myself a glass of water. "What new business do you have? Is Salvatore coming?"

"Yes, he—"

Salvatore arrives, his usual disheveled self in his rumpled, brown outfit. That's his strength though - with his appearance, people easily discount him, but he's a shark. "James, Luca." He sets his briefcase on James' desk and sits next to me.

James informs us of his plans. "We presently rule the drug trafficking in the north, and there's demand in the east, so I'm thinking of expanding. Luca, what do you think?"

"I don't know anything about the east. Are there small drug dealers operating there? I'll have to send Alessandro or John to investigate. We can easily regulate uncharted territory. Smalltime drug dealers can be pushed out within weeks or fall under our payroll. And we have to make sure Leggia's men aren't doing any business in the east," I advise.

James nods his head in acknowledgement. "Salvatore?"

"I say let John do some digging around. We will need new offshore bank accounts to discreetly manage the cash flow."

"Let's put it in motion, gentlemen," Salvatore resolves.

CHAPTER 12

Fallon

Luca calls me every night until our date. Sometimes we talk for half an hour. Sometimes we talk for only five minutes, but I have come to anticipate the evening calls.

Promptly at six on Friday night, Luca knocks on my door.

Opening the door, I say jokingly, "Did you just stand outside the door until it was six and then knock?"

Luca's lips curve in a crooked grin. "No, I'm just punctual."

"Well, it's creepy," I throw back. Luca's looking dashing, as always, in his black jeans and silver grey button-down shirt with the sleeves rolled up to his elbows, his handsome features strengthened by the gleam in his eyes. I motion to him in full length and state in a sarcastic tone, "This is casual?" He texted me last night to dress casual.

"It is for me."

I look at myself - in dark jeans and a turquoise shirt that hangs casually over one shoulder, hair contained in a low side-knot – and frown.

Luca tilts my chin up to him with his finger. "You look beautiful, *dolcezza*. Don't frown like that. I come bearing gifts." He beams.

"Dolcezza?" I question.

"An endearment."

"Not 'baby,' I hope?" My brows crease, hoping he did not just call me baby.

Luca laughs. "No, more like sweetheart."

"I like that, sounds sweet."

He leans down beside the door and holds out a white, square box.

I show him a sincere smile and peek inside: an entire dark chocolate cake, dessert from our first date. "Do we have to go out? I'd rather stay here and eat this." My eyes widen in delight, and I lick my lips.

"You can eat it tomorrow." He leans down and pecks me on the lips. "Since it's still a workday." Luca grasps my hips. "Although I think you can eat carbs any day. And you *are* eating carbs tonight for dinner."

"Fine. Come inside," I demand quickly and put the cake on the kitchen table.

Luca walks over to me and takes my face in his hands to let his tongue trace my lips. Every brush of his tongue brings a surge of excitement, causing me to breathe heavily and tug at the hair at his nape as he continues to taste my lips.

Luca pulls back a fraction and heat flashes across his eyes. "I'm taking you to my place. Pack some clothes," he announces seductively.

***

After changing into a comfortable dress, I'm wandering barefooted on the hardwood floors of his penthouse - which has a magnificent view of Chicago from the floor-to-ceiling windows - as Luca runs down the street for some groceries immediately after we arrived. His penthouse is decorated in warm off-white and brown colors that must've been done by interior designers because everything matches perfectly.

As I head back to the living room, the elevator doors open and Luca steps out with a grocery bag. He places the groceries on his solid black granite-top kitchen island.

I join him in the kitchen and peek in the bag. "What did you get?"

I'm tenderly pushed aside and led to sit on the bar stool on the other side of the island. "No peeking. You sit while I busy myself with dinner." He takes out the groceries one by one: eggs, parsley, bread, and wine.

"What are we eating?"

"Pasta, of course."

"You forgot the pasta." I lean my elbows on the island.

Luca shoots me a disapproving look. "We're making fresh pasta." He points his thumb behind him over his shoulder. Next to the refrigerator is a chrome-coated steel pasta machine. "None of that store-bought pasta in my house. You and I are making tagliatelle."

"I thought *you* were making dinner, and I only had to sit here?" I tease him.

Luca gets a cutting board and flour from the cabinet behind him. "*You* are only permitted to help with the pasta, then you need to sit back down."

"Yes, boss," I salute.

Luca stills for a split second, but I catch it and frown at him. He disregards my questioning frown. "Come."

I stand next to Luca, and he pulls me in front of him, his body heat warming my back. His hand skims down my arm, removing the beige elastic band I always wear - in case I want to put my long hair up - from my wrist. "Never thought a beautiful woman would be prancing around my home, barefooted." He then pulls my hair into a ponytail and presses his lips softly to my neck.

I rest my head back on his shoulder. "I don't believe that. Plenty of women have been here, I'm sure."

Luca palms my face, forcing me to turn my head and look at him. "That's not what I said *or* meant. Don't belittle this moment. The thought of you waiting for me here turned me on, but my fantasy wasn't as promising as the real thing. You in this white lightweight dress - no shoes, no make-up, just the real you - is enough to make me hard." He's rubbing his stiffening length against my backside.

"Thank you." I bow into him and he takes this as an invitation to run his hands along my cleavage.

"I want you so bad it hurts," he groans in a breath that caresses my face. Luca massages my breasts in his warm hands while his lips search for skin to touch. "What do you want, Fallon. Do I need to feed you first?" he asks while kissing my shoulder and trailing his hand down to cup me between my legs. My legs open wider, and he buries his hand in my panties, ever so slightly circling two fingers.

I push back against him. "No," I answer with conviction because I want him. I want to feel all of him.

I'm spun around lightning fast and smothered by a forceful and claiming kiss when he strips my dress off of me and flings it across the kitchen as if he can't get me naked fast enough. His look is feral as he stares hungrily at my bare breasts. I place both my palms on his solid chest and into the V of his shirt and smile teasingly. He cocks his head in question right before I rip open his dress shirt, making the buttons fly around the room and clank on the floor. I've always wanted to do that.

My arms come around his neck when his sexy smirk is close to my mouth, and he lifts me onto the cold counter. Luca unfastens his belt, and I slide his boxers off with my feet to take his erection in hand. He growls into my mouth, and I help him strip my panties and then stroke him as he continues to kiss and bite down my throat, yanking me forward to the edge. He gets a condom from his pants on the floor and quickly rolls it on. Luca hisses as I center him at my entrance, rubbing the head of his shaft up and down myself.

Our hooded eyes lock before he pushes into me, stretching me inch by inch, slow and deliberate, allowing me time to adjust to his thick length.

He groans, feeling how I open up to him. "Fuck, Fallon, you're so tight. I want to fuck you hard." And his eyes close while he attempts to compose himself.

I watch his muscular body push into my soft flesh and shoot him a luscious smile. "I want you to fuck me hard, Luca." I lie back on the counter as he rests my legs against his toned chest, kissing my ankle.

He makes a low guttural sound, barely holding his control, and eases in and out unhurriedly while watching me, allowing himself to enjoy the sensation when he pushes all the way inside. His pumping increases while he hooks my legs under his arms, pushing my knees toward my chest, and starts to ride me. It feels delightfully raw when he kisses me hard on my mouth, jawline, and then bites my shoulder, his powerful strokes enticing me even more. I whimper when he pinches my nipple. There's nothing tender about what we're doing, but it still feels intimate to me. My eyelids fall closed as he takes my body without mercy.

He slows his pumping. "Look at me, or I slow down," Luca hoarsely demands.

My eyes snap open to look up at him as he's pumping ferociously into me, changing his angle. Luca adjusts my body slightly under his strong grip, moving me into a position where I can only feel the pleasures of his strokes. My orgasm rips through me, and the heat burns at my core, instantly traveling through my entire body. My inner walls clench around his erection, my back arches, and I feel him going in deeper, prolonging my pleasure. He sensually kneads the soft flesh of my breast, and I scream his name once more before I can look at him again through half-closed eyes. Satiated, I slowly drift back from my high.

Luca pulls up my legs again and lets them rest against his chest. His throaty groan through clenched teeth warns me of his impending release. His groin is pressed between my legs, and all I can do is take what he gives me. I feel his erection growing and twitching as he thrust a few more times. Luca's hands trail down my outer legs and hips as he releases himself with a low, "Fuck!" His thrusting slows and he falls on top of me, his hand on my hip caressing upward to cover my breast.

We lie there panting for a while, deliciously exhausted.

Luca lifts himself off of me and we lock eyes; the same look of pleasured souls is reflected in our gaze. "I was planning to feed you first," he confesses with a mock smile.

I'm still floating back from this unexpected and extremely satisfying momentum.

He ghosts his lips over mine and covers my body again, letting our flushed skin touch. "If you want to lie here while I'm cooking, I'm not complaining. I'm just getting started with you, *dolcezza.*"

I laugh and push him away. Luca's eyes cut to my breasts and his hand wanders over my stomach. "I'll get up, chef. I'm suddenly famished." Before he can make a crude remark, I mumble, "For food." I'm stuck to the counter from our sweaty activity and slowly rise up.

He places my dress over my head, constantly touching any piece of bare skin he can get his hands on.

After we wash our hands and clean the cooking area, Luca stands behind me again and places the flour on the board to make a well. "Now for the pasta. Crack four eggs into the well," he instructs.

I get a fork from the drawer and crack them neatly into the flour.

"Now we whisk the eggs until they're smooth."

I do as instructed. We do this all with me trapped between his arms. I sigh contently.

Luca traces the spaghetti strap of my dress. "Aren't you cold?"

"No, I like wearing lightweight, comfortable clothes, and I'm never cold. I look at him sideways. "You're distracting me, chef."

A deep rumble leaves his chest. "*You* are distracting, my sexy student." He kisses my bare shoulder and eyes the eggs. "Good. Now we mix it."

Luca covers my hands with his and shows me how to incorporate the eggs with the flour. "Use the tips of your fingers to mix it a little at a time."

Together, we combine the eggs and flour. "Finally, we knead the pieces together into one smooth lump of dough." He kneads it himself; smashing, pulling, and reshaping the dough. Then he releases it for my turn. "Keep kneading until it's all smooth; no lumps."

I bash the dough continually, which is fun. This could be good anger control. When you're angry, just bash some dough. I laugh at my own thought.

Luca catches it. "What's funny?"

"I was thinking, if you need to get your anger out of your system, bashing dough would be good therapy."

His lips curve into a smile. "Very true. With little casualties," he adds distractedly. He still lingers behind me and observes my movement.

I feel my biceps working. "This is hard work."

Again, he covers my hand with his and together we knead, our fingers entwining in the dough. Our cheeks side by side, his closeness is irresistibly tempting me to kiss him.

As if reading my thoughts, he traces his nose over my jaw. "You're pulling me in," he mutters in an anguished tone.

"What?" My fingers are sticking to the dough too much, pulling it apart instead of smoothing it out. "My fingers are too sticky."

Luca straightens. "Rub some flour on your hands."

I do as he says and smooth the dough out. "Done."

"Perfect. It needs to rest for thirty minutes." Luca rolls the dough in a circle with both hands and covers the ball with a large overturned bowl.

"I want to use the pasta machine," I announce while rinsing my hands.

"You're an enthusiastic student," Luca remarks, smiling.

"I didn't know cooking could be this way. With Teagan, I get screamed at when I do one thing wrong, and then she bans me from the kitchen. I hate cooking with her." I wiggle my eyebrows. "With you, it's kind of a turn-on." I turn to check out the pasta machine. "Um, this looks brand new, Mr. DeMiliano. Are you just showing off for me?"

Luca shows me a hint of a playful grin. "What if I was? Are you complaining? I'll use any excuse to wow you."

"Definitely no complaints." I slip back onto the bar stool.

Luca dazzles me with a lazy smirk. He offers me a glass of red as he starts chopping garlic and parsley.

"Who taught you to cook?"

"*Mi zio.* First night with him, we made pasta together. I was sad and didn't want to talk. He understood and just let me make a mess with dough."

"He sounds so nice. Does he have any children of his own?"

"No. He had one love, but her family didn't want her marrying my uncle. This was back in Italy. He never married. As

113

far as I know, he never had a serious relationship while living here."

I taste the wine. "He lives alone in Venice?" The wine has a deep, rich taste which is astoundingly dry, yet delicious.

"He has many friends and some family members. He isn't lonely over there."

I hear a vibrating sound, and disapproval paints Luca's face as he checks his screen and types a short message.

I've already finished my second glass of wine and feel lazy and warm. I'm not in the mood to make the pasta anymore. "Luca." I smile at him. "I think you can make the pasta much better than me so maybe you should do it." I slip off the stool and sink into the soft couch cushions.

He humors me. "Of course." Then adds, "I'm sure it has nothing to do with the fact that you just want to hang on the couch."

"I'm sure it doesn't." I laugh him off.

I've dozed off and am awakened by Luca's soft voice near my ear. "*Dolcezza*, dinner's ready." He's squatted before me on the couch and pushes my hair out of my eyes.

I sit up and see that he has the dinner table set up with candles.

Luca holds out my chair and plates up the food. "You make a mouthwateringly good shrimp pasta with garlic and parsley," I commend him.

"I don't cook often, so I'm pleased you're enjoying it."

"I never thought I would say this, but no dessert for me tonight." This pasta is filling.

"Never thought you'd say that either. Are you positive?"

"Quite positive," I confirm. "Are you busy this week?"

"A little."

"It's my birthday soon," I hint.

"I know."

"How?"

"I checked your Facebook," he admits quietly.

"So you do like Facebook—"

"No, I only checked yours. That's all."

"Yeah, right," I throw back. "Well, when you're not busy this week, you can stop by my apartment after work."

"I definitely will. I'd rather be busy with you than work." He smiles wickedly.

CHAPTER 13

Fallon

And that's what we do for the next few months, busy ourselves with each other. Always planned dates.

I give Luca an unplanned visit after I've had a meeting with a client three streets from his penthouse. I try persuading the reception to let me go on up, but they're unyielding in checking with Mr. DeMiliano first. They're strict here. I get clearance to go up after they've phoned Luca, and he greets me at the door.

"Hi. I was in the neighborhood and wanted to see you."

"Hi, Fallon. I wish you would've called; I'm actually working." Displeasure is carved in his features.

Taken aback by his rigid, unwelcome posture, I try to look past him into the apartment. Luca has never been anything but courteous, and his discontented manner warrants my suspicion. Normally Luca is in tight control of his emotions to the point that it's sometimes challenging for me to interpret his reaction. "That's fine. I just wanted to say hi. I'm obviously interrupting." I want in that apartment because my instinct is screaming at me to check it out. "I'll just grab a bottle of water, and I'll be on my way."

Luca's brows crease - he knows I'm on to him and whatever business is going on in there.

I shoulder him out the way and stride to the kitchen. There I'm greeted by the guy who was waiting impatiently outside the coffee shop the second time I met Luca. He has pitch black hair and dark brown eyes, but he has a kind undercurrent about him. His hair is longer than Luca's, falling over his ears slightly and curling at the nape.

The guy stands from his seat at the kitchen island. He's dressed in a tailored grey suit, so he obviously shares Luca's love for the finer Italian suits. "Hi, I'm Adriano. Luca's business partner. You must be Fallon. I've heard a lot about you."

Luca *is* actually busy with work. Adriano's here and I see the two laptops on the counter. "Hi, Adriano. I've heard significantly less about you."

He feigns a hurt expression when Luca - who is still not acting like himself - enters the kitchen. "Luca, *stronzo*, you don't tell your girlfriend about the most important man in your life." He points at himself.

Luca provides him a bored look. "Don't flatter yourself."

Adriano returns his attention to me. "Anyway, I'm his best and *only* friend." He slaps Luca's back. "I'm the only guy confident enough to be this Mr. Universe's friend." He offers a wicked grin.

Adriano's comical attitude has eased the stiffening air between Luca and me.

"If you're my only friend, that means you're my best friend by default," Luca chides.

Adriano shrugs. "I'll take that."

Luca and Adriano have an endearing brotherly bond. I smile and retrieve a bottle of water from the fridge. I hold the bottle up. "Anyone else?" As I turn back around, I catch a strange look being exchanged between Luca and Adriano.

"No," Luca answers.

"I'll be right back," Adriano informs us and walks down the hall to the guest room.

Taking the cap of the bottle, I take a swig while keeping my stare locked on Luca. "What's wrong, Luca?"

Luca cocks his head in question. "Why would anything be wrong?"

I close in on him standing next to the kitchen island. "You don't like surprises? You haven't even kissed me."

A lazy smile pulls at his mouth. "You came here for a quickie, Ms. Michaels?"

"Maybe—"

Heels are clicking loudly on the floor. Someone is descending the stairs. Then several things happen that bother me. Luca takes a step back from me. Adriano opens the guest room door and comes out looking contrite. And I see a woman is heading toward us with a smug look on her face.

Shocked, I ask Luca, "Who is that?"

The woman takes a stand beside Luca, effectively making me the outsider in this equation. Annoyance reflects behinds his eyes.

Attempting to defuse the situation, Adriano responds tersely, "This is Gina, a friend of mine." His irritation deters her from opening her mouth.

Gina - with her obvious fake breasts, painted face, acrylic nails, and plastic high heels - stands there glowering at me.

My eyes are glued to Luca, and I completely ignore her. If she's a friend of Adriano, why is she being possessive over Luca? Is his annoyance directed at me or her?

It's directed at her because as she touches his arm, he shrugs her off and anger brims inside him. Luca relays something to Adriano without any words; they only lock eyes briefly.

I stay quiet, too curious to see how these men are going to weasel themselves out of this awkward situation.

Adriano speaks up first. "She's in some trouble, and I told her to come here. I'll take her home now." He's anything but gentle in handling his lady friend. Adriano practically bulldozes her out of the apartment.

The front door closes, and I tip my head to the side for Luca to start talking.

He wipes his hand over his mouth. "Say something." Luca takes the water bottle I've been clutching and places it on the counter.

I release a deep breath. This entire encounter has me speculating what's going on in his life. "Who's she?"

Luca steps forward to touch me, but his hand stops mid-air when I glare at him. "She's a friend of Adriano's. She called him while we were working." He gestures toward the laptops. "Look we *were* working, Fallon. Adriano told her to come here. She got here a few minutes before you arrived. She was freshening up in the bathroom, and Adriano was taking her home after we settled one last e-mail."

"Why was she all over you if she's only a friend of Adriano? You know her too?"

"Yes." A curt reply.

"You know what I mean. Don't play coy with me now. How *well* do you know her?" I'm asking if he slept with her.

"I'm not attracted to her, Fallon." No answer is an affirmative answer. He steps forward and I immediately step back. Luca's eyes soften in culpability and defeat.

"I knew by your reaction to my visit that something was wrong. And then I find a woman in your apartment—"

Luca casually interrupts. "Adriano was here too. I wasn't alone with her, Fallon. Don't make this bigger than it is."

"Don't make it bigger? I felt the tension, Luca. I felt something was off, and the way she wanted to mark her territory with you is unsettling. And don't think I didn't notice you evading my questions until I literally spelled it out for you." My voice mirrors his frustration.

"You want to know?" His voice rising. "She's a stripper. Adriano is the idiot who befriended her. We had business to finish, and it was easier for her to come by here because Adriano couldn't leave yet. This is exactly what I wanted to prevent." He waves to the distance between us and expels an exaggerated breath.

My annoyance has risen to unbelievable heights after the stripper confession. "This is not sitting well with me, Luca. Are there other situations where you don't want to upset me and therefore you omit things?" Moisture pools in my eyes.

"I want to protect you from any harm." Luca's gradually advancing on me and tries to palm my neck.

I shake him off. "Harm? What are you talking about? I'm not quite sure you're getting my point. You will not find a random man – someone you don't know - in my house when you decide to visit me."

I swear I see guilt and anger battling in his intense green eyes. "I'm trying here, Fallon. Don't overreact."

"What? Are you serious? You think I'm overreacting?" I say sullenly. "You shouldn't trivialize this."

Luca paces back and forth. "Yes... No... Fuck!" he mutters.

I cross my arms over my chest. "I'm upset and I want to be away from you right now." The unsettling thoughts haven't been negated by our talk. I desperately need to leave. "I'm going home."

Disappointed, Luca implores, "No, stay. Don't go like this." He closes the distance between us and touches my face. I stop him and move his hand away because I don't want to be softened by his touch.

His disappointment fades and pure fury blisters to the surface at my rejection of his touch. He's not used to hearing no. Luca grabs my shoulders vehemently, forcing my gaze on him. "You are not going anywhere like this."

My brows shoot skyward at his directive tone, making me defensive. "You don't decide whether I stay or go." I throw the water bottle in my purse and dash out of his house. As I close the apartment door, I hear Luca cursing a string of profanities.

One unplanned meeting between us has planted the seeds of mistrust in me. There's a small voice in the back of my head shouting to be acknowledged.

CHAPTER 14

Luca

I did not handle that well. I fist my hands in my hair.

Fucking Gina has some nerve.

This is why I don't allow people in my home. Only because Adriano couldn't leave immediately to get her, did I permit her coming here. Adriano's soldier was supposed to pick her up and take her to the house, but we put him on another assignment last minute. Gina's as stupid as she's fake. I cringe at the memory of fucking her. She's one of the reasons why I don't drink too much anymore.

All I wanted was to finish our business quickly and visit Fallon. That plan obviously failed. Adriano left without his laptop, but I'm not positive Fallon perceived that as sketchy. We opened the laptops when the reception notified me that Fallon was downstairs.

Adriano and I own a software development company. The company develops and implements special requirements software for businesses worldwide. We act as silent owners, and the office is located in The Loop. Of course the software developments are used for the Syndicate to breach firewalls and government systems. Apart from being the silent owners, Adriano and I are also the investors – which is how we legalize the profit from the drug earnings, making it appear that we are just two noble and successful entrepreneurs. Usually once, twice a week, Adriano or I visit the office to sign documents and answer e-mails or prepare for audits. Every detail has been covered to ensure this company looks legitimate. We have operational, sales, and finance directors who manage the day-to-day business, and we have managed to stay behind the scenes as much as possible. The three directors are associates on my payroll, not true Syndicate members.

To the outside world, we're entrepreneurs who avoid the media; not that uncommon. One of the most important aspects of our Syndicate life is to uphold the façade of being a contributing member of society. None of the high-ranking men have a criminal record. Once you have a criminal record, you can never be anything more than a soldier in any Syndicate, whether it's New York Syndicate, Chicago, or LA. This is our strength. Soldiers are never seen in public with *made* men. *Capo crimine*, underbosses, *Consiglieri*, and *Capi* are artists, entrepreneurs, politicians, journalists, police men, all with clean records and no run-ins with the police or ties to any criminal activity that is documented by the government. Chicago Syndicate is the largest and most influential venture, devoted to regulating the drug traffic in Central Chicago and now expanding to East Chicago. Crystal Lake and some other small areas have been sold because they weren't beneficial enough for us. We have smooth-running drug trafficking procedures set up that benefit all parties. Even though Leggia's now in charge of Crystal Lake, we still own the veto right to the Chicago territory, which means that James can still overpower anything Leggia does in Crystal Lake if it affects our business. The other Syndicates will not interfere as long as it benefits the status quo: nobody is exposed or incriminated or linked to criminal activity. James has always been careful about expanding because expanding also brings along more intricate planning and risk of exposure.

We we're discussing Leggia when Gina called Adriano. I made a snap decision for Gina to wait here because I had to update my *Capo*.

I can't control Fallon, which irks *and* intrigues me. She has a mind of her own, a free spirit that doesn't consent giving into me. Waves of fury and excitement swished through me at her dismissal of staying here. She's a challenge, and she's reeling me in.

First, the hindrance, Gina, will be dealt with. She made the wrong move in coming between Fallon and me. I text Adriano on my way out.

Where are you?

Riding around the area still. I'm guessing Gina won't be going back to the house.

```
Meet me at the park, all the way in the
back.
```

Gina's smugness has vanished. All I see is fear written all over her while they pad across the grass.

Adriano joins me on the bench while Gina keeps her stance before us.

We both glare at her as I speak. "Where is her boldness now?"

Adriano moves his head from left to right slowly in mock disappointment.

Gina begs, "Luca, I'm sorry. I wasn't thinking. You know... I thought you liked me too."

Never have I given her the time of day except for that one time we fucked, which I barely remember. What's left of my conscience obligated me to let her stay after our fucking since I was partly at fault. But she doesn't know when to shut her irritating trap. Gina's manipulative and vindictive. A woman scorned could pose a problem for me personally, though I'm sure she wants to live, so she'll disappear quietly. She isn't a danger to the Syndicate because she has absolutely no incriminating information on us. Holding up my hand, I hush her.

Adriano says, "You don't belong with us, Gina. You are not to come to the house anymore."

She trembles and cries, "What about my stuff at the house? I don't have any money."

"Your stuff will be sent to you. Adriano will give you some cash."

"Luca, Adriano, please, I want to stay with you. I'm so sorry."

"You should've thought about that before you decided to interfere in my life," I reply.

Adriano rises. "See you at the house?"

I nod briefly.

"Come." He yanks Gina with him.

***

I'm palming my phone, ready to call Fallon, but I need to let her cool off. "Camilla, can I have water?"

She gets a bottle from the fridge behind her and hands it to me. "What's on your mind, Luca?"

Propping one foot on the foot rest, I sit forward. Camilla might be able to help me get back into Fallon's good graces. "A woman," I reveal.

She swipes a cloth over the bar counter and stops at my confession. "Well, I never. Has a woman finally captured your attention beyond fucking?"

"Stop working; sit with me. Nobody is here anyway." The room is deserted while I'm waiting for Adriano.

"Let me just clean the counter. Do tell, Luca." She stops across from me.

"I need to make a woman stop being mad at me."

"Is she special?"

I confess, "Yes." I pause, unsure whether to tell this to her. "Every time I'm with her, something cuts short or ruins our time together."

Camilla smiles tentatively, knowingly. She stays quiet, allowing me to continue.

"I'm tainting her with my presence."

"How?" she questions.

I angle my head sideways. "You know more about what goes on around here than any of the other women, Camilla. I see how you're unobtrusively absorbing this lifestyle."

"Does she know about this?" Camilla waves her hand around.

"No. She was untainted, but now she's been dragged in without even realizing." I've said too much to Camilla. Changing the subject, I add, "It's her birthday Sunday. I have a gift, but I need something extra."

"What did you get her?"

"A few books."

Camilla scrunches her nose up. "Books?"

The corner of my lip turns up. "She'll love them."

"What does she like, except for books?"

My mind tries to think of everything Fallon's told me. "Mostly books…theater, movies." I screw the top off the water bottle.

Camilla's eyes start to glow. "I have an idea. Get your laptop - we can arrange everything online. You have a budget?"

"No budget, give me your best idea."

CHAPTER 15

Fallon

I lie awake as the sun comes up the next morning. This quiet voice in my head is screaming louder and louder that Luca is holding back from me. I've fallen for him, but some things don't add up. Am I overanalyzing this? Could be; that's what I told myself last night. That woman in his house and the way he and Adriano reacted has made me wary. His explanation could be true or not. However, my questions about Luca aren't stopping me from pursuing this relationship. I check my phone, and just then Luca texts me that he's coming over. Not ten minutes later, I buzz him in and leave the front door open before crawling back into bed.

I'm lounging in bed when he appears in the doorway with a silver box in hand. He sets it on my nightstand. "Morning."

"Morning." I turn on my side to face him.

The dark circles around his eyes betray he had a rough night. Luca takes an encouraging breath, preparing himself for an apology. "Fallon, I'm sorry about last night. Gina's truly nothing to me."

I wasn't even worried about the woman per se. It's the situation that had me upset. "I believe you. The situation was just awkward and it made me apprehensive to believe you."

Luca edges closer to my bed. "I truly get that. It won't happen again."

He removes his clothes until he's in just his boxers and joins me in bed.

Before he gets the chance to open his mouth, I cut in, "Can I open my present?"

He nods with a tentative smile.

I turn to the table and Luca slips in behind me. His arms encircle my waist. "Can we forget about yesterday, Fallon?" His palms wander over the inside of my thighs, forcing my legs apart.

I greedily lift the top off of the box and remove the silver tissue paper. My heart skips a beat. "Oh, my... What... How?" I trace the three volumes of *The Count of Monte Christo*, each with a dissimilar hardcover.

Luca's lips warm the side of my neck. "Good?"

Amazed, I glimpse at him over my shoulder. "Good?" I almost yell incredulously and point to the books. "*This* will get you laid."

He grins and kisses my cheek.

"Wait. It can't be coincidence that you just happened to get me the ones with the covers I didn't have yet."

"I checked to see which volumes you had. You told me the second time we met in the coffee shop that you purchase your favorite books with all the different covers, and you haven't completed your *Count of Monte Christo* collection yet."

I'm still riveted by my new additions, and Luca grants me this moment in solitude. Luca apologized and I'm not in the mood to fight, so I lean back against his chest.

His fingers trace the sensitive skin on the inside of my thighs. "Fuck, Fallon. Your skin feels peachy soft." He grunts appreciatively. "Your luscious body is playing tricks on me. You're consuming my thoughts. All. Day. And. Night."

I'm pleased I'm not the only one starting to feel that way. "Same goes for you."

He lets out a quiet laugh. "I have another gift for you," Luca whispers while still hugging me to him sitting in his lap. "You haven't noticed the envelope in the box underneath your books."

I clap my hands in eagerness before rummaging through the silver tissue paper until I've found a black envelope. Tearing it open, I take out tickets to *The Phantom of the Opera* on Broadway. I've always wanted to see that show on Broadway in New York. I frown when I see the date: my birthday, tomorrow. My eyes cut to Luca's. "Are we—"

"Go pack your bags. We're flying to New York to attend *The Phantom* matinee."

I shriek in delight and throw myself at Luca, peppering kisses all over his face.

***

The Phantom was two-and-a-half hours of sublime theater. Luca and I slept in the Grand Suite at the ideally-located Peninsula, and we have to check out at noon.

When I come out of the bathroom dressed in only my towel, he's on the phone in the living room. Music is playing, but as I step closer to him, I hear his words.

"Don't start. I'll take care of it tonight. No, I'll call you later," he replies in an authoritative tone to the person he's talking to.

I walk up to him and loop my arms around him. His anxiety edges off of him.

He hangs up and turns in my embrace. "Hmmm, your addictive scent... I was waiting for you. I don't like to be kept waiting," he mumbles into my neck.

"Well, that's how relationships work. Sometimes you wait. Better get used to it," I retort while lacing my fingers through his hair. My nails softly scrape his skin, making him growl in appreciation.

He lifts his head and looks down his nose to stare at me, shocked and amused. "Is that a challenge, Michaels?" he counters with a mischievous smile.

"Absolutely," I breathe.

"I love a good, feisty challenge," he says seductively.

I look up at him amiably when he strokes the inside of my thigh with the back of his forefinger and snatches the towel off of me, leaving me standing naked in front of him. A cold rush of air sweeps over my skin as I take in his dark expression. The darkness isn't fueled by lust. There's a menacing undertone on his handsome face. "Are you okay?" I search his eyes for some light.

He hugs my naked form and breathes me in. "I hate that this weekend with you has been interrupted by my work."

"Well, you don't have to be this upset and mad about it." I try a lighthearted tone.

The guitar intro music notes of 'Brown Eyed Girl' by Van Morrison start to play from the speakers.

"Do you have to leave now, or can we have dinner in New York tonight?" I sway my hips to the music as his hands trail down to my behind.

"No," he growls. "We can stay in New York for a couple more hours." Luca takes in another sharp breath.

Grabbing his hair, I pull back his head and softly sing along, meeting his eyes. *"Hey where did we go?"* I twirl around Luca. Standing behind him, I rake my nails over his chest, down his abs to the top of his khaki-brown slacks, smiling roguishly at him when he shoots me a sidelong glance.

He catches my hand and swivels me around to him. Luca clasps my left hand in his right while he holds me to him by my hip and joins my dance. His left hand slides up my side to stroke the underside of my breast with his thumb and then back down my hip. He leads me in our seductive dance, never missing a beat.

We sway together from left to right with smiles on our faces. Our dance has blown away the tension in his body. His intensity shattered by little me. I'd like to believe that I'm the only one that reaches him on this fundamental level. Luca's eyes lock with mine as he mouths along with the lyrics and dips me low. My mahogany locks touching the ground.

He kisses me hard and hungry and spins me facing away from him, pushing me against the glass window and pinning my hands above my head. A shudder resounds through me as my hands contact the cold glass, and he gazes at me in the window reflection. "Keep them there," he orders. My hips are pulled back slightly, and my back arches when Luca's fingertips glide down my spine. Palming my behind, he massages the swell of my ass in both hands. The heat radiating off of him is absorbed by my back as he leans in close to place a kiss between my shoulders. Going down into a kneeling position, he traces his nose down my back, stopping twice to leave a rough kiss in his wake. Luca bites both cheeks and releases a low growl before he starts licking me from front to back with the flat of his tongue. All the while his hands keep cupping my behind. "I want to hear you, Fallon." His throaty voice barely reaches my ears over the endnotes of 'Brown Eyed Girl.' His tongue traces my folds and the inside of my thighs, and then he sucks the bundle of nerves into his warm mouth. Finally, his tongue moves inside me, tasting my inner walls and making my muscles tighten in sweet anticipation. I close my eyes, thinking only of him on his knees.

Unfastening his pants and pushing down his boxer briefs, Luca picks me up by my legs – without turning me around - and his strong, warm hands hold my behind up easily. He shifts my body with my knees pushed up and holds it steady against the window as if I weigh nothing. "It's going to be hard and fast, Fallon," he groans and pushes into me in one hard thrust from behind, filling me completely, making us one.

My back curves more to take him in deep, and I spread my arms wide, palms flat against the window.

He whispers dirty words in Italian while he takes me hard. A low, rasping sound escapes him as he keeps up his punishing strokes until he spills inside me and then holds himself still, his lips grazing my shoulder, as our breathing regulates. As he pulls out slowly and places my feet back on the floor, he tightens a fist around my locks, forcing my stare forward. Then Luca takes my left hand and spreads his come around with our entangled fingers. "Rub it in, Fallon," he whispers against my temple in a hoarse tone while locking eyes with me in the window. His look is blazing with lust, love, and promise. Promise of how I'm his and he's mine.

"Now I have to shower again." An eager grin pulls at my lips, hinting for him to join me.

He scoops me up under my knees and saunters to the bathroom. "I'll clean you, my brown eyed girl."

In the bathroom, I'm seated on the shiny white counter - after he places a towel over it - and rub my hand over Luca's unshaven jaw before pulling his shirt over his head. Now we're both naked.

"I need to shave," he comments while rubbing his palm over the underside of his jaw.

"No, don't shave. Do you have a trimmer with you? I like the scruffy look on you."

He checks his carry-on and comes back with a trimmer in hand.

I tap my fingers on my lips and ask him, "Can I trim you?"

Uncertainty glimmers behind his eyes. "Okay… But I'll set the trimmer size and show you how to do it first."

My eyes round in enthusiasm that he'll let me do it. "Yes, yes. Show me."

He plugs the device in and lets it graze over his jaw to neatly shorten the hairs.

"That's so easy. Let me," I persuade and lift my hand to the trimmer.

Luca hands it over but doesn't release his hold. "Don't go too fast. Or too slow. Just be careful."

I refrain from rolling my eyes at him. "Mr. Control Freak, I won't kill you with a trimmer." I tug the device out of his hand and let it slide over his jaw, but it isn't shaving as effortlessly as when he did it. My brows furrow in concentration.

Luca's trying to contain a smirk.

"Don't move your lips," I warn and finish trimming quickly.

Luca checks his reflection in the mirror, smoothing his hand over his jawline. "Good work, Michaels." He wedges himself between my legs and places both hands on the counter on either side of me. "Are you happy with your gifts?" he asks softly.

"Of course I am." I rear back slightly to look up into his earnest face. "This isn't necessary to make me happy, though. Don't get me wrong. It's a wonderful gift." I look around. "But all I want is you. We have to enjoy the little things in life. The musical, this hotel, it's all great. But *this* is my happiness," I mutter as I reach up and place my hand over his heart and my other hand over mine. "Spending time with you makes me happy."

Luca's lips turn up and while usually his smile doesn't reach his eyes, this time it does. He folds me into the warmth of his arms, and I cross my ankles behind him before we step into the shower.

***

For the rest of the day, there's a restlessness in his behavior, so I ask him several times if we should leave in order for him to take care of his business, but he assures me he can handle it on Monday. Luca's attentive, but his mind is clearly somewhere else.

We eat Spanish tapas in a small dining room near our hotel, but at the restaurant, it becomes clear to me that he's even more troubled than I realized. As he makes a visit to the restroom, I start toward the glass case at the bar to inspect the desserts.

A man at the bar takes this as his cue to flirt with me. "Hello, pretty lady."

I barely acknowledge him with a faltering smile.

Yet, he continues. "Can I buy you a drink?" The guy is in his early thirties maybe. He has a distinctive scar above his right eyebrow that cuts through it, giving him a creepy look.

I glance at the restroom and quickly say, "I'm actually with someone. No, thank you."

His unnerving laugh washes over me.

Of course he saw I was with Luca because he must've seen our intimate pose at the table. Feeling uncomfortable, I head back to my table, but the guy grabs my arm - forcing me to turn - and then, just as suddenly, releases me. I'm startled, and before I have the chance to say something, Luca's standing beside me.

He looks me over quickly and takes a protective stance between me and the other guy. "Everything okay?" he asks me in a soft tone, however I sense the rage vibrating off of him. His customary cool façade falters, the darkness threatening to come out, which makes wonder if he usually masks his true nature from me.

"Y-Yes... I was just checking the desserts."

He rubs his hands up and down my arms to calm me. "Go to our table." His tone is gentle, yet demanding.

Still in a daze, I step back and sit down. Because I'm too curious to know what's happening, I turn and see the two men in a heated conversation. Luca towers over the guy, speaking to him in a hushed tone. The guy stands up on shaky legs, but Luca doesn't move an inch as the guy tries to step away and leaves. Luca rolls his neck and paces back to me.

"What just happened?" we simultaneously ask.

"I went to check the desserts. That guy offered me a drink. I said I was on a date, and when I walked away, he stopped me by the arm for a second right before you showed up. I was just startled. That's all. What did you say to him? Do you know him? He looked scared."

Luca relaxes a little. "I told him to never talk to you again. He should be happy I let him walk out of here. I came back and saw his hand on your arm." Luca gives me a disconsolate look.

I suddenly feel defensive. "I didn't do anything to encourage him to start flirting."

Luca sighs in exasperation. "I know."

I blow out a heavy breath while stillness surrounds us. "Maybe we should just go now?" I softly suggest. "We'll be a little early at the airport."

His eyes snap up to mine. "Don't you want dessert?"

"No, I would like to go home, Luca. You've been on edge all day." I stand up.

"Fallon, if you want to go, we will." Right after Luca settles the check, we head to the hotel to retrieve our carry-ons and continue to the airport.

I'm not sure where our weekend went from perfect bliss to annoyed frustration. Luca's preoccupied and something is obviously weighing heavily on his mind. I don't even want to know now. Ignorance is bliss.

**

We pick up his car where we left it at Chicago O'Hare and drive immediately back to my apartment. He stops the car at the front entrance of my condominium, so I guess he's not staying.

"Fallon, are you angry?" Luca asks me point blank.

"No, I'm not," I admit honestly. "I'm disappointed that you've been distracted today."

"I'm sorry that I've been unfocused. I have to be in Michigan for the entire week, and I won't see you again until Friday. I don't like that." Luca rests his hand on my thigh.

"Me either."

He cups my face and kisses me firmly. His tongue probing my mouth open, demanding me to let him in. "I'm planning to be with you the entire upcoming weekend," he whispers between kisses. "Call me whenever you want."

"I will. Thanks for a wonderful weekend and for my gifts." A smile overtakes my face.

"Good night, *dolcezza.*" He traces his nose down my cheek and throat, sending a delightful shiver down my spine.

I run my hand through his thick hair as he places one kiss on my collarbone. "Good night."

Luca doesn't leave until I'm inside my apartment. I turn on the light and move to the window to wave and watch as he drives away.

***

The following morning I'm awakened by a lovely incoming text message from him that makes my heart flutter.

Good morning, Fallon. 'There are two
ways of seeing: with the body and with the
soul. The body's sight can sometimes
forget, but the soul remembers forever.' -
your favorite: Alexandre Dumas

CHAPTER 16

Luca

Forty-one minutes flashes on the display of the treadmill. Adriano and I work-out together three times a week at The Blackhall gym. It's a fully-equipped gym, only accessed by the residents. I did talk the manager into getting Adriano a membership, even though he isn't a resident. In the morning it's usually quiet; most of my neighbors work out at night or not at all. A handful of people are also in the gym now.

Adriano wipes the sweat off his forehead with his towel as his sprint slows down beside me. "How was your weekend? I'm not used to talking to you only once an entire weekend."

"She took up all my time."

"Did Danny try to contact her again?"

"No. He only called her that one time in the coffee shop. She never returned his call." This has become much more than an assignment to retrieve information. "James wants me to focus on Leggia. The two other *Capi* have been ordered to find Danny asap."

"Luca, what now? We don't need her; she has nothing of importance. You think you can build a relationship with her? How many lies have you already told?" His voice lowers.

"There's a perfectly good reason why we agreed to not bring innocent outsiders into this."

"I can't back off anymore," I answer.

"You can. You choose not to."

I stop the treadmill and turn to Adriano. "What is it with Camilla that has you going back to her over and over again? She's the only constant in your life, beside me."

Adriano also stops and we step aside. "That's an entirely different situation."

I pull my towel over my neck as we head to the incline bench. "The circumstances are different; the situation is similar. Why do you need her? You fuck everything in sight with a skirt on. Do you really *need* to fuck Camilla too?"

"I do. I'm an asshole, and I can't stand it when one of the other men eye her. I want her to want me. She makes me... I don't know exactly what."

"Human?" I fill in.

"Yes."

"I'm starting to understand your twisted logic. I can't walk away anymore because I'm in too deep. I crave her presence after I leave our fucked up world at the end of the day. She's giving me back some of my humanity, but I'm also conflicted sometimes - conflicted between being Luca, her 'normal' boyfriend, and Luca, the underboss. How long can this go on? With her I can just be. Just be." I lay my white towel on the bench before lying on it.

Adriano sits on the shoulder press machine across from me but doesn't resume his work out.

I take the dumbbells off of the floor, arms hanging straight down, and raise them to shoulder height, the thumb sides of my hands facing up. After eight reps of the Y raise, I rest. "And there are more complications now."

He leans against the machine, waiting for me to elaborate.

"In New York, one of Leggia's men - I don't know his name - was either following me or her. I had a suspicion someone was tailing us, but I couldn't pinpoint anything unusual. The guy was good because until the next day - in the restaurant with Fallon before we left for the airport - I didn't notice anything peculiar. After visiting the restroom, I came out and he was chatting her up. I ran up to her so fast." It's been a long time since a situation panicked me, but I can only categorize my reaction as sheer panic when I saw a Mafia member talking to my girlfriend. Panic was quickly overridden by rage and an obsessive need to protect her. "He has a scar on his right eyebrow - find out who he is."

"I will do it today," Adriano confirms.

"He was taunting me, asking me to share the hot piece of ass. The moment Fallon went back to her seat, I threatened him to back off. I couldn't think straight, and I reacted too quickly, ruled by my anger. By threatening him, he now can report back that she's my soft spot. I put her in more danger."

Adriano agrees, "How did she react?"

"We had a disagreement. It irked me that she even talked to him."

Adriano laughs. "That girl's bringing out the jealous beast in you."

"Don't I know it." I stand back up. "I need her followed by one of us because I'm positive Leggia will be tracking her moves from now on, if only to rile me up."

"*We* can't do it this week. Do you want one of the soldiers to do it?" Adriano inquires.

"No, they'll ask too many questions. I'm not sure what - if anything - Leggia will do with the information that I have a girl. James doesn't know anything. Nobody knows except you, and I wanted to keep it that way." My lips thin in annoyance of the unknown.

"What did you tell her about this week?"

Adriano and I have business to take care of regarding settling deals in the east. "I told her I would be in Michigan all week."

Who could keep an eye on her for me?

"Let one of the associates you trust do it. What about that guy who also drives Camilla around when she buys the club inventory?" I ask.

"David? Yes, he's trustworthy."

"He's to safeguard her constantly, without her knowing and at all costs," I demand. "You done working out?"

"I was done after the treadmill." Adriano takes his towel in hand.

"Let's go."

CHAPTER 17

Luca

After a work week of missing Fallon and constantly worrying about whether anyone would harm her, I was thrilled to be home with her so that I could keep her safe myself. I'm crazed with desire for her, and tonight signifies an important change in our relationship; it's the night I realize I've fallen in love with her.

While I'm cleaning up the mess in *her* house, she's nagging me to leave the dishes and come sit with her on the couch. She's eager to tell me some news, but I keep on clearing the dining room table. She grabs a pillow from next to her on the couch and throws it at me.

"Fallon," I warn without looking at her.

She throws another pillow at me, but I duck and then calmly place the plate in my hand back on the table. Fallon gets up quickly and bolts to the bedroom, almost tripping in the hall while she grabs the doorframe to turn toward her room. I'm right behind her and just as she enters the bedroom, I catch her waist from behind, laughing freely.

"Luca," she speaks quietly, out of breath. "I've never heard this unrestrained laugh from you before."

She's right, I feel free and uninhibited because of her. Slipping my hands down to the waistband of her skirt, I let my palm stroke her stomach, sidling up to touch the heavy curve of her breasts. My other hand is crawling up to palm her throat, and I lightly trace her ear with my lips. "Fallon, you can run, but you can never hide from me." My fingers dig into her soft breast, and our hips are crushing into each other as our breathing increases. I walk her forward to the bed. "What did you want to tell me?"

She lets out the sexiest gratified moan. "I got a promotion. You're touching the breasts of the Head Copywriter now."

I smile against her ear. "That's fantastic and well-deserved. Your writing is remarkable. I'm glad they acknowledge that." I reach down and push her skirt and panties off all together. Then I speedily strip her shirt and bra because I want her naked right now.

She turns around to unfasten my pants while I grab the back of my shirt to pull it over my head. Her nails rake up and down my taut muscles. I love her soft hands always exploring me.

I hiss and stop her eager movement by taking her wrists in my hands. If she doesn't stop, I'll blow before I'm inside her. "This is about you tonight, Fallon."

She shakes off my hands, and I allow her to turn us around and push me to the mattress. I'm rock-hard looking up at the shape of her sexy body and flawless, glowing skin and stroke myself twice to tempt her.

She wets her lips and flicks her thumbs over her rosy nipples. "This is about *us*." She pouts her lips, and all I can think about is having those beautiful lips wrapped around me.

I growl when I lunge forward eagerly to touch her. "Then we're tasting each other. Get on here," I order and point to my face while scooting back on the bed until my head lies on the pillow.

With fluent elegance like only she can move, she starts to crawl over me and her center is pushed on my face.

Fucking sweet.

She moans and throws her head back when I firmly cup her ass and trace my tongue everywhere between her thighs, because I missed her taste. My left hand crawls up to wrap around the tips of her hair, and I pull her head back slightly, letting her arch more into my mouth. I continue to pull and release her hair, adding more pressure with my tongue every time because I want to hear her moan louder.

My raging hard-on is flexing against my stomach. She strokes me up and down and leans forward to take me into her luscious mouth. I release a low groan when she starts to circle the head with her tongue and takes me in all the way to the back of her throat while grinding on my face.

I press my thumbs to her sensitive spot as she's squirms above me, so I squeeze her bottom firmer, rubbing harder, and plunge my tongue in. Fallon circles her hips on my face, and I can tell by the volume of her moans that she's going to come soon. Her head bobs up and down fiercely as my balls tighten. Tasting her while I come into her wet mouth, I feel her inner walls contracting and suck harder when her violent shudders pull me into a soul-wrenching climax.

She moans noisily. My little screamer. Fallon swallows and groans loudly, her unguarded sexual drive linking me even more to her.

I leave a kiss on her center. "I love it when you swallow," I inform her in a possessive tone.

She sits down on the bed, facing me. "I know," she throws back sweetly with a dreamy look about her.

"I came so hard, and I'm still fucking hard for you," I let her know in a hoarse voice and sit up to close the distance between our bodies.

She wraps her fingers around my hard-on. In this intimate moment where we share so much through our eyes without speaking our thoughts, she wants to tell me how much I mean to her. Her emotions are written all over her beautiful face. My indulgent eyes encourage her, but something holds her back, and she hesitates.

I sink my hand into her hair. On rare occasions, I have true contentment in my smile. Usually my mood is blackened by a dark nuance I know she can't decipher, but in this moment, the tinge is blocked out by pure ecstasy. I share my true gratified smile with her and sit back against the headboard, coaxing her to straddle me.

"I love you," she mentions the three words I've wanted to hear as she slides down easily.

I bring her forward, her lips hovering an inch from mine. *"Ti amo."* I love you. Her hair curtains around us, and I warmly caress the strands out of her face and trace the back of my hand down her cheek, over her pink lips.

Fallon places both of her hands on my chest. My eyes penetrating tantalizingly deep into hers, lost in a world where only she and I exist.

I nuzzle her neck – loving the smoothness of her skin against my lips - up her jawline, and caringly rub our noses together while I absorb her sweet ambrosia scent. I long for the softness of her hipbone beneath my palms when she starts to move extremely slowly.

All I want is her, every day, every night. *"Ti amo solo tu, dolcezza."* I love only you. I bite her lower lip and suck it into my mouth.

As she starts to round her hips, we groan together. I've come to crave her body and her taste. I kiss her firmly and trail down to suck on her throat.

Her head falls back when both my hands dig into her, and I move her back and forth to ride me. I need to see her face as she comes. I need her to see only me as she comes, so I palm the back of her head and force Fallon to look at me. "Stay with me," I command in a voice thick with lust.

We come together passionately, never breaking our stare.

I need to be more careful to keep her safe from the Syndicate. I am not about to give her up.

CHAPTER 18

Fallon

The wet and wild season of spring turns into an unprecedented hot and humid summer. Luca and I have become even closer the last couple of weeks. After the Gina altercation, nothing out of the ordinary has happened, and the seeds of mistrust have been quelled. Luca has been spending a lot of time at my place. We decide to spend a weekend at a cottage in Lake Forest. Unfortunately, my parents are on vacation again so we won't be able to visit them.

I wear a thin, short white strapless dress, but Luca has the air-conditioning on the coldest setting so my nipples are rock hard in the car, even though it's hot outside. "I'm cold." I point to my nipples, making sure he notices my sideways grin.

Luca glances at me, then back at the road, then whips his eyes back to my chest area. "You have no idea how much I've fallen in love with you. Every day you obsess me a little more."

I affectionately shove his cheek to force his gaze back on the road.

He smirks as his right hand cups my left breast underneath the dress, and he groans. "It makes me hard in a split second when you don't wear a bra." Luca grazes his fingertips over my nipple.

I moan when his touch heats my skin, but I push Luca's hand out and pull my dress back up to properly cover my breast so that he can concentrate on the road.

We manage to arrive at the lake without any accidents. During the summer, the lake is swamped with people and today is no exception. Even finding a vacant parking space seems to take forever.

I want to find a place in the shade, so we walk to a more secluded area and locate a spot under a tree only fifteen feet from the water. After I lay out our towels, I remove my dress to reveal my bikini underneath and Luca removes his shirt. His taut body glistens in the sunlight. I move my pilot glasses on top of my head to soak in the sight of him. Through his sunglasses, I see his gaze is also trained on me.

His lips twitch up as he lies down on the towel and takes me with him. Removing the sunscreen from the bag, he starts to rub it on my stomach, arms, and legs. "Turn over." Luca rubs an excessive amount on the insides of my thighs and swell of my behind. "You want to come, Fallon?"

My head snaps up. "People are going to see." I look around suspiciously, but nobody is within a few feet of us.

"No, relax. I'm blocking you with my body. I would never allow anyone to see you come." A shudder sparkles through me as he meets my eyes, and I wonder whether that was a threat or a promise. Luca massages down my back and his hand disappears in my bikini bottoms.

Luca groans when his middle finger trails down my behind and between my legs, rubbing softly in a circular motion for minutes before he pushes in two fingers.

"Shh." When I start to moan, he smothers my cry with a kiss until my peak subsides.

Satisfied, I keep my eyes closed and enter dreamland.

When I wake, the sun is hanging low in the pale blue sky and Luca's not lying next to me. Rubbing my eyes, I stand up to search for him and check my phone. I've been asleep for almost an hour, and it's less crowded now. I scan the lake from left to right but can't see Luca.

Searching for my water in my bag, I groan from thirst when I can't find it. The bottle must've fallen out. My mood turns cheerful, however, when I do find the car keys in the bag, so I pack my towel and head for the parking lot.

I choose a different path through the opulent green trees to walk back to the car. It's eerily silent at this part of the lake around this time. I hear a rustling behind me and have the distinct feeling someone is watching me. As I turn around quickly, I see nothing out of the ordinary, but I can't shake the feeling someone is trailing behind me. I pick up my pace and search for my phone in my bag to call Luca. Of course, my phone has fallen out of its compartment. My rummaging is becoming increasingly frantic because unidentified noises are closing in on me. At the bottom of my bag, my hands finally touch the smooth surface of my phone. I'm relieved to find it and press to call Luca.

Thankfully, he answers on the first ring. "Fallon."

"Where are you?" I hiss.

"We forgot our drinks. I went back to the car, but I can't find my car keys—"

"They're in my bag. I've got them." I hear the crunching of branches behind me. I look sideways. Nothing.

"What's wrong?" Luca asks, concerned.

"I'm heading back to the car to get a drink. I'm walking through the trees, and I hear noises behind me." The unease in my stomach is growing.

"Where are you?" he barks. "Why didn't you stay put?"

"I don't know how to explain where I am." Fallen branches obstruct a clear view of the pathway. I'm confused about which way to head.

"Fallon, from where we were lying, did you head left or right toward the trees?"

"Uhm…." The rustling is coming closer, igniting my anxiety, and I pick up my pace.

"Fallon!" I hear Luca screaming from the phone dangling in my hand beside my hip as my legs race toward the parking lot. "Motherfucker!"

I'm still unsure which way to run. I swirl my head around and spot some vague movement in the distance.

"Fallon, answer me, now. Answer me!" Luca shouts.

I recognize three entwined trees on the left and remember that way leads to the lot. I bring the phone back up to my ear. "I'm almost at the lot." I'm dripping in anxious sweat, mixed with the heat of summer.

"Where? And don't you dare hang up on me or stop talking!" he orders loudly.

I flinch from his harsh tone of voice. "From the left of the parking lot where we parked."

I turn to the left and then straight ahead. Breathing heavily, I spot a parked silver SUV far ahead: the parking area. I keep walking hurriedly, my focus ahead on reaching the lot.

"I see you, Fallon. Keep coming toward me." I recognize Luca's silhouette stepping in front of the silver car. He seems so small, so far away, but Luca is an excellent sprinter and reaches me quickly.

He takes me into his arms and places my phone in his pocket as he holds me tightly. "You're safe, *dolcezza*. You're fine. You're fine," he keeps repeating more to himself than to me. Luca pushes me away, holding me at arm's length, giving me a once over. "Are you hurt?"

I shake my head, trying to catch my breath. "That was such a scare." I hold up my trembling hand for him to see, and I let out a weak laugh when I realize that I probably overreacted. "I just had this eerie feeling someone was watching me."

Luca's eyes narrow as he stares behind me and pulls me back into the protection of his embrace.

We're both breathing heavily, our chests heaving in relief.

"Come, *dolcezza.*" Luca takes my bag and slings it over his shoulder, tucking me into his side and guiding us to his car.

I crane my neck to look back.

"Don't, Fallon," Luca orders and holds me tightly, his voice trembling. He must've been scared too.

"Nothing happened; I'm okay." I try to ease him and caress his stubble-covered jaw as he tightly closes his eyes.

CHAPTER 19

Luca

I lie awake at two a.m. with Fallon in my arms and my eyes trained to spit fire at the ceiling. She's draped over me, her head resting on my chest. Hugging her securely to me, I push my lips in her hair.

My heartbeat accelerates thinking about this afternoon. I should've been more careful. She was having a peaceful sleep at the lake, and people were around us. She was supposed to be safe. I ran to the car and forgot my keys, and then she called me saying the words I've been dreading to hear. I'm fuming that she walked via an isolated path. She needs to be more aware of her surroundings. I've told her this before.

I ease out from under her, and she stirs and turns on her other side to continue her deep sleep. I drive my hands through my ruffled hair and get up from the bed as soundlessly as possible and head to the chair where my clothes are folded in a pile. Taking my disposable phone from my pants pocket, I read Adriano's text message.

Damian has him. At the warehouse within 10 min. You coming?

I'm coming now. Do not touch him.

While I'm dressing, my gaze is set on Fallon lying on the bed. She has pulled me in deeper than I ever thought possible. Buttoning my pants, I search for my gun out of habit before I remember I've stashed it in the car; I can't risk her discovering my handgun. I drop on the chair to watch her sleep some more. The rise and fall of her chest has a calming effect on me. The last month I've been putting in a lot of effort to gain her trust and not have her exposed to anything Syndicate-related. That has given us a chance to build a relationship. I've been delegating more work to my *Capi* in order to have free time with Fallon. But this Leggia business will force me away from her for the next couple of weeks. James and I need to know what Leggia is up to, and it's my primary duty as the underboss to find that out as soon as possible.

She's fine, but for how long?

I will do anything to keep her. I'm prepared to do anything to protect her.

Earlier, I texted Adriano to come to Lake Forest with Damian. They were at the house, which is not far from here. Like Lake Forest, the house is also situated up north, bordering the suburbs. Adriano was to drop everything to find the man that frightened Fallon. It must have been one of Leggia's men. The spy we have in the Leggia Syndicate - one of my *Capo's* soldiers - was ordered to find out which of Leggia's soldiers was assigned to Lake Forest today. Adriano had confirmation on whom and his whereabouts within three hours.

Fallon wasn't followed the week I was in Michigan. My man was watching her around the clock that week. Leggia's sending me a message by having his soldier following her when she's with me - first in New York and now here. Although I'm not sure what the message is, yet.

She's usually a deep sleeper; I hope she doesn't wake during the night. If she does, then I'll cross that bridge when it happens.

I take one set of keys that hang next to the front door and sneak quietly out of the wooden cottage.

***

Within fifteen minutes, I'm at my destination. Adriano and Damian are already present.

Damian lets me in. "First room. Ramón Vasquez."

I immediately make my way to the first concrete-floor room on the right. Adriano sits on a chair beside a square wooden table and a sink on my left, smoking his cigarette. The hideous orange paint on the walls is peeling off. Dangling on a hook – on a steel bar that hangs from left to right in the back of the small six by five room - with his wrists tied together is the man I was looking for: Ramón Vasquez. The man who was also watching us in New York. The man with the scar through his right brow. His feet hover an inch from the ground.

I commend Adriano with a swift nod for catching him this fast. "Well, well. Ramón, I distinctly remember telling you what would happen if you were in close proximity to my woman again." I stand before him with my hands folded behind me for a long minute while his harsh breathing fills the room. I can see a will to fight in him, even though his body is hurting and his face is beet red from his painful position.

"I-I was hoping to get into Fallon's sweet little pussy," he tries to taunt me but stutters.

A layer of sweat gathers on my forehead from reigning in my fury.

Adriano lets out a laugh at Ramón's attempt to still act tough and hints his cigarette toward the tools he has set out on the table: a hammer and a crimper.

Next to the crimper is a folded, sheer plastic hospital gown which I throw on to prevent staining my clothes. I grab the medium size hammer from the table and wrap my fingers tightly around the handle. "You just signed your death warrant, Ramón." I was already wound up from this afternoon, and he threw fuel on the fire by speaking about her like that.

Ramón's eyes extend in fear. "No, no. I was kidding. I was only hired to follow her, nothing more. I'm sorry."

I close my eyes and roll my neck. When I open them again, I can't hold back. "Too little." I bring the hammer up slowly to make him aware of how far he's pushed me, and then I smash it down on his right knee. "Too late."

I hear the crunch of Ramon's bone breaking as his body bangs against the wall and his earsplitting screams dance around the room.

Throwing the hammer on the floor, I drive my fist into his nose, over and over, pouring my entire wrath into my hits. The blows splinter through my knuckles, and I relish it. His blood scatters on my face, and his head smashes against the wall behind him as it slouches back from my fists. Son of a bitch thinks he can scare Fallon. "Nobody threatens Fallon. Look. At. Me." I fist his hair roughly.

Ramón's eyes focus on me, blood trickling from his nose and mouth. Suddenly, I smell urine and look down to see him soiling himself.

"Don't you wish you knew when to shut the fuck up instead of taunting people when *you* are the one tied up?" I bang his head against the wall and bring the hammer back up to prepare for another blow to his knee. "Have you had enough?" I spit through my tense breathing.

"Pl-please….stop," he stammers pathetically.

My arm falls down beside my body when I look at his battered face, and I decide that it's enough. I toss the hammer into the sink – out of breath - turn on the faucet and clean it, then my face. Removing the plastic gown, I check to ensure I'm clean of any blood. "Am I spotless?" I ask Adriano to check my face.

He scans me up and down. "Yes."

"Come," I order.

Adriano accompanies me to my car. "Leave him hanging there until morning. Then burn his body. Let Leggia wonder what happened to Ramón."

"Harsh," Adriano mutters.

My head shoots to him in annoyance. "He came too close to her, Adriano."

He sighs. "I know. But, Luca, I've never once seen you lose control. Tonight came fairly close."

I brace my neck, trying to ease the tension out. "I don't know how to keep her safe without eliminating all the threats."

Adriano changes the subject. "Where's James by the way? I haven't seen him in two weeks."

"James is too busy with organizing everything behind the scenes for our business in the east. He and Salvatore have to set up the financial routes. *I* even barely speak to him, which currently suits me fine. I don't know how long I can keep him in the dark about Fallon." I open my car door. "I have to get back before she wakes up."

***

The cottage is still dark, and Fallon hasn't called me. In total, I've been gone forty minutes. Slipping back into the house, I step out of my clothes in the hall and open the bedroom door. She's sleeping in the exact same position as when I left her. I fold my clothes and leave them on the chair as they were before and step into the bathroom to check one more time for any blood remnants.

I slide in behind her warm body, and her hair tickles my nose. She's only wearing panties, nothing else. I sift my hands over her soft skin, a little too roughly in my still decreasing furious state. Her fragrance evaporates my demons of this night.

Fallon rouses, curls into me, and throws her leg over my hip to push her core over my boxer briefs.

I feel and smell her arousal, and I harden instantly.

Her eyes flutter open. "I'll be quiet," she promises in a sugary sweet tone that makes it impossible for me to deny her.

Sliding my hands over her hips, I pull down her panties to take them off. I trail my fingers back up the inside of her thigh and hook her leg higher over my hip as I glide my lips over her cheeks while she moans softly.

I probe between her legs, circling her wetness with two fingers.

She pushes down my boxers and strokes me with her addictive touch.

I pull her closer by the leg hooked over me and rub my hard-on over her wetness. Then I drive inside her in one hard thrust, swallowing her soft cry with a kiss. Her head rests on my extended arm on the pillow, and I cup it to push her into my kiss. The other hand grips her ass and pulls her into me to fuck her hard.

"Luca," she groans.

My eyes close. Visions of Jack, Ramón, and the first associate I ever killed invade my head. I shake my head to lose the thoughts as I respire my actions of tonight, my exertion of our fucking, and my love for her into the hollow of her neck while driving myself into her sweet and tight body.

"Luca. Luca." Fallon's hands rest on my chest. "Luca, where are you?"

I keep my thrusts brutal with eyes secured shut.

I won't give her up. I need to protect her.

Her hands aren't resting on my chest anymore. Now she's pushing me away.

"Luca," she whisper shouts. "Stop it." Two warm hands cover my cheeks. "Open your eyes. Come back to me."

Her soft voice breaks my trance. My eyes open and I meet her worried ones. I still immediately, blinking and burying my head into her cleavage as I pull out of her.

Fallon hugs my neck. "Where did you go, Luca? Come back to me."

"I'm back," I assure her and look into her eyes as I brush her hair away with my fingertips.

"What happened?" Her look is earnest with concern. "You were a million miles away."

"I'm scared of losing you, *dolcezza*." Partly the truth.

"I'm fine." She takes my hand and holds it over her heart. "I'm fine. We had a scare today, I didn't know it bothered you that much. You should've talked to me." Her fingers trail down the side of my face.

"Ti amo così tanto." I love you so much. I press my lips into her hand. "It scared the fuck out of me."

"Me too, initially. I love you too. We're together and I'm fine, and that's what I keep reminding myself." She pauses in thought. "Is something else going on?"

I can't tell her how I handled her stalker. "I'll keep reminding myself of that too from now on. Let's sleep."

My actions of earlier are another vision added to the nightmares that haunt me. Only my nightmares not only haunt me by night, but also by day.

She's in danger by association with me now. I should've stayed away from her.

We keep our position, our bodies intertwined, trying to fall asleep.

CHAPTER 20

Fallon

A shift in our relationship follows. The days Luca leaves it's becoming ever more problematic to reach him. He doesn't answer his phone or it takes hours for him to return my calls, and his absentmindedness alarms me once in a while. He has woven a carefully crafted façade of quiet confidence; one that's always preserved except for the few times I catch him unguarded. In those moments I wonder if I'm enough for him. Maybe he's becoming bored with me? But then he manages to make tender love to me that restores my faith in our relationship.

Until I catch him in lie after lie. Until I realize that our slight altercations when we first met were signs I should've never ignored. Until I realize I never knew him at all.

***

Saturday morning, I'm warming up to go running. I choose seven a.m. or else it will be too hot in the blistering heat of summer. Luca's away for business this weekend.

Instead of my standard route, I'm being spontaneous and take another one. With my earbuds in and my bottle of water in hand, I start jogging to the park. The park is fairly busy, so I run to a more secluded area and pass by several churches where I decide to take a break. Out of breath, I cool down a little and take a drink of my water as sweat trickles down my spine. Churchgoers are exiting the church across the street and the church bells are ringing loudly, announcing the end of the service. I'm jumping up and down slowly in my spot and halt promptly when I see a familiar face coming down the church steps. I remove my earbuds and quickly hide behind a tree before Luca has a chance to see me. He's supposed to be out of town. My nails dig into my damp palms.

Luca steps aside to let the other people stream out and puts his sunglasses on. A priest walks up to him. He kisses the priest on the cheek and says something in his ear all the while gripping the priest's head. Luca's right hand slides into his jacket pocket.

Is he gritting his teeth?

Luca steps back and raises his brows, waiting for an answer. The priest nods and leaves hurriedly, obviously upset. Luca then scans the street and steadily heads to his car.

Like a stalker, I follow his every move until he drives away. As he turns and drives by the tree I'm hiding behind, I round it so my position isn't discovered and watch his taillights disappear. I'm lightheaded from all the thoughts raging inside me.

What is he doing in a church with a priest? Is this the first time he lied about a business trip?

I'm still perspiring, not from my run but from the shock of catching him. It takes me well over thirty minutes before I'm standing at my front door – feeling numb. The unknown is hitting me hard.

Once inside, I become angry and call Teagan. Dazed, I seat myself at the kitchen table.

"Babe, I was asleep. This better be good," Teagan answers in a sleepy voice.

I'm silent.

"Fall? Are you there?" she asks, louder now.

"Yeah. I'm here." Why was she sleeping? It's midday in London. "Isn't it the middle of the day there?"

"Yes, but I'm lazy. Fall, what's wrong?"

"Oh, I'm not sure." The first tears are falling.

"Sweetie, what happened? Are you crying? Are you okay? Are you home?" Typical Teagan, firing questions at me all at once.

Her worry envelops me in a warm hold, making me feel loved. "Yes, I'm home. I'm fine physically. I caught Luca twenty minutes from here at a church, when he's supposedly out of town."

"Um… You caught him? You mean with another woman?" Teagan probes.

"No, not with a woman. I caught him in a lie. He's supposed to be on a business conference out of town since yesterday, but I just saw him, this morning, here in town." I can't even wrap my mind around it yet.

"That's weird. He told you he would be away for the weekend? What did you see exactly?"

"Yes," I retort, exhaling tersely. "I was so shocked at seeing him. It blindsided me. I couldn't confront him right there. And now I'm pissed at myself because I should've put him on the spot then and there. I was running and saw him exiting the church. He talked to a priest. They had - what appeared to be - an intense conversation and then he left."

"I don't know. Maybe there is a perfectly good explanation. Is he religious? What was he doing at the church?"

"As far as I know, he isn't religious. And why would he keep that from me? If he was, I wouldn't mind." I play with the edges of a paperback lying on the table.

"True."

My anger is not dissipating but increasing. "I thought about calling him now to check and see if he would lie about his whereabouts."

"Do that," she agrees.

"I wanted to talk to you first before my anger took over. First, I'm going to shower, then I'm calling him."

"Okay, let me know what he says."

"Go back to sleep, babe. Sorry for waking you."

"Don't," she warns. "You can call me any time. Look, I don't know him, but from what you've told me, he really loves you."

I make a noncommittal sound of disapproval and palm my forehead to lessen the pain of my headache. "I have no idea what's going on. I need to talk to him. I'll talk to you later. Night."

"Night."

Not a minute later, after just staring ahead, I hear my phone ring: Luca. I take a deep breath to compose myself. "Hi."

"*Dolcezza*, what are you doing?"

He's still in his car. I recognize the background noise. "I was just about to jump into the shower. Why?" My lip quivers, but I sound calm.

"I have a surprise for you," he declares.

"Okay…"

"I'm back already."

Interesting. "In town?" I'm not divulging that I caught him yet.

"Yes, I was actually close-by you to drop something off. I grabbed a quick bite, and now I'm on my way to you. I missed you."

I release a sigh, both pleased and displeased. The insecurity and distrust have taken root in my mind. Why did he have a heated tête-à-tête with a priest? Luca's dark mood is for once emulated by me. If I confront him now, I'm positive he won't be completely honest. My gut instinct is telling me to store this for later, to not let him know I saw him at the church. Let him think I'm none the wiser. My mind is screaming at me that he's telling a half-truth. My heart is shouting to believe him. I hate myself for my overruling thought. Everything is clouded by my thought of how much I love this guy. Feeling confused and distrustful, I realize I don't want to see him now. "Luca, I already had plans for today. After my shower, I'm leaving."

He's disconcertingly silent, letting on he's surprised by my reaction. "Will you be gone the entire day?"

"Probably."

Luca's considering his reply. After another silence, he asks in a severe manner, "What do you have planned?"

Not having any plans, I utter the first thing that comes to mind that could be remotely true. "Jason."

"Jason?" he repeats and waits for me to elaborate.

"I'm going to a new book store. Jason, my colleague, offered to accompany me." Nervousness fills my stomach because of another awkward silence that ensues. Desperate to be alone with my thoughts, I continue. "I have to shower and leave. We'll talk tonight?"

"Fallon." There's a desolate tremble in his voice.

"Let's talk later, okay?" I persist and end our conversation. I rear back in my seat and gaze up at the ceiling. An unnerving feeling cuts through me. I bite my bottom lip in frustration before heading toward the shower.

I stand under the scorching heat of my showerhead for a long time, letting the water cascade down on me, hoping it will cleanse these overwhelming emotions of wariness. Stepping out of the shower, I'm not feeling any better and shriek when I enter my room after drying off.

Luca is sitting on my bed with his elbows resting on his knees, hands folded together, looking down. His gaze snaps up when I shriek.

I clutch my chest. "You have got to stop scaring me like that." I blow an irritated breath through my lips.

He doesn't talk.

I'm completely naked. Hesitantly, I go to him. We both know something is wrong. Is he lying, or am I misjudging the entire situation and ruining our love?

Luca palms the back of my thighs to pull me closer to him and leans his cheek against my abdomen. I lace my fingers through his hair as he draws in a long, tormented breath and rubs his stubble-covered cheek against the soft flesh of my stomach. "What's going on, Fallon?" Luca asks in that desolate tone.

"You tell me," I counter.

Hands on my thighs stiffen momentarily, and he looks up into my eyes as his eyes narrow in suspicion. *"Cosa intendi dire?"* What do you mean?

When Luca's pissed or passionate, he has the tendency to switch to Italian. My brows crease at his defensive tone and obvious discontented physical reaction. Normally, he's a master at hiding those reactions.

I stay quiet, and he sighs in defeat. "I have to leave again tonight. I came to spend time with you, and you're angry for some reason. *Perciò dimmi, cosa c'è che non va?"* So, tell me, what's wrong?

I step away from him, and he tries to hold on, but I pry his hands off of me. I put on my panties and bra and unleash my disgruntlement on him. "How come it's difficult to reach you when you're away? When we first started dating, you were always available, or at least you had the decency to text me when you'd call back."

He's stunned by my question. "That's what this is about? I have businesses, Fallon. Sometimes I'm in meetings where it would be rude for me to text. But if that bothers you, I will from now on," he says with guarded gentleness.

I'm pacing in front of him. When we first met, there were several occasions where I questioned Luca's honesty. I found it vague that he isn't on Facebook. I found it vague when Gina was at his place and the way he and Adriano reacted. The business trips he goes on are suspicious. That voice of doubt is yelling at me to open my eyes.

Ask your question.

I try to encourage myself and meet his eyes. "Is there something else you're not telling me?"

He stands up in one quick move and grips my face in both hands. *"Ti amo. Esisti solo tu per me."* I love you. You're the only one for me. "You're my pleasure, my sanity, my calmness, my home. My positive counterpart in every negative characteristic I own."

"Then why do I have this distressing feeling that you're always holding back?"

He rests his forehead against mine. "It hurts me when you're hurting." Luca negates my comment. "How do I make that feeling disappear?"

"I don't know," I reveal honestly and take a step back to disentangle us. Utterly confused about this situation, I decide I need to be alone so I continue with my lie. "I have to dress and go." I deter my gaze.

Concern takes over his expression when he sees me shutting him out. "Do you want me to leave?"

"Yes," I answer evenly.

He stops me by the arm as I make my way to my closet but doesn't say anything. The hurt in his eyes grips at my heart. Only that hurt is swiftly replaced by his mask, his controlled concealment of emotions restored. And it's this change in him that has me petrified something bigger is going on here, so I turn around to my closet.

Luca stands there for several minutes staring at my back, and then he leaves after quietly closing the door.

***

I stay home alone the entire day, coming to the conclusion
that I have nothing substantial to base my suspicion on. Luca
doesn't call or text. Maybe, just maybe, he's telling the truth?
My first mistake is that I chose to believe him. Time and time
again, I chose to believe him. I appeal to my common sense and
call him that night. He answers on the first ring, and I ask him to
come home. Within an hour, Luca's at my apartment. He uses
the key I gave him days ago for the first time to enter 'our'
apartment. Most of our time is spent in my apartment; it feels
like ours now.

I'm half asleep in bed, lying on my stomach when Luca
returns home and flips me over caringly. His shirt is already off.
He unfastens his pants and slides into bed next to me in his boxer
briefs, facing me. I tentatively touch his troubled face, his skin is
ice cold while it's been a warm day. The temperature must've
plummeted. I hold open my embrace as a peace offering, and he
buries his face in my neck and, as always, inhales my scent to
calm him down while entangling our legs.

"I'm sorry," I mumble.

"You don't have to be," he replies agonizingly soft. "I love
you so much." His arms around me tighten to press our bodies
closer together as if we're one, and we drift off to sleep in this
embrace.

I wake a few hours later needing to use the bathroom and untangle myself from his grip. As I return to the bed, I pick up Luca's discarded clothes from the floor to throw them in the laundry basket behind the door. The collar of his white shirt is covered in red-brownish blotches. My eyes widen as understanding dawns on me that his shirt is stained with blood. Not a good sign.

Luca stirs and sees me with his shirt in my hand.

I sit down on the bed next to him and show him the stains. "What's this?"

He avoids my eyes and answers in a sleepy voice. "Nothing, Fallon."

"Luca, did you fight tonight?" I cover his hand with mine in reassurance that I wouldn't be mad. However, I do want to know why there's blood on his clothes.

"I was upset and some guy was goading me," he admits with a sorrowful look.

"Oh Luca, I'm sorry you were so upset about us. I shouldn't have left things unresolved. Are you hurt?" I ease back in the crook of his arm and rest my left hand on his chest. My first reaction of concern is swiftly replaced with more doubt.

He's lying.

He holds me, his hand caressing up and down my left arm, and kisses me on the top of my head. "I'm fine now that I'm with you again. *Tu sei il mio mondo.*" You're my world.

"Weren't you supposed to leave town again tonight?" I ask, not letting on that I think he's lying to me.

"Yes, but I need to stay with you more, *dolcezza*." He comforts me, and we fall asleep, holding tightly onto each other.

CHAPTER 21

Luca

Her breathing evens out, her grip on me loosens. She's asleep. Today was a close call. My hand traces patterns across her bare shoulders.

The priest is Leggia's priest, Father Eli. I had to pay a visit to Father Eli today and then travel east to meet James. Leggia is a religious man that goes to confession. I need to discover more about him because the moment will come when he tries to blackmail me with Fallon. He has started to play a game with me, and she is his leverage. Father Eli is easily pressured with money and his love for young men, which he desperately wants to keep hidden from his wife and the community, but my *Capo*, Adriano, can find out the dirtiest of secrets.

I told her I would be gone for the weekend. I went to confession with Father Eli and gave him an ultimatum: get valuable information on Leggia - information he doesn't want anyone to know that will hurt him, or I will expose the photos I have in my possession of Eli in compromising positions with several extremely young men.

I was supposed to visit the priest and then be on my way to James, but I spotted Fallon immediately when I left the church. I'm trained to notice everything unusual. Someone staring at me and retreating behind a tree quickly is clearly unusual. I wore my sunglasses to prevent her from seeing the alarm in my eyes. Damage control was needed, but first things first. Father Eli hurried down the steps after sending me away without accepting my offer. They always tell me to fuck off first, and then run after me with their tail between their legs. Eli couldn't take the risk of me exposing him. My gun was in the inner pocket of my suit jacket, and I aimed it at Father Eli, giving him two weeks to report back.

When he left, I got in the car. I needed to think about how to handle Fallon because this was bad. She's become progressively distrustful lately. My first plan was to tell the truth, well, part of it. I was expecting for her to demand an explanation. When she didn't mention that she caught me, I was unnerved and only left because I was thrown off by her secretive behavior. The fact that she didn't tell me means she's growing even more distrustful. My anxiety doubled in her dismissal of me.

I contacted James and told him that I couldn't make it tonight, but he was too busy to ask why. I met up with Adriano, who was having trouble with an associate. I must be more careful because I never noticed the bloodstains - of the associate Adriano and I fought with - on my shirt.

Even though I'm marginally reassured and glad Fallon called me, her behavior is a sign that it's only a matter of time before she finds out who I really am.

I could've stayed away. I didn't do it then, and I'm in too deep to even consider it as an option anymore. Although, it was never *really* an option.

Leggia has me on edge constantly. This dispute he has with our Syndicate is eating into my time with Fallon and has interfered with the relaxed life I've built with her, and that's making me hostile. I need some space to cope with Syndicate business.

CHAPTER 22

Fallon

Another shift has occurred in our relationship. After the first time I confronted him with his dubious behavior in my room, Luca has been distancing himself from me for days. I feel it in the coldness of his kisses. I feel his unfriendliness when he comes home. He's with me physically, but mentally he's worlds away. Somewhere I can't reach him. No matter how hard I fight, he's slowly drifting away from me. I catch glimpses of him when we're making love, but those fleeting moments aren't enough to sustain this relationship. On the other hand, those fleeting moments are constantly pushing me to keep fighting for us, even though I know something is wrong - something he isn't sharing with me.

I ask Luca to join me for lunch on a random Wednesday. He's reluctant to accept my invitation, but my irritation at his refusal persuades him to meet me at the deli.

When I step into the deli, Luca's already waiting impatiently. "I don't have much time, Fallon."

I slide into the chair. "I rarely see you, Luca. You can't spare five minutes for me?"

Luca sighs. "I can, *dolcezza*. It's just a busy time."

"I get that and I'm trying to be supportive, but this is not healthy for us." I'm completely in the dark about what's going on with him.

"I'm not in the mood to argue," he throws back.

"Who's arguing? I want us to talk, communicate," I explain.

"It's only work, Fallon. We are fine." He doesn't budge.

I let out an exasperated breath. "Let's order."

We eat within ten minutes and head back out.

Luca reaches out to stroke the side of my face, pushing my hair back. "*Ti amo, dolcezza. Non ti preoccupare.*" I love you. Don't worry.

That does not appease me at all. Talking to him when he's not ready is like pulling teeth.

As our eyes burn into each other, the usual sparks of love and lust are now replaced with sparks of mistrust when we say goodbye. Luca will be away on business again for the next two days.

Stepping onto my floor, I diligently work for half an hour until Alex interrupts me. "Can I see you in my office?" he demands coldly and strides back.

I get my notebook and pen and follow him in for more workload.

***

I'm emotional, nervous, and confused. The next night I'm not feeling any better. For once, I'm glad Luca's away on business. He's already texted twice and called once today asking what I'm doing. I'll text him later because I need to think. I need to be alone with my thoughts; however, sitting home alone is making me ever more worried. Luca can tell me with so much conviction that nothing is wrong. Everything is wrong. Maybe I should end this now? Maybe I'm not in too deep yet? I'm torn between ending this because of the unknown and continuing in the hopes that I'm wrong about Luca.

In the kitchen cabinet, I find an old bottle of vodka that Teagan left. I hold the bottle up, unsure whether to drink or not.

"Screw it." I'm about to open the bottle when the doorbell rings.

I check the peephole and unlock the door. "How did you get in the building?"

Jason shows me his white teeth. "Neighbor let me in."

I open to door wider for him to enter.

"I was going to meet a friend two streets from here who canceled five minutes before our appointment, so I thought I'd come by to see you. You were not in a good mood yesterday, but I was so busy, I didn't get a chance to talk to you." He plops down on the couch.

Getting the vodka and two shot glasses from the kitchen, I pour two shots. "I feel like crap. I don't want to talk."

Jason takes his shot and clinks it with mine. "I'm a guy, you don't have to tell me *no talking* twice. I prefer that too." His lips stretch into a boyish grin.

We take our shots and refill immediately.

Jason is searching the coffee table after our third shot. "Where's your remote?"

The alcohol is warming my body and slowly numbing the growing unease in my heart. "I have no idea. Give me one more shot."

"You're going to regret it in the morning. You'll be stinking drunk within minutes if you continue."

I turn up my nose. "No more shots for me then." This is hitting me hard. My head feels heavy. "I didn't have dinner."

"In that case, definitely no more for you." He's walking toward the TV, searching for the remote. "Did you freaking eat the remote?" He turns around impatiently.

"I never watch TV. Let me check." I stand up and hold my arms out in front of me to steady myself.

Jason laughs at me. "You can't even handle a few shots."

I smile at him. "I already feel a little drunk."

"I can tell from that ridiculous smirk on your face."

I reach him and open the drawer of the entertainment center to rummage around. "Do you really need to watch TV? Read a magazine." Grabbing a magazine from the drawer, I throw it at him.

He catches it and flings it onto the table. "That's it." Jason strides toward me and starts to tickle me because he knows I'm extremely ticklish.

"Stop it!" I yell through my giggles, trying to capture his hands and curl down to stop him from reaching my underarms.

I twist on the floor as Jason lies on my back. "St-Stop!"

"You needed a good laugh and to unwind." He's trying to wiggle his hand under my down pressed arm. "Come on, little one."

"Shut up," I croak in between exhausting laughs. "Stop!"

My front door swings open. Jason and I turn as one to see Luca running at us and hauling Jason off of me, flinging him onto the living room table.

Jason grunts after he falls with all his weight back on the wooden table.

Luca's silently fuming. "What. Is. Going. On. Here." He towers over Jason and grips his shirt.

I snap out of my astonishment and jump up. "No. It's only Jason."

I yank Luca's arm to let Jason go.

His glower is in full force and turned on me as he looks down into my eyes. "The colleague?"

"Yes, let him go," I plead.

"Dude, I was only tickling her," Jason pipes in.

Luca's grip tightens briefly and Jason holds up his hands in defense while Luca keeps his scathing eyes on him before he shoves him away. "Leave. Now."

Jason adjusts his clothes. "Are you okay, Fallon?"

"Yeah, I'll be fine," I placate and nod toward the door for him to move out of here.

He strides out as Luca spins his aggravation on me.

Jason mouths, "Call me." And he closes the door, leaving us alone.

"Where have you been all day?" Luca asks in a dead calm tone as if nothing happened just now.

The alcohol is slowing down my reaction time. "What?"

"Where have you been all day?" he repeats and glowers some more at me.

"Home."

"Then why couldn't you send a text back or answer your goddamn phone?"

"I- I was going to later, but…" I sigh in frustration. "I'm just sad about everything between us," I honestly tell him. "Jason deserves an apology."

"He'll get one," Luca counters. "I need you to answer your phone from now on."

"Yes, okay." In my foggy mind, I remember that he isn't supposed to be back until tomorrow. "Why are you home early?"

"Because I can't function when we distance ourselves from each other." Flashes of anger and sorrow flicker across his face.

"*You* distance yourself from me," I mumble.

Luca's eyelids drift shut, and he takes my hand and kisses my fingers. When they open, his pupils have dilated, making his eyes terrifyingly indistinct.

"Luca—"

His lips crash down on mine, and he forces me backward until he pins me against the wall and lifts me up, parting my thighs around him. His straining erection is pressing against my dampening heat as my skirt rides up my hips. Without breaking our kiss, Luca unbuttons his pants and tears my panties off while arousal floods me. He slams inside me to the hilt. My back curves to take him in. The fullness of adjusting to him erases the empty feeling that has been lingering since he left, and I gasp in delight. He bites my lips and pushes his tongue into my mouth, desperately seeking mine. My back is scraping against the wall as he vehemently thrusts into me. Both his hands powerfully palm my ass to hold me up while my nails are digging into his shoulders and breaking his skin. My head falls back in heady ecstasy, and I scream in pleasure and pain while my alcohol-induced body is already tingling from a pending orgasm. I'm unsure whether his arduous thrusts are meant to punish me or himself. Luca's relentlessly fucking me. He buries his face in my cleavage with hints of a growl in his rasping tone. A rush of heat is flooding my lower abdomen, and I revel in my orgasm when it hits me in full force while Luca keeps up his pace.

Mere seconds later, he withdraws and places me on my feet. "I need to come on you," he demands in a dangerously low voice, and he tears open my blouse and unclasps my bra.

I kneel in front of Luca before I wrap my hand around him. He presses himself to the swell of my breasts. My hand slides over his silky arousal, pumping frantically, and I look up at him as he cups the back of my head with his left hand. His right hand steadies him, palm flat against the wall.

Our eyes lock as his erection twitches, and he shoots his semen on my breasts with a satisfying groan. Luca slows his thrusting in my hand to ride out the last drop. With his erection in his own left hand now, he spreads his load over my breasts. Marking me. Pacifying his jealous tendencies.

I can barely keep my eyes open because the alcohol and sex have tired me.

Luca steps out of his pants and picks me up, cradling me to him as he walks to the bedroom and lays me down in my bed. He takes off my clothes and cleans me with a warm bath cloth.

I manage to pry open my eyes and watch him tenderly take care of me.

As if he senses I'm awake, he looks up into my eyes. His handsome features are saddened by a grim look. He tries to smile, but it doesn't reach his eyes. *"Dormi, dolcezza."* Sleep.

I turn on my side. Moments later Luca slips in behind me and tucks me against his sculpted chest. He fingers my hair back from my face and nestles my neck while holding me tightly around my middle. *"Ti amo, amore mio."* I love you, my love.

I can't say it back.

CHAPTER 23

Fallon

The average person lives 80 years. The average person lives 29,200 days. When I come to realize *that*; an average life, in days, seems infinitely small. Only 29,200 days. A whole lifetime of memories, of love lost and love found exists within 29,200 days. Shouldn't I strive for happiness in those 29,200 days? Shouldn't I stop worrying about inconsequential matters? Shouldn't I relish in every moment of every day? I probably should and keep repeating that to myself. Only my mantra loses its power when every day that voice inside my head screams to be acknowledged. I can't keep deluding myself that I'm worried about inconsequential matters. What may have started as inconsequential has turned into a very consequential matter that's slowly tearing us apart.

Teagan doesn't understand my reasoning because she hasn't gotten to know Luca. It's frustrating for me to get my point across, so I just tell her we're fine.

I'm stuck in a cycle I don't know how to break. I put up a wall of protection, and Luca can't reach me anymore. The entire situation is about to blow up. My anxiety is reaching a breaking point. We've both been progressively distant.

One night I arrive home late from work, and I find him pacing my living room. He hurriedly slips a phone into his pocket that's not his current smartphone. It was definitely an older type of phone.

He has another phone?

As I see it, I can react in several ways. One - I ask him directly about the phone, which I'm quite positive he'll lie about now because of the way he inconspicuously placed it in his pants. Two - I can be hysterical and demand an explanation, which I won't get. Three - I can wait until I get my chance to check the phone myself. I choose option three.

Luca strides determinedly toward me as I enter my apartment, looking me over intently. "Where have you been? I've been trying to reach you for hours." Annoyance reflects behind his eyes.

I take my time removing my sandals. All I want is to unwind and jump into the shower after working in the sweltering heat of this August day since the air-conditioning broke at the office. We're hosting the yearly orphan charity event in two days, this Friday. I've told him that I would be busy this entire week with last-minute preparations and writing the speeches for Alex.

"Fallon!" Luca crowds me.

Turning around to him, I say in an aggravated tone, "I told you I would be busy this week. I didn't have time to check my phone."

Luca's hair is in disarray, falling over his forehead. He's obviously worried and infuriated. Apprehensively, he approaches me. "I asked you to always answer. I need you to abide by that promise. Especially now," he almost yells at me, throwing his hand in the air. His usual self-control wavers.

I don't let him intimidate me. "What the hell are you talking about? Abide?" I spit the word with malice. "Lose the attitude."

His breathing is labored from trying to restrain his emotions. As he clenches his hands, his strained biceps ripple through his dress shirt in contained rage.

I hold up my hands in surrender. "Let's calm down here."

"Are you leaving tonight or staying in?" he demands to know.

It takes me a minute to grasp his sudden change of subject. "I'm staying in."

He heads toward the door, passing and ignoring me.

"We're just going to leave everything unresolved again, Luca? We never talk about this and just continue on. If you walk out on me now, don't bother coming back." The threat I don't mean leaves my lips without my thinking clearly. I try speaking in a calm tone, but my shivering bottom lip reveals my edginess.

He catches my eyes and grits his teeth. "I need to leave now and calm down. I don't want to say anything I'll regret." Luca opens the door and disappears.

I clutch my stomach in agony.

He has another phone?

Why was he so upset about not reaching me? Every question causes more doubt in my mind. I'm still standing in the exact same place while my mind tries to comprehend what's happening to us. Confounded, I go to my bedroom and crawl into bed. I can't believe Luca would betray me, but that scenario is becoming more plausible with every day that passes. I don't understand how I can sense that his love for me is so deep yet we're still drifting apart. Unless I'm feeling things that have been long gone?

I fall into a restless sleep.

***

He didn't come back to 'our' home last night. My apartment has been our home for weeks. Everything here reminds me of him.

I take my time in the shower, realizing I can't afford to call in sick with this year's biggest event in two days. I refrain from calling him. He left. Maybe he doesn't want to hear anything from me? Maybe it's over? Feeling miserable, I dress myself.

As usual, I first head to the coffee shop for my Lady Grey tea before taking the fifteen-minute walk to work. I'm reliving the past several weeks over and over in my head while standing in line to place my order. What did I miss? Have I been naïve and ignoring signs?

"Excuse me... Excuse me."

I'm jarred from my thoughts by a customer behind me. The guy reminds me that I should order.

"I'm sorry," I state, distracted, and move forward to order my tea. I'm fumbling in my purse, swallowing back a wide array of emotions.

The man behind me gently touches my elbow. "Is everything okay?"

I look at him but can't find any words.

He orders a coffee and pays for both of us. Taking our drinks, I follow him to his table. I don't join him as he takes his seat. "I'm sorry. I'm having a bad day. Let me pay you back."

"Don't worry about it. It's on me. I noticed you seemed distracted. Please feel free to sit if you want," he mentions nicely.

I hesitate at first, but I should calm myself before heading to work and decide to accept his offer.

Before I even get the chance to sit down, the front door opens loudly and Luca advances in, stalking determinedly toward me. Luca with the same furious eyes as yesterday. He leans in close to my face. "Can I talk to you?"

Because of the uncompromising lines of his hard profile and my need to avoid a scene in here, I agree. "Thank you. I'll see you around," I greet the guy.

Luca pins him with a displeased look.

"It was my pleasure." He doesn't back down under Luca's scowl.

I smile timidly at the guy when Luca places his hand at the small of my back and guides me outside. The door closes and I spin around as soon as I step over the threshold, eyes narrowing. "Happy now that you've marked your territory?"

His jaw clenches. "No. Trust me, *that* was me being civil."

Suddenly a disturbing thought crosses my mind. "Were you following me?" Luca knows I first have a tea before walking to work, but this morning I'm almost an hour behind on my regular morning routine.

"Yes," he confesses without any remorse.

"What?" I refuse to cry and suppress my hurt and surprise at his confession. "You said you would come back, and *you* didn't. I'm going to work because I don't want to talk to you now."

"Fallon." Luca softens his voice and tries to palm my face with one hand, but I avoid his touch by taking a few steady steps back. Luca rushes forward and almost stumbles over a steel chair trying to reach for me, his tightly leashed self-control breaking more and more.

"No. Do not follow me!" I march away before I change my mind, leaving him behind.

***

Still aggravated, I arrive at the posh, glass building, greet the receptionist behind her desk as my heels click on the tiled floor, and I take the elevator to the third floor. The building has over fifty floors, so it's always crowded in every one of the nine elevators during rush hours. Standing in the full elevator, I'm glad when the door opens on the third floor. Our floor has five offices, but most of us sit together in the open space. The floor-to-ceiling windows and the black tiled floor give the space a simple, yet elegant, style. We each have a laptop and can seat ourselves at any white desk of our choice. It's all highly informal. When in need of privacy, every employee is allowed to occupy one of the offices.

I'm relieved one of the offices is unoccupied so that I can grant myself a few minutes of privacy. I let out a terse deep breath when I enter the small office. It's simple and understated, white and grey walls with a black floor. I arrange my laptop on the white desk. Throwing my bag on one of the two chairs on the other side, I power up my laptop and plant myself in the desk chair.

I swivel to glare outside. With my hands clasped together on my lap, I peer down to hundreds of people running through the streets. Everybody walking in the different directions that life takes them. Masses of people who each have his/her own individual story. Some might be joyful, some might be sad, some might be lonely. Among all the people across the street, there's one person standing immobile, looking right at me. I need to know what his story is. Everyone steps around him. Green eyes that would always capture my attention in a room filled with thousands call to me, pulling me to him. The tiny hairs on my arms rise as his stare is locked on me, his impeccable suit in contrast with his anguished gaze. Neither of us relents, both of us observing, thinking, and anticipating what to do now?

Alex enters the office without knocking; I see his reflection in the window.

Forced to concentrate on work, I twirl back around.

"Good morning, Fallon. Tell me the speeches are done?" He sits in the vacant chair across from me.

I open the document in Word and print the two speeches I've prepared for tomorrow evening. Handing the documents to him, I emphasize, "They're finished."

"Anything else you need to tell me?" he asks in a derisive tone.

"No," I retort curtly.

Alex's lips turn up into a sardonic smile. "We'll talk later."

I spin back around in my chair to the window, only Luca's gone. My laptop notifies me of incoming messages. I need the distraction and focus solely on putting the finishing touches to all the written communication for tomorrow. I check the menus with all the accompanying texts I wrote and send the final menu to the printer.

The day proceeds in a blur of last-minute arrangements in need of some extra help. Tomorrow, we'll all be at the venue the entire day. The event is being hosted at the Silver Dahlia Hotel. I turn off my laptop at eight and see that I have several missed calls from Luca and texts from my parents and Teagan.

During my walk home, I call my parents and Teagan. My parents always encourage me to enjoy the events after my months of hard work. Teagan needs reassurance that Luca and I aren't fighting. Not wanting her to worry on the other side of the ocean, I lie and tell her we're fine.

At home, I take off my dress and heels in the living room. Fatigued, I drop face down on the couch and fall asleep without eating dinner.

Later that night, I wake when I hear the door opening and closing. I turn my head to see Luca standing in front of me, his thick, dark hair neatly combed back. His jaw, covered in a light, neatly-trimmed beard, never fails to enthrall me. This stunning man that chose to love me - the only man I've ever loved – is slipping away from me. It was all too good to be true.

He crouches before the couch, bringing us face to face. Gently, he tucks my hair behind my ear and coils his fingers in my tresses.

Tears are burning to explode, but I hold them in. Despondency is mirrored in our eyes.

"Am I losing you?" he whispers sadly while ghosting his fingertips down my spine.

As much as I want to give him a hopeful denial, I can't. He *is* losing me, and I'm losing him. Only I'm clearly the one left in the dark as to what exactly is going on.

I move up as Luca sits on the couch and motions for me to sit astride him. He cradles my neck in both hands, pulling me close. The familiarity of his minty breath and citrus cologne used to comfort me, now it saddens me. I lock eyes with him. "What's happening to us? I'm lost." Even though I've grown to love him, I need to take care of myself and open my eyes. I need to end this carefully. Guilt sparkles in his eyes, spinning with pain and regret in his dejected appearance. I lean forward against his chest to hug my arms around his waist because the memories we've created together aren't easily forgotten. I want to stand up, but Luca holds me firmly around my waist, afraid I might leave. "I don't know where we go from here," I confess in a muffled voice.

"Let me just hold you, please, Fallon. I just need to hold you." He kisses the top of my head and stands up, so I circle my legs around his hips as he carries me in his embrace to the bedroom. He lays me down on my back before undressing, and then he slips in beside me under the covers. Luca flips me on top of him to softly stroke my back and sides.

That familiar voice in my thoughts telling me that his secretiveness is fueled by something far greater than I can fathom has finally been accepted.

CHAPTER 24

Fallon

The next morning and afternoon is hectic. We're set up at the Silver Dahlia. Our guests arrive at six. The event is simple. We start with a seven-course dinner that we sold per plate, then an independent filmmaker will present a short documentary he filmed about the increasing numbers of orphans worldwide, and several vacations will be auctioned. The chef and the artists all volunteered, and we paid half the price for the venue and the vacations. Apart from the proceeds we'll make from the tickets and vacations, our guests can donate money the entire night.

I return home to shower and change at four and wear my silk, blood red floor-length dress with an open back and a thigh-high split. My hair is up in a tight bun secured high on top of my head, and I'm putting my lipstick – the infamous red lipstick – in my golden clutch when I hear my front door unlock. I check the time: five fifteen.

Luca strolls into my bedroom and halts to gawk appreciatively at me. Standing behind me, he strokes the back of his forefinger down my spine. *"Sei bellissima, dolcezza."* You're stunning.

"Are you still coming with me?" I thought - with all the struggles of the last few weeks - he wasn't joining me at the event. My plan to be apart more is backfiring on me. The moment *I* try to create a distance, he stops it and suddenly has time for me again. Maybe he's onto me?

He steps out of his shoes and unbuttons his shirt. "Of course. I want to be there with you," he clarifies pragmatically.

I don't have time to think about this now. "Hurry. Shower."

He takes off his pants in the bedroom and jumps into the shower. "Going."

I check my dress in the mirror, and my eyes wander to his pants lying in a heap on the floor.

Should I check it?

This is my opportunity. The bathroom door is half ajar, fragrant steam rising from the small opening.

I hurriedly kneel and feel in his pockets. First comes out his smartphone and then another phone.

I knew it!

Throwing his pants back on the floor, I take the other phone and run through the hall, past the kitchen, and into the living room. It's the phone I saw him slipping into his pocket the night he couldn't reach me. It seems to be a disposable one. This is definitely an old model; it doesn't even have a color screen. It's a simplistic black cellphone with press buttons and a tiny display. He doesn't have any contacts stored in it. I walk past the couch to the windows and glance warily back at the hall. The shower is still running. My hands are perspiring as I hurriedly search the cell for any useful information. I click different buttons but can't find any messages. After entering another menu, I find them. There are messages from unknown numbers - no names - because none are stored in the phone. One message reads: 'button.' I wrinkle my nose in confusion while checking the next one. I can only read part of the message – 'make a marriage' – when a poised voice interrupts.

"What are you doing?"

I spin around, shocked.

Luca stands at the opposite end of the sofa with a towel wrapped low around his hips and his damp hair attractively disheveled from towel drying. I hate that I have to fight to avoid being lured by his charm. The phone in my hand catches his attention, and his eyes snap back up to mine while he takes a defensive stance, bracing himself for my reaction.

An array of feelings including hurt, sorrow, betrayal, and curiosity sting me. Hurriedly, I try to decide what reaction I want him to see. My curiosity and determination to find out what exactly has been happening the last couple of weeks wins.

I need him to open up to me. How do I handle this?

I throw the phone at his chest, and he catches it clumsily when it hits him. "You are married? Married?" I comment in a rising tone.

Luca looks stunned. "Fallon, what did you read?" He sounds shaken, but it's well-hidden. He glimpses at the phone and places it on the kitchen counter behind him.

"Does it matter? I knew… I knew you were lying to me. I've been suspicious for weeks." I peek at him. My behind is leaning against the couch to keep me standing.

His impatient voice rings out, "Fallon, what are you talking about?"

My lips thin into a straight line. "Don't you dare deny it. I read a message about marriage." I bring my clamped left fist to my mouth. Grazing my teeth over my knuckles, I replay the last few weeks in fast forward through my mind.

Luca cautiously approaches me. "Fallon, it's not what you think," he denies. "There's nobody else."

My eyes turn into slits. "Why do you have another phone? Why do you go on so many business trips?" I take a step back, not wanting to be near him.

He tries to reach for me again, but the hurt stemming from my shaking body halts him in his tracks. My back is slightly pressed against the window.

Luca stands in my previous place at the sofa. He drags his hand through his hair. Sighing heavily, he pleads, "You're wrong. I'm not married—"

The buzzer rings, signaling the cab is waiting downstairs to take me to the venue. I carefully avoid Luca and walk past the coffee table to tell the cab driver I'll be down in a minute. All I want is to stay home, yet that's the last thing I want. I head toward the bedroom to fix my makeup. With a cotton stick, I remove the smudges of mascara from under my eyes.

Luca follows me. "Should I wait here for you?" he asks tiredly, seating himself on the edge of the bed.

I put my makeup and phone in my clutch, and I leave. "No."

My casual response jolts him and Luca runs up to me, still in his towel. "Fallon, we need to talk." His left arm shoots out against the wall, blocking my way to the front door.

"Not now," I hiss.

"I'll wait for you here then," he says resolutely.

"No," I repeat. "*You* leave my house."

Exasperation gleams in his dark eyes. It's those darkening eyes that warned me I should guard my heart from this man. "Fallon, you have to give me a chance to explain. Tomorrow? I'll come tomorrow so—"

"You'll answer all my questions?" I interrupt fiercely. "Nothing will be left unresolved. That time is over. I want to know everything."

"Yes." His eyes narrow in doubt. "I'll be here early, and I'll call you later to ensure that you're home safe."

I sigh in defeat. "I probably won't answer." My brows rise in enragement when his impatience grows.

But he's not intimidated by me in the least. "Answer your phone," Luca demands, refusing to budge. In a kinder tone, he adds, "I would do it for your peace of mind if the roles were reversed."

I sidestep him.

Luca's fingers encircle my upper arm as I open the door.

I barely glance at him over my shoulder.

"Good luck tonight. I'm proud of you," he expresses in a soft tone. "I will give you all your answers tomorrow."

Amber collides with equally sad green before I close the door.

***

I arrive at the Silver Dahlia only fifteen minutes before dinner is served. Most of the guests are already seated. The restaurant has sixty round tables decorated with silver tablecloths and centerpieces of painted blue roses. I'm placed with my colleagues at a table for six next to Jason, who is looking dashing in his tux.

"Everything okay?" Jason notices my distressed state.

I nod as I sit down. "Yes, small disagreement. He's not coming." I glance at the empty seat next to me that is reserved for Luca.

Jason frowns. "He's not coming because of a disagreement?" he asks, not suppressing his judgmental tone. Jason's date, our co-worker Alexandra, overhears him and shows me a supportive smile.

I wave him off. "I don't want to talk about it. Let's enjoy our night." I'm unable to talk about Luca without bursting into tears, so I try to stay in the present when the first course is served, but negativity engulfs me. Doubt is a treacherous feeling.

Will he ever give me straight answers? Have I naively fallen for a man who has woven an intricate web of lies to be with me? What has been true the last few weeks?

Incapable of eating, I excuse myself from the table to visit the restroom.

Jason follows me. "Fallon, go home if you're not feeling well. I'll cover for you if anyone asks, which I highly doubt. Our work is done. We should be enjoying ourselves, and you obviously can't. Go talk to Luca."

Eyeing the restaurant, I only hesitate for a second. I regret leaving Luca and should talk to him now, before he has an entire night to come up with new lies. Jason hugs me, sensing my misery.

"Thanks, Jason. I'm going now. Go back to your date." I watch him return to his seat.

At the front entrance of the hotel, Alex is mingling with guests. I want to avoid him and search for another exit in this huge hotel. I go through the foyer, into the hall and to the kitchen in the rear. I know - from spending the morning here - that only the main kitchen is being used. The fire exit opens into the backstreet behind the hotel. I enter another hall that's actually prohibited to guests. There are two doors - I check the first and it's unlocked. I sigh in relief when I find myself looking into the empty rear kitchen. There's only a small light on, and I scan the room and spot an exit at the far end. For a supposedly small kitchen, the room is remarkably spacious. I press the handlebar down to open the door. Unlocked again.

The door indeed opens into the alley which is barely illuminated by a flickering light. I can't see the street, so I have to walk through the alley and round the corner to access it. I open the door further to step outside, but a second before the door slams shut, I hear a faint *thud* and - in reflex - my head follows said noise to the back of the dim alley.

Everything happens in fast forward from that point on. Two silhouettes are standing ominously over a body that slouches to the ground next to the dumpster. One of the men has a gun in hand, angled at the person falling to the ground. The door behind me slams shut, and both of their heads spin around to me. My eyes enlarge as waves of panic grip me, so I quickly search the door - no handlebar on the outside. It only opens from the inside. The men are maybe ten steps away from me at the back of the alley. I pivot and will my legs to sprint toward the street. My heels are clicking urgently against the asphalt, and I don't dare to look back. I lose my footing and misstep halfway to the street, falling with my palms flat in front of me, scraping my knees open and pushing myself back up as quickly as possible.

Not one step further, I'm raised off my heels with an arm around my waist and a hand sealing my mouth. I scream futilely. The guy jerks my face to the side, and I struggle in his hold, kicking out into the night air. He drags me toward the back of the alley, past the fire exit door, and stops at the dumpster, joining the other perpetrator. There's blood seeping from the victim's torso onto the ground. To my astonishment, I recognize this dead man. He has stopped by at work often to visit Alex. My stomach heaves from the pungent smell of blood and trash.

The man restraining me says against my ear, "Stop. Struggling." With the silencer pointed to my temple, I hear the click of a gun. The disgusting smell of liquor on his breath enhances my nausea.

I signal that I will stay quiet, nodding my head to the guy in front of me and the one at my back.

He moves his hand an inch away from my mouth, and the other man arches one brow, waiting for me to panic and start screaming again. The one behind me kicks the back of my knees so I fall forward, the impact with the concrete burning my already-bloodied knees.

Both men stand before me now. Tears induced by my physical pain trail down my cheeks. I can't see the men clearly in the darkness of the alley, but the one that kicked me has blond hair and is fairly short; the other one has copper or brown hair. Both are dressed in suits. I don't look away as they both glare at me and then at each other.

The blond guy palms his mouth in frustration while keeping his gun aimed at my forehead. His eyes are trained on me when he addresses his partner. "What do we do?"

"Take her. We have to leave now." The other guy, also holding a gun, stashes it under his jacket.

Blond guy clutches his hair with one hand and then backhands me in my face. The force of the blow resounding through my head.

Then I'm propelled into unconsciousness when the back of his gun knocks me out cold.

CHAPTER 25

Fallon

I'm startled by angry male voices that I hear far away. I want open my eyes, but my eyelids feel sewn shut, too heavy to open. No matter how hard I fight, my eyes stay closed. I try to focus on the voices. Slowly, I feel myself drifting away.

No, don't drift, stay conscious!

Is someone shouting? I can't feel anything - not my hands, not my legs. But I'm awake; I'm sure of it. Again, I will my eyes to open… Nothing. My frightened state is increasing as the seconds tick away, and I'm stuck in my head with only my thoughts.

I faintly hear the male voices speak up. "When will she wake up? She's been out for long. This is not a good sign. What the fuck went wrong?"

"*Maybe* we shouldn't discuss that here and now in case the girl can hear us."

"Fine. This bitch better wake up soon because we need to get rid of her anyway. Can't we just dump her body somewhere?"

Oh god, no. Who are these people? Where the hell am I?

"Are you fucking kidding me? We don't know who she is or what the fuck she was doing there. We need answers before we make another move."

"We also need to get out of here as soon as possible before someone finds out we brought her in here. I have to admit, she's a cute little thing, gets my juices flowing. Can't we have a little fun with her?"

"No! Where do you suppose we move her? Do not touch her until we figure this out."

The voices become quieter.

"Frank, go check and see who's arriving at the front door. Don't mention the girl yet."

"Fucking hell, I *am* mentioning the girl. We could use her."

I hear footsteps of someone walking away and a door slams, startling me.

"Fucking little shithead!"

Silence.

I suddenly feel a warm gush against my ear and someone whispers, "Did you just move, girl?" Then everything fades to black and I lose consciousness again.

***

I wake. Coldness surrounds me. My head is heavy and aching as I try to move, and I grimace when my bound left wrist restrains me. It's cuffed to the bed railing above me in this small room with four off-white walls, no windows, and a light bulb hanging in the middle of the ceiling. The bed is against the wall in the corner. I touch the cold wall with my right hand. There's a door on my left, a few feet away. I sit up, dragging the cuff to the middle of the railing. Black spots overtake my eyesight for a moment. My dress it torn, my knees covered in dried blood. An almost imperceptible noise catches my attention in the upper left corner of the room. A device turned - it's a camera.

The door opens suddenly and bangs against the wall with a loud crash. I sit up on the bed because I feel less vulnerable sitting than lying down. It's him again: the short, blond guy that hit me. He stammers into the room, drunk. I swallow deeply, and my throat hurts from the dryness. His predatory walk ignites my distress, and his daunting smile makes me shiver in fear. Instantly, I move back on the bed, even though I know I can't hide.

"You look scared, little lady." His eyes are blazing with malicious intent.

I *am* scared, but I just stare at him. I will not let him goad me, even though I want to cry because he's going to touch me. There's nothing I can do, but I will fight him any way I can.

"I think you need a good fuck. You were messing with business that has nothing to do with you, and you caused me trouble. You owe me."

I don't acknowledge his words and try to sit still as a statue.

He stands before me and tilts his head. "I like my women to scream. I think you would scream when I fuck your ass. Wouldn't you?" he insults.

He fists my hair and hauls me up. The cuff on my left wrist rattles against the bed railing as I'm being forced to rise. I squeeze my eyes shut to keep from screaming out because of the pain burning in my scalp. I will not give him that satisfaction.

This must be a horrible nightmare, and I'll wake up any minute now. But this is my reality. This is happening. I'm going to get raped in this room. The tears I've been desperately wanting to hold back wet my cheeks.

I will fight him. I need to fight him.

His hold on my hair loosens involuntarily. The smell of liquor lingering around him informs me he's drunk and obviously can't access his full strength. He quickly recovers and tightens his fist again while I make a fist with my right hand.

I will fight this. I will fight him.

With all my power, I punch his nose, forcing him to sway back.

His hand goes up to his bleeding nose. "You fucking little bitch!" he spits and comes at me in full force.

We stumble back onto the bed, and my scalp collides with the railing. I'm dizzy and see dozens of white and black stars for a moment, but I start kicking like a madwoman.

Do not let him take off your clothes.

I want to exhaust him. He's drunk, and he should get tired soon. With my left hand restrained, I kick and scream, trying to kick him in the balls, but I miss since he's holding me down on my back on the bed.

"Stupid bitch." He punches me in the stomach.

All the air is being ripped from my lungs as I gasp for the breath that's been beaten out of me. He leans his entire body on me, and presses his arms on mine while he sits on my legs. I let my eyelids close for a second to avoid the blood that is dripping from his nose in my eyes. My insides are wrenching with terror. My left arm bends in an awkward position because of the cuff as pain cloaks my wrist, arm, and shoulder. I cry out because the pain is excruciating, but it miraculously spurs me on, and I don't allow myself to wallow in it. "Get off me, asshole." I maneuver my whole body and refuse to lie still. Although he's much stronger than I am, his drunken haze has indeed made him weaker. I wriggle one leg free from underneath him and frantically jerk my hips up and down to get him off me. The last pins in my hair fall out and strands of my locks obscure my view. I blow them out of my face harshly. His strenuous breathing causes him to hyperventilate. I keep moving my body uncontrollably and manage to push off the bed with my right leg. He's growing weaker, so I look down my right side to kick him again. Then I see his phone falling out of his pants pocket onto the bed, and I hurriedly push the phone under the covers with my leg. My right arm is free again, and I lift my right side off the bed with my leg and arm, throwing him off me.

He falls down on the floor, and the back of his head hits the concrete. "FUCK!" he yells.

I'm frozen in shock, afraid I've caused even more trouble for myself.

Our labored breathing echoes off the walls.

"I will have you later, stupid cunt." He gets up from the floor, rubbing his head, and then slaps my face with the force of his fury.

I recoil from the sting and close my eyes until he leaves. I keep my eyes closed and my body unmoving until I hear the door close. I force myself to stay still for a few moments to make sure he doesn't come back, counting to thirty in my head.

I'm trembling. I'm hurt. I'm crying. I'm terrified. Every area of my skin is covered in sweat. I can't think about anything but calling for help.

After reaching thirty, I quickly try to find the phone. Then I remember the camera in the room. I vainly breathe in to calm myself while I search for the phone under the covers. A sob escapes me when I can't locate it, but then my fingertips touch something cold. The phone is near my behind. Using my ass, I push the phone into my hand and turn on my right side, covering what I'm doing from the camera while ignoring the pain in my left arm that the movement causes. It's a smartphone with touchscreen. I hold it close to my eyes and dial, and misdial the number. I can't get my fingers to stop trembling, so I dial again, almost getting the numbers correct this time, before I hear a noise outside the room.

Someone is coming.

The door opens, and I immediately let the phone slide out of my hand onto the pillow and hide it under my hair.

Shit. Did he see the phone? Did he see me move?

Footsteps approach the bed while I'm sweating profusely and using all my power not to shudder in fear.

He's coming back for his phone.

"Can't let you have my alcohol, bitch," the same guy who tried to assault me says.

I don't remember him coming in with a drink or a bottle. I'm motionless with my eyes sealed shut as my tears fall on the pillow. I hear the slosh of liquid in a bottle. He's taking a swig, standing behind me while I'm lying on my side, concealing the phone under my hair and partly under my head.

Please, please, please leave!

I've been holding my breath since the door opened. Too panicked to even breathe. He turns but still stands there.

He must've seen the phone. He's toying with me.

A long stretch of silence ensues. No movement…

After what feels like an eternity but must be mere seconds, he strolls out. The door closes and I let out the breath I've been holding in. My breathing is erratic from the panic boiling in my blood. Yet again, I force myself to wait before grabbing the phone with my perspiring hands. My vision is blurred from my tears. I get the phone and sit up facing the wall, but I can barely control my right hand before I get the number correct and press dial, holding the phone up to my ear. "Please, please pick up quickly," I murmur with an unsteady voice. My left arm is strained under the angle I'm holding it at, but I ignore the pain. My entire body stills when I hear the ringtone outside the room. I look at the phone, confused, and then hold it up to my ear again. The ringtone becomes clearer. Then the door of the room unlocks. The ringtone is in the room with me now. My head spins around with the phone still pressed to my ear and my world stops.

The adrenalin that has been shooting through my veins since the blond guy entered my room recedes. Every molecule in my existence is drenched in stunned silence. Time moves on but stops in my mind while I'm wearily trying to comprehend what's happening. As I face the person standing in the doorway, the phone slips out of my hand lifelessly and drops to the ground with a loud crash. The ringing of the other phone stops that instant.

CHAPTER 26

Luca

Gravel creaks beneath the tires of my car as I approach the circular driveway. I park next to two BMWs - one is Adriano's sapphire black M3. Sitting in my car, I glare at the house for a few minutes. This place, this life I've wanted to keep hidden from Fallon. How do I tell her? I have the entire night to prepare myself. Hating that she didn't want me waiting at her house, I drove back here. I still have no idea how I'm going to reveal everything. I was so desperate to hang on to her that I practically begged her to meet me tomorrow morning.

On the drive back here, I relived those few minutes repeatedly. There was something mysterious in her reaction.

When everything one wants slowly slips away, a person can amaze himself by how far he'd go to keep it. She's everything I want, but she's the one I deceived most. It was the only way to keep her safe, away from my merciless world.

As I pass the front guard, he dips his chin to greet me. I arrive in the house feeling exhausted. Standing in the foyer, I hear commotion coming from the basement and a door slams, resounding loud between these walls.

Can't these guys be quiet for one fucking moment?!

I need to wind down in seclusion, so I ignore the sounds and march up the grand stairs. I want Adriano to brief me on his guys' assignment tonight. Chances are, he's enjoying himself with Camilla. I quietly visit the 'strip club' to check out what's going on there. I push open the door and see Adriano getting a lap dance from a topless woman - not Camilla - on the couch. As I lean in the doorway on my shoulder with one hand in my pocket, the woman sees me first -when she lifts her head from his groin - and freezes. A frown crinkles my forehead, and I nod my head toward the other exit, silently demanding her to leave. She quickly scrambles away.

Adriano lifts his head and buttons his dress shirt.

"*Buonasera,* Luca, care to join us?"

"Us?" My brows draw together.

He scans the empty room and snorts. "Well, I guess the men have all retreated to a private room."

"Adriano," I calmly say. "Come to my office. I want details. *Now.*"

While walking in silence to my office on the other side of the second floor, Adriano calls Damian and then informs me when he hangs up. "He's coming. He was in the basement."

Damian was making that noise.

"You didn't talk to him yet?" I'm annoyed that Adriano didn't debrief his own soldier, but I don't show it.

"No, Damian didn't call in," he confirms.

We enter my office, and I immediately sit in my chair behind my desk. I grab a stack of paperwork to place it in my left drawer and close it.

Adriano falls into the seat across from me. "What's wrong?" My friend obviously senses my mood. "We'll talk later." I open my laptop, type in my password, and immediately access the live feed of the entire house.

What's going on in that basement?

I push the button under my desk to open the door after Damian knocks.

Damian enters, distraught. He has been sweating, which is not a good sign. I lean back in my chair and signal for him to sit. "What happened?" I rest a hand on my desk.

Both Adriano and I stare at him - Adriano with an irritated expression, and I with a blank expression.

I evenly repeat, "Damian, what went wrong?"

His face jerks toward me. "We killed the associate, but there was a witness."

Not good.

Adriano's becoming more irritated by the second. I discreetly lift my hand toward Adriano for him to cool down, for now.

Damian continues. "She saw the shooting. I didn't know what to do. Frank panicked. He had an order for that one kill—"

"What exactly did she witness?" Adriano interrupts.

"The kill," Damian confesses.

Adriano and I briefly glance at each other. We realize the enormity of this screw-up.

"Damn it, Damian. A woman? What did you do with her?" Adriano demands to know.

"I brought her here. I had to think quickly. Frank screwed up!"

"Did Frank kill his target?" I need to know if we've bound Frank into silence. If he killed the associate, he can never break the code of silence and secrecy, *omertà*, without facing murder charges. In other words: we have him by the balls now.

"Yes," Damian answers.

Good.

We tested Frank on his skill at espionage, obedience, and discretion. He succeeded, but the most important skill that is required to ensure a membership in our Syndicate – kill mercilessly and without any witnesses – he failed at.

"Did you dispose of the body? Or did you focus all your attention on the witness?" I scowl at both Damian and Adriano. Adriano introduced prospect Frank and thought he would be a valuable member.

"Body is disposed of and crime scene is clean. She's the only loose end," Damian carefully answers.

I cover my mouth with my left hand.

"I'm sorry I brought her here, *Padrino*," Damian apologizes in a weak voice.

"You should be." My tone isn't giving away any indication of the thoughts roaring through my mind. Stroking my fingers over my chin, I ask, "What was your plan after getting her here?"

"I don't know. I…" He takes a deep breath.

Damian's concealment of information is starting to worry me. "Tell me exactly what happened. What are you withholding?" I command with thinning eyes.

He rubs his hand over his forehead. "I smelled booze on Frank."

Adriano and I share a surprised look - that he even had the nerve to show up on assignment drunk. "He was drunk?" I calmly probe.

"I think so. His aim was unsteady," Damian informs us.

"You fucking moron. Why didn't you call me? And where the fuck is Frank!" Adriano yells.

"I think Frank knows he's in big trouble. When I came up from the basement, he was sitting in the living room," Damian expresses quickly.

I let Adriano handle his soldier, and I wipe my hand over mouth. Glancing at my laptop, I see there's a woman lying on her back in one of the rooms in the basement. I zoom in and my blood turns ice cold. My pulse is pumping furiously in my ears. Sweat immediately forms on my forehead as I gaze at her. Adriano's yelling becomes distorted and fades away as my vision is focused on the screen, and everything else goes black instantaneously. There's a bruise on her face, below her left eye.

Her dark hair is a mess, her beautiful red gown is ruined, and the skin on her knees is damaged. Frozen in place, I gaze at Fallon. I blink a few times and zoom in closer, hoping my eyes are deceiving me. But I'm positive it's Fallon, lying unconscious on the bed. They shackled her. My two lives collide. My heart is being held in a death grip that's smothering me. Ever so slowly, all my senses come back to me. Shouting invades my ears.

"*Idiota!* Get Frank. Now!" Adriano's still screaming at Damian.

Damian hurriedly leaves the room.

Adriano shifts his attention to me as I undo a few more buttons on my dress shirt because I feel suffocated. My brain is trying to comprehend what I just saw. My fist tightens on the desk while I'm transfixed by the image of her unconscious body on my screen.

"Luca. What is it?" Adriano hesitantly asks.

I run my hand over my face. Standing up, I say, "It's her. *Il mio amore.* She's the witness." And grit my teeth before turning the laptop screen toward him in a violent shove.

His eyes widen the moment he recognizes Fallon. "Fucking shit!"

I head to the table next to the door to get a drink. Taking the top off of the decanter, I pour a shot of whisky and toss it back, grimacing as the liquid burns down my throat. A million thoughts race through my mind while I need to think and ensure that neither I nor she is endangered further.

I order Adriano, "Follow Damian to find Frank." Frank is becoming a liability.

Adriano gives me a chagrined look. "I told you this would bring trouble," he mutters as he gets up to leave.

I stop him by his arm and look him dead in the eye. "Make sure no one has access to her until I figure out what I'm going to do."

Adriano returns my steady gaze. "I can change the code after I've found Damian and Frank. Until we've talked to them, we can still hold off questions. But, Luca, think good and hard before you do anything unwise. As your *Capo*, but mostly as your friend, I'm telling you to not act on your anger now."

Sighing, I let him go.

As soon as the door closes, I exhale a tormented breath and grip the glass in my hand while anger crawls over my skin, faster and faster. I let my eyelids fall, but all I see are visions of Fallon chained to the bed downstairs. My eyes open, and I hurl the glass across the room. It hits the opposing wall and splinters into a thousand pieces.

This night has gone from bad to horrific. Fallon finds my other phone and concludes that I'm married. I was supposed to be at her event tonight to ensure her safety, but I couldn't press my luck with her. She would never have taken me with her after finding the phone. She was already too suspicious of my behavior the past few weeks and that damn message ruined everything for me.

This power struggle with Leggia has taken up almost all my time, forcing me to be on more business trips away from Fallon, which has increased her suspicion. The image I've built around myself to keep her love was already filled with cracks, but the cracks have now expanded into one huge problem we might not overcome.

When she wouldn't answer her phone, I would risk everything and put all business on hold to personally ensure that she was safe. Everything I have done has been a desperate attempt to keep her love for me untainted. This work has taken away more and more time I've been craving to spend with her. I just never imagined Fallon would be a witness.

Why the fuck wasn't she inside?

I could let her go right now because James hasn't been informed. Only Frank, Damian, Adriano, and I know we have a captive. But she will go to the police, so I must expose myself to her. I press my thumb and middle finger to my temples as I sit in my chair. With my elbows on my desk, I cover my mouth with one hand while my stare is locked to that basement room that holds the only positive thing in my life. Her body stirs, and I zoom in. My fingertips trace Fallon on the screen, eager to touch her in any way possible. Her legs twitch, her head jerks, and her eyes open and blink to adapt to the light in the room. Her petrified expression shatters me beyond repair. I can't look at her and think straight, so I walk up to the window, and rake my hands through my hair, clasping my fingers behind my head.

I told her to be more aware of her surroundings. What the hell was she doing in the back alley alone? I'm furious at her, at myself, at Damian, at Frank. No, I'm not furious at her. She was never supposed to know.

She will leave me.

As I turn around, disorder on the laptop screen catches my attention. I hurriedly angle it up to get a better view and grip it harshly. "Motherfucker!" I bellow. The sheer rage and fear boiling inside me bursts into flames. This is exactly what I was afraid of. Fallon is wildly pushing Frank off of her. I storm to my door, but when I reach it, I take a deep breath and remind myself to not raise suspicion with anyone. I can't slow down. I'm risking everything. Panic and dread fill me. I crash my door open and don't even bother closing it. I will fucking kill Frank if she's hurt. Pins and needles are cutting through me while I sprint through the long hall. The house seems to have gotten bigger.

Adriano blocks my way as I reach the first stairwell and asks, concerned, *"Cosa è successo"?* What happened? "Calm down, Luca."

"Get the fuck out of my way," I whisper yell. I jostle him away with both hands, but before I descend the stairs, I look back at a stunned Adriano. "Go close my office door. *Subito!*" Now! I race down but halt mid stairs when I spot James at the bottom.

What is he doing back already?

He wasn't supposed to be in until tomorrow. Grasping the railing, I'm agitated and ready to blow.

Stay. Calm.

I roll my neck as my head is pounding in unease. "James," I greet as evenly as I can, meeting him at the bottom of the steps.

James studies my nervous state. "Do we have a problem? I overheard Damian in the living room." James points his thumb over his shoulder toward Damian, standing in the doorway - who fires me an apologetic look.

Shit! James knows. Now I can't release her tonight anymore.

I glance at the door to my right that leads to the basement and see that door closing; someone just walked in or out. "No, I'll talk to you tomorrow."

James eyes are focused on his phone screen as he distractedly says, "Fine." He looks up. "You okay?"

Sweat forms on my brows. "Tired as hell."

"Me too. I'm going up. Let's meet at nine in the morning, son."

I nod as he disappears. The front guard enters the living room on the other side of the foyer. "Fuck," I whisper while clenching my jaw. I wait until the door is closed so nobody can see me going into the basement. The guard shuts that door immediately, leaving the foyer finally empty. I run to the basement door and take the few steps two at a time. Fallon's in the last room. Ignoring my ringing phone in my pocket, I race to the last room and key in the code to open the door. Frank's gone, and Fallon has her back to me, a phone pressed to her ear.

She turns around, her gaze latches on to mine, and the shaken expression on her face tells me that she was calling me. I swallow back my rage when I see blood on her nose and mouth. The phone she's clutching slips out of her hand and falls to the ground when I inch closer to her. She's in shock. Her fearful eyes follow my slow movements. Her eyes dart to the phone and then quickly back up to me. She's going to reach for it because Fallon's instinct is telling her, correctly, that I'm not here by accident.

Is that Frank's phone she's managed to get hold of?

We both dash for the phone, and I snatch it up before she touches it. Her bound left hand restrains her, and I close the door quickly before turning back around. She edges away as I stalk toward her. "Fallon." I approach her like I would a scared child. "I'm here to help you." Her look of terror and confusion magnifies. My chest achingly heaves from the displeasure simmering below the surface at seeing her in this state.

I didn't get to her in time.

Her entire body is trembling and shaking. "Wh-what's happening? Why... What are you doing here..."

How do I get her to trust me? "Fallon, I did not have anything to do with you being here. I didn't know it was you in here until a few minutes ago."

She keeps staring at me. Her shocked expression aimed solely at me. Every negative emotion glints in her fearful eyes.

"You're bleeding," I say quietly and slowly approach her.

"Don't come near me," she warns in a broken voice.

I drag my hands through my tousled hair. "Fallon, you're bleeding. I want to check your injuries." I need to examine the cuts on her knees and the bruises on her face.

She touches her nose and looks at her bloodied hand. With her bottom lip quivering profusely, her mouth falls open but nothing comes out except for an almost imperceptible gasp. Her eyes are stricken with consternation.

Resting my forehead on my clenched knuckles, I try to calm myself because I need to regain my composure for her. "Fallon, we don't have much time."

"Why...? What? I don't understand anything." Her eyes are overflowing with unshed tears. "Are you getting me out of here?" she asks in a nervous tone.

I see her mind desperately trying to put together a scrambled puzzle of which she's missing all the essential pieces. She knows I'm part of this, somehow. Her fear is tangible in the vast silence while she waits for my answer.

I close the distance between us and splay my hands on the wall on either side of her head. "Listen to me carefully. There are cameras watching this. Do not let on that you know me. That will not work in your favor."

232

She recoils, thinking I'm threatening her. Good. I need her fear to force her into submission now. "You are part of this?" Her voice is infinitely small.

My brow creases. "No, not the way you think. I can and will help you, but you have to trust me for now." I ease back to watch her reaction.

Fallon's probably going in shock because she's staring ahead at the door, and her eyes glaze over right before she faints. I catch her and lay her on the bed, lowering myself in front of the bed to check the blood on her face. Frustrated that I can't find where it's coming from, I wipe the already-dried blood away with my sleeve. Thankfully, she's not cut. My barely contained rage storms within me when I stroke the welts on her face.

"Luca, I'm coming in." Adriano keys in the code and opens the door. He hands me a first aid kit. "The camera is turned off in here. The house is almost empty. I'll stand watch at the basement door."

I accept the kit, never looking anywhere but at Fallon. "*Grazie*. Leave the door open."

Adriano leaves, and I start to clean Fallon's face, neck, and hands. My eyes wander over her body. I swallow heavily when they fall on her battered knees and immediately clean the cuts and gently apply antiseptic. She stirs – jerking her left arm - and rejoins our world. "Shh." I caress her hair. A deep sense of sadness overwhelms me when her fearful expression meets mine and realization of her situation sets in as the last couple of hours flood her memory.

"What happened?"

"You fainted. How are you feeling?"

"Luca, what's this room? What's going to happen to me? Please tell me. I'm scared." The anxiety is rising in her tone.

I exhale curtly. "Tell me how you're feeling first, Fallon."

"Confused."

"Physically, how are you feeling physically?"

"My knees hurt and my cheekbones too."

With all my power, I keep my fingers entwined to prevent from reaching out to her. Relieved that no other parts of her body hurt, I deliver her answers. "I'm not married. You misunderstood that message on the phone. Make a marriage simply means a business merger." I pause to take in a deep breath. "I'm part of the *Cosa Nostra.*"

Fallon gasps.

"I'm the underboss of this family. You witnessed a hit. My men are never allowed to leave witnesses so they took you. I've been protecting you from this life."

"Protecting me? By lying to me from the start? Protecting me or yourself?"

"It has always been about protecting you, *dolcezz*a." I reach out to her face but she winces.

"Are you…" She swallows. "You going to kill me?"

Her question saws at my heart. All the trust we've built in the last months vanished by this one night, by these couple of hours that have guaranteed my loss of Fallon. "No, Fallon. I need to find a way to get you out of here."

"How do I know this isn't a ruse? How can I trust you?" Her tone is painted with belligerence.

The entire night is weighing on my mind, and I don't have time for her defiance now. "You have no choice, do you?" I counter, unnervingly calm.

Distress colors her eyes again. She's smart enough to keep quiet now.

"I know you must have many questions. Ask them now." Adriano is guarding the basement, and since the house is empty, I want to be honest with her. Maybe with honesty I can provide her a sense of security. I move to sit beside on the bed with my fingers interlaced between my knees.

"I don't know where to begin." She pauses to formulate her inquiry. "Where am I?"

"You're still in Chicago. About one hour from The Loop." I don't tell her she's up north, near Lake Forest. "This is the basement of a house. It's our headquarters."

Fallon licks her dry lips. "Was it all a lie?"

"No. My work was partly a lie. My feelings, never doubt those."

She's holding in a snort because of her fear. "Who are you?" She never breaks eye contact, but the tremor in her speech is a constant reminder of her fear.

I reign in my emotions to lay it all out for her methodically. I'm only willing to disclose this information once in order for her to comprehend the seriousness of her predicament. "I'm part of the Chicago Syndicate. James is the *Capo crimine, the Don*. I'm his underboss. We rule the underworld. I have *Capo* regimes that work for me and James; they handle the day-to-day business. All the *Capi* report to me, as the underboss, and I report to James. Adriano, my friend you've met, he's one of the *Capi*."

"Syndicate?"

"Mafia, *Cosa Nostra*. We prefer the term Syndicate."

Stunned, she tentatively probes, "So you don't have your own company?"

"Yes, Adriano and I are silent partners in a legit company." I pause to check her reaction. "But that company is used to launder money too."

"But what exactly do you do for this...."

"Syndicate?" I fill in her words. "I can't disclose everything, Fallon. It's for your own safety that you don't know the details."

Her hand covers her mouth as tears leak down her cheeks. Her gaze snaps to mine. "Are you his son? This James' son?"

I privately laugh at her comment. "No, we're not technically family. We're a Chicago Crime Syndicate. Contrary to common belief, ranks and affiliations are not hereditary in the *Cosa Nostra*. None of us are blood related."

Fallon shakes her head. "I have so many questions now, but everything is blurred. I'm too shaken up. I'm too scared of what's to come. What's going to happen to me?"

"I need you to fill in some blanks, Fallon."

Confusion clouds her face.

"Do you know what time you were taken? What were you doing in that alley?" I keep my voice focused to not betray my disapproval.

"How do you know I was kidnapped in the alley behind the venue? What time is it now?"

"Focus," I remind her sternly. I told you my men seized you. I already spoke to them; that's how I found out you were the one taken captive." I glance at my watch. "It's almost ten p.m."

Caution is clearly perceptible. I'm silently thanking god that she has always been easy to read and wait patiently for her response, although I can't refrain from touching her anymore. When I lean forward to massage her cuffed wrist, her eyes narrow, but she allows my touch so I let my other hand rest below the bruise on her cheek, my thumb softly stroking the purple-covered skin. In this vital moment, we stare at each other, both realizing our entire relationship has changed forever.

Never will we go back to just being Luca and Fallon.

Never will she trust me again.

Never will I have her full devotion again.

She breaks from the intensity of our stare and faces the wall. Without looking at me, she speaks. "I wanted to talk to you, so I decided to leave the charity around seven, maybe seven thirty. Alex was crowding the front entrance, which is why I used the back exit. I opened the door and saw two men shooting another man. The door closed, and you can't open it from outside. They saw me. I ran, fell, and scraped my knees. The blond guy caught me, hit me, and knocked me out with his gun." Fallon's tears trickle onto the pillow.

I stiffen as she summarizes the events of this horrible night.

"I heard the two men talking about how they screwed up when they thought I was still unconscious. When I woke up, that blond guy came in here – drunk - and tried to rape me. His phone fell out of his pocket without him noticing, so I snatched it and hid it under the covers, and my first instinct was to call you." A disillusioned look is thrown at me.

Fucking Frank.

I'm secretly proud of Fallon. She's obviously telling the truth because her story lines up with what I witnessed on the camera. *Somewhere* she does still trust me.

The usual light in her amber eyes is missing. Her eyes that sparkle in the daylight, illuminating her gorgeous face. Those eyes that have lured me since the night we met. Those usually innocent eyes, filled with so much love for me, are now haunted by hurt. I will kill Frank for ever laying one hand on what's mine. My hand hasn't ceased massaging her wrist.

"Luca, can you undo the cuffs? They cut into my skin."

I tightly shut my eyes to refrain from undoing them. I want to so badly, but she wants to be released to fight me. I know this. She has just learned disturbing news and is trying to manipulate me to escape. The human mind will always try to escape these circumstances. I stand back, bracing myself for the disappointment that will radiate from her. "I can't. I'm sorry, Fallon. I need to find a way to get you out without endangering you more."

Fallon is startled by my reluctance. "Are you going to leave me here?" The incredulous look she shoots me powers me backward.

I need to leave before I undo the cuffs and create more problems for us.

"Luca, Luca." Fallon scrambles up on the bed and lunges at me. With her left arm pulled behind her, attached to the bed, she touches my chest with her right hand. "Luca, you can't leave me alone here. What if he returns? What if someone else comes back? What am I supposed to do? I'm so scared. Please, please don't go." She fires all of this at me at once.

I cover her hand on my chest. "Nobody will come here. I can promise you. See that camera?" I point to the camera in the corner. "I will watch over you every minute, Fallon."

"You're going to leave me alone here?" she cries, clutching my hand. "Please don't do this," she pleads.

I blink back my emotions because my control is crushing, and I place my hands on her face. "I promise I will come back as soon as possible. Do not let on that you know me, okay?"

She buries her head in my neck, and I inhale my Fallon to calm my nerves. Fallon's right arm comes around my waist, tugging me to her. "Please, please don't leave me alone."

Her anguish is like acid pouring over me, her fear scalding my skin. I kiss the top of her head and remove her hand from my waist as I turn toward the door. After closing the door, I can still hear her saying my name repeatedly. Anger and guilt fill my mind.

CHAPTER 27

Luca

Adriano and I stride back to my office through the currently almost-empty house. I immediately turn on the camera in Fallon's room, and she seems so small standing there in the room, looking lost. I rub circles over my tired eyes and throw the phone on my desk. "You sent Damian with Frank? Why weren't you with them, Adriano? You, as the *Capo* of your soldiers, should've been there to prevent this. My hands are tied now, Adriano. Either way, we're screwed. I have no idea how James will react when he finds out I've been dating her. And why did Damian agree to take her? Your men screwed up." I'm furious about this entire situation.

"Luca, if this was any other girl, you wouldn't be upset," Adriano replies evenly. "Damian did not screw up. Would you rather they killed her there on the spot? I sent Damian because he's my first soldier. He made sure Frank was carefully tested."

"Frank fucked up. Do you think I'll agree to his membership now? I'll never allow it. Do you know what he did?" Adriano sits down as I keep my standing position behind my desk, constantly checking my screen. "He tried to rape her."

Adriano's expression hardens. "When?"

"When I ran downstairs. Frank has already proven to be a
liability before he was accepted. Do you realize how ignorant he
is? He's not capable to be a soldier. I want him out." I motion to
Frank's phone lying on the desk. "He lost it when he struggled
with Fallon."

"I will take care of Frank."

"No. I'll take of care of him." I sit down and rest my elbows
on my desk, intertwining my fingers. "He touched her. He beat
her." I can't even express how enraged I am. How badly I want
to unleash my fury on Frank.

"Luca, we don't torture one of our own. You know the rules.
We don't take any chances. Finish him quickly, and then we
need to come up with a plan for her. Frank is the least of our
worries."

Keeping my eyes on my screen, I fight between the need to
hurt him badly and the need to prioritize in order to regain some
control of the situation. "I know," I finally say. My need to
control this situation wins. "Adriano, check one more time to
make sure everyone has left." I steadily give my order, even
though I know Adriano - as my only friend in this organization -
must know I'm all but calm right now.

"Is she worth it, Luca?" My *Capo* has always stood behind
me. He's the only man in this ruthless world I trust indisputably.

"Without a doubt," I answer immediately.

"What is it about her?"

The memory of seeing her for the first time in the club, with her full, soft mouth and her striking brown hair flowing around her flawless face and petite frame comes to mind. Her innocence, the quietness that surrounds her character has attracted me like no other woman has ever attracted me before. "She makes everything worthwhile."

"What are you most afraid of, Luca?"

I'm afraid of losing her love, but I don't say it out loud. All I can think about is her. Remembering the first night I met her calms me. Thinking about my two worlds colliding infuriates and terrifies me. This is not how it's supposed to be. Damian and Frank fucked up. "Where's Frank?"

"Passed out in the living room. Damian's making sure he doesn't leave the house."

My sight isn't moving from the security feed. "I'm giving her a sleeping pill. Meet me downstairs in five. We'll take care of Frank tonight." Fallon has lain down on the bed. She's staring right at me, directly into the camera - eyes haunted with a mixture of anger, fear, and disappointment make me question my sanity.

Opening the left desk drawer, I take out two sleeping pills to crush and stir them in a glass of water in the kitchen.

With the glass in hand, I enter Fallon's room. She struggles to sit up. Hopeful that I've come to end her nightmare, but I'll destroy her hope. "Drink this. I don't want you dehydrated." I lower myself onto the bed.

She eyes the glass. "I don't want to." Fallon surprises herself with the venom in her tone.

I don't want her up all night worrying. "It's only water, Fallon. You must be thirsty?" I ask her gently.

After moments of nothing, she timidly takes the glass and gulps it down. She doesn't spare me a glance and lies back down with her back to me.

My hands long to soothe her. I want to gather her in my arms, but she has erected an invisible barrier around herself. The sleeping pills will allow her to sleep the entire night.

I lock the door with the new code, making certain nobody can access this room.

CHAPTER 28

Luca

I step into the living room, just when Adriano's placing a black plastic bucket of ice cold water on the table. As Frank lies passed out on the couch, Adriano drives his fist into Frank's nose.

Disoriented, Frank almost falls off and touches his bloodied nose. "Fucker. Wh- what—" He stops mid-sentence when his gaze meets Adriano's enraged face.

Damian and Adriano take hold of Frank by his upper arms and jerk him up.

"Stop it," Frank spits with blood.

Damian twists Frank's arm back as Adriano mirrors the action and clutches Frank's neck, hovering him above the bucket and plunging his head in. Frank's body spasms and he kicks his legs out in front of him under the table. His head bangs against the side of the bucket as Adriano keeps him underwater and then brings him back up.

Frank gasps for air. "Damian...no..."

"Shut up!" Damian roars. "You fucked up. Now you pay."

Water's thrashing over the rim when they dip him in again.

The memory of Fallon fighting to avoid being raped explodes in my mind. Of *him* on her. I move to stand in front of Frank. When I signal my hand up, Adriano hauls Frank up.

Frank spits out water and sucks oxygen into his deprived lungs.

"Look at me, Frank."

"*Padrino*, I don-t…know what I did wrong," Frank sputters.

"You should not force yourself on women - for one. Two - you should never touch what's mine. You should never even look at what's mine." I reach for my gun that's tucked in my pants. "Let's play a game." I attach the silencer, which I also had on me, screwing it on while locking eyes with Frank. "Run."

The two men let him go, and Frank jumps up unsteadily toward the back exit.

"Well, at least he's smart enough to not run right into the chests of the front guard," Adriano jokingly says.

We follow Frank's trail through the kitchen and out the back door. The garden perimeter of this house isn't fenced, but there's nowhere to go. There are no other houses for miles, and Frank's running toward the river.

"This guy runs like a drunk girl." Adriano keeps insulting Frank. "He's not even that far away yet."

I hold out my firearm, aiming for his knee. And fire once.

Frank falls down with a loud scream of agony.

We approach him and the three of us tower over Frank lying on his side in the grass. He's clasping his ass.

"Uh-oh, in the butt," Adriano observes and slaps me on my back. "You took *nip it in the bud* too literally. Aim is off, Luca."

I shake my head at Adriano's lighthearted ways, even in the worst of circumstances. "I was going for the knee," I admit.

"Please...Please give me a second...argh," Frank yelps when Damian pins him on his back with the sole of his shoe.

I cast my head down to look Frank in the eye. Another man lost in this cold-blooded world. Targeting for his heart, I pull the trigger and end him instantly before my rage gets the upper hand.

"Throw him in the river. You know the drill," I order Adriano and Damian. "Do you have her purse?" I ask Damian.

"Yes, it was this tiny thing with only her phone and keys," he informs.

"Give it to me when you come back."

Keeping my promise to watch over Fallon, I return back inside the house. I bring my laptop with me to my private room here. I'm not going to my penthouse as long as she's in the basement. I toy with the idea of bringing Fallon with me since the house is deserted. I don't trust anyone in this business except Adriano and James. Only because I knew the importance of capturing Danny - and everything would be risked to silence him - did I not let James in on my involvement with Fallon.

However, I can conclude that Fallon will be of no help in leading us to Danny, nor is she essential in our quest for him.

I lie awake after hours of insomnia while my strategy is materializing in my head. Nobody in this Syndicate would dare touch her if they thought she was my wife. Alessa – James' wife – has been kept out of everything. She's always protected, and she doesn't know that she's constantly being guarded. Now that I've had time to think about everything that's happened and organized my thoughts, I'm starting to discover that the biggest problem here is probably Fallon. How do I convince her to trust me and stay with me? First order of business tomorrow is to tell James about my relationship with her. It's only a matter of time before everything comes out anyway. It's best to have him in my corner. Fallon's already an indirect part of this Syndicate because of her affiliation to me. I just need to make sure she doesn't contact the police. She can go home, and I'll give her time without letting her out of my sight. If I keep her here, she'll hate me forever.

What also has me worried is Leggia. Leggia has been quiet over the last week, which is unlike him. He has been openly taunting me for weeks.

I throw my legs over the side of the bed. I'm the damn underboss of this Syndicate, and I want her in *my* bed not in some cold basement.

I trudge downstairs in my sweatpants and key in the code. Fallon's stirring. Damian handed me the keys to the cuffs before he left. I free Fallon's wrist and sit her up to cradle her in my lap. Her eyes are unfocused as she struggles to stay awake. Sifting her hair out of her face, I revel in the feel of my Fallon. Her perfume is different. Her usual sweet smell is faint, a faded remembrance of her before she was brought in to my corrupted world. She looks up, and by the devotion in her eyes, I can tell she's too sleepy to recall where she is. Desperate as I am to give her some sense of security under these corrupt circumstances, I smile at her.

"I…" She wets her dry mouth. "Don't feel good."

I swallow back the brick that's lodged painfully in my throat and kiss her forehead. "I'll take care of you, *dolcezza*. Sleep." And I hug her to me tightly, not knowing if it might be last time I'll ever be this close to her again without the animosity emanating from her. Pushing my lips into her hair, I leave several hard kisses while breathing her in as the fear of losing her love grows with every minute of every hour.

Her smooth skin is blemished. My *dolcezza* with an admirable spirit to fight despite her fear.

Her bruises will heal.

The cuts on her knees will heal.

The scars on her soul and mind have just begun to form. Those scars will become deeper and deeper with time. Those scars are now feeding her hatred for me. I'm desperate to avoid the day when all that's left is pure hate and contempt for what I allowed to happen to her.

I bring Fallon to my room. Carefully, I lay her on the bed and run back down to close the basement and reenter the original code. I take a glass of water and some fruit back up with me, and I lock the door to my private room, storing the key in my pants pocket. From my drawer, I choose a clean white t-shirt to change her into. Fallon's sleeping peacefully on my bed, and serenity overcomes me now that she's with me again. Caressing her hair back from her face, I touch her lips after removing her dress and bra. I pull the t-shirt down over her head and lay her back down under the covers.

I don't know if she'll ever be able to trust me again. I don't know if she can accept my lifestyle - even in time - but I will do anything to keep her safe. I'm not deserving of her love, but I need it. I want it, and I will not give up on us.

Laying myself next to her, I place her head on my chest. Resting my chin on her head, I enfold her into my body because I need to feel her warmth and hear her breathing.

CHAPTER 29

Fallon

I'm in that dream moment where I slowly sense I'm waking. Warmness surrounds me as my spirit wakes. Luca's familiar scent fills my lungs. Pushing my nose into his chest, I grimace when my face hurts, and my eyes fall open. I try to turn onto my back, but Luca holds me to him. My eyes drift up, and his eyes are intently focused on me.

I take in the grey colors of an unknown room, and my memory overflows with my situation.

The event.

The shooting.

They took me.

Luca's part of the Mafia.

I'm held captive.

Again, I try to move, without success.

"Calm down, *dolcezza*. You're in my room. You're fine. How are you feeling?"

I was in a basement when I fell asleep. The fear crippling me last night is less distinguishable this morning. I hate that he makes me feel safe. Last night replays in my mind. Violated. The sour taste in my mouth sickens me. I feel disgusted and want to shower, wash away the vicious memories of the previous night.

Luca sits us up, and I gasp in pain when the skin on my knees tightens. He tries to pacify me by caressing my bangs to the side. "We need to clean you, *dolcezza.*"

I twitch away from his touch. "Please don't call me that."

Taking in the room – twice the size of my own bedroom - I make mental notes. To my left is the door, probably locked. To my front is an en suite bathroom. There's an adjacent walk-in closet. To my right are two huge windows decorated with golden curtains. Next to the door is a black dresser with five drawers.

His posture tenses and Luca's movement in my hair stills. "We have to shower," he comments as he stands up.

Are we just going to play happy couple?

"Come, Fallon," he urges.

I follow him to the enormous, spotless, white-tiled room with a toilet, two sinks, and a shower with two shower heads. Uneasily, I stand in the middle of the room and catch my reflection in the mirror, not recognizing my pale skin with a purple bruise. Hesitantly, I touch the swollen skin under my eye.

Luca places his hands on my shoulders. "We'll talk later."

Talk? I need to escape.

"I want to shower alone," I whisper.

"Fine, but the door stays open."

I beg him with my eyes to leave me alone, to no avail.

"Shower however long you want, Fallon." He pauses, searching for his next words. "Look at me, Fallon."

My gaze whips to him.

"I'm not going to hurt you. I'll clean your injuries after you're done." Luca wants to add something but decides against it.

The silence is weighing around us and neither of us moves.

Finally, he reaches into the shower and turns on the faucet. Luca dismisses a heavy breath and leaves the bathroom, keeping the door open while sitting on the bed, facing me. That's all the privacy I get.

I strip out of the shirt - that smells like him - and my underwear. Stepping into the shower, I cry when the hot water connects with my cut open skin.

"Are you okay?" Luca inquires.

I don't speak. The steam of the warming water is clouding the shower stall. Luca and I can still clearly see each other. His eyes are stained with repentance. Mine are teeming in tears. With just his stare, he forces the happy memories we've created over the last months to the surface of my mind.

I tear my gaze away from him and scrub my body clean while trembling in pain. The physical discomfort isn't as bad. The bruising on my face is more uncomfortable than painful. Standing straight under the showerhead with my head tossed back, I let the droplets rinse my face and try desperately to achieve some calm to arrange my thoughts.

I was almost raped. Luca's part of the Mafia. I'm kidnapped. What will happen to me? What will happen to us? The last question pops up and instantly certifies my anger. I will not think about us. There's no *us* in this situation. Least important is my love for this man. Most important now, is for me to focus on getting out of here. Luca has already started to provide me with answers. Pushing my hurt, confusion, and anger aside is easier said than done. So many emotions swirl chaotically in my tightly-wound body. I exhale a deep breath and turn off the faucet. Boxer briefs and a clean black t-shirt have been placed on the sink for me to wear.

Luca's rummaging through his drawer. "Sit on the bed, *dol*—Fallon." He comes over to me and crouches before me to apply antiseptic to my knees and cover them with a bandage. He uncaps Arnica cream and lotions the discoloration under my eye.

My eyes drift shut under his affectionate touch. I hear him heave a sigh but refuse to meet his gaze as he's too close. The pad of his thumb wipes my bruised skin, but my hurt and fear are far greater than this lone bruise implies.

"I'm going to shower quickly. I must take care of some business before you and I can talk."

My eyes pop open. "You're leaving me alone again?"

"Listen. You're safe here. Do you understand?"

I just stare at him.

Think. Think. Being alone is perfect, gives me time to find a way to escape.

"Yes," I answer to appease him and don't move an inch from the bed as Luca showers and dresses quickly. I lean forward to

watch him dress in the walk-in closet, just in time to see him
stash a gun in the back of his pants.

He has a gun? Did he ever carry it when he was with me?

He comes out of his closet wearing navy dress pants and a
white dress shirt without a tie. "Are you hungry?"

I shake my head, ignoring my empty stomach.

"Try to drink the water and eat the apple or orange." He
points to the nightstand. "I'll bring more food later." Luca laces
his fingers through my still wet hair. As much as I want to pull
away, I let him. "Nothing is going to happen to you, Fallon. I'll
explain everything tonight." His hand slides into his pocket to
retrieve the room key, and he heads out without looking back at
me.

Immediately, I jump up and press my ear to the door -
listening to his receding footsteps - and click the door handle.
Locked. I race to the other side of the room and check the
window frame. Where does it open? There isn't a single handle
on these windows. Nothing to see outside, only land and trees
and a river in the distance ahead. No neighboring houses. The
sun is hanging low in the baby blue sky, so it must be early
morning. I look down and see that we're pretty high up - not on
the first floor of this house. It's impossible to jump down
anyway, so I give up my effort to open the window and head to
search the drawers. First one is filled with men's underwear. The
second has first aid kit material. The other ones are empty. Next,
I search the bathroom but come up empty also. I don't know

what I expect to find. Maybe a weapon to defend myself, if needed.

The closet is my last hope. It's a small room with several of Luca's tailored suits hanging on the rack. Shirts and pants are folded in square compartments next to the suits, and two pairs of shoes are on the floor. I check all the pockets - the pocket of every pair of pants and suit jacket. Nothing. Disheartened, I throw myself onto the bed to glare out the window.

What to do now?

CHAPTER 30

Luca

I hear Fallon running to the door as soon as I close and lock it behind me. Pinching the bridge of my nose, I compose myself after dealing with her cold behavior. She needs time to process everything.

After my discussion with James, I hope to tell her that I'm taking her home. I need to convince James that she won't contact the police. A soldier or I will guard her at all times until I've gained her trust again. And she *will* trust me again. I'll make sure of that. I still feel her love for me through the animosity and mistrust. Our love hasn't been overpowered by her current hate for me - yet.

On the second floor, I knock on James' office door.

"Come in."

"James."

"Good morning, son." James pours me a cup of coffee and places it on his desk as he leans against it. "Let's cut right to business; we have a busy day."

I take the leather chair and sit down.

"Luca, I need to commend you for being on top of everything these last few months while I've been arranging our new ventures in the east. I'm, as always, content with your smooth and swift execution of all businesses and liabilities."

I rest my ankle over my knee and lean back. "You're welcome. I'm pleased you're still content." I decide to cut to the chase. "I have to talk about a private matter."

"Sure."

"I met a woman."

James smiles.

"You know of her too."

James brows knit together.

"It's Fallon Michaels."

"Danny's girl?"

My lips thin in irritation. "She's *my* girl. But yes, Danny's ex-girlfriend."

"And you've been dating her?"

"Yes. At first it was only to find out if Danny had contacted her - he hasn't. There hasn't been any communication between Danny and Fallon except for that one time he called her, which she never returned. She's of no importance in regards to catching Danny." I look him in the eye and instead of disgruntlement, I recognize fatherly pride. "There's an additional complication. She witnessed a kill last night - by accident. Frank screwed up and kidnapped her. Adriano and I took care of Frank after he tried to rape her in this house. She's up in my room now. She didn't know about the Syndicate until yesterday. She loves me and I love her. After her initial shock wears off, I know I'll persuade her to avoid contacting the police."

James slides into his chair. "Hmm. I'm not happy you didn't tell me about her from the start." He pauses and cracks one knuckle. "But I do get it. I never told you how I met Alessa, did I? She was a friend of one of my girls." He scratches his chin. "When I saw her, I was a goner. I was in a similar situation. I didn't tell anyone about her because I thought it was the only way to keep her. To this day, she doesn't know all I do, but over the years she has found out things that made her question her love for me. Luca, not every woman is cut out for this world. Is she trustworthy? Can you vouch for her? I protect Alessa by keeping her in the dark. Fallon has now been exposed to our Syndicate."

Leaning forward with my elbows on my knees, I vouch. "She's trustworthy. She's smart. It will take time for her to trust me again. She won't go to the police if I ask her not to." I relay all this as if it's a done deal, but it's not. Many of Chicago's police officers are on my payroll anyway. I can make her statement disappear if that's needed.

James taps his pen on the desk. "I trust you. If you believe she's worth it, then you have my blessing. She's your responsibility," he stresses. "From now on, she'll be under the protection of the Syndicate. Our Syndicate needs to be informed that she's your partner. So I presume she's coping well with all that happened last night?"

"She is," I lie. "Like I said, she's a calm and intelligent woman."

"Good, good." James pauses and adds, "I call you 'son' because you *are* a son to me, Luca. I've always wanted you to find someone. A good woman will make this life bearable. We can be ruthless men. That doesn't mean we don't deserve the love of a good woman."

"I just don't want all of this to change her."

"It *will* change her. This life changes everyone, Luca. You can still be happy with her, though. I've had a suspicion you met someone. There was a distinct change in you, and it hasn't been a negative change. I *am* disappointed you didn't entrust me with this earlier. I would've backed you. I've chosen you as my underboss for a reason."

"There was so much going on, James. I wanted us to focus purely on the east. "

James nods. "Ensure it doesn't happen again. You only get one second chance with me. You settle things with Fallon."

"I'm taking her home tonight."

"Good. It's better that she's not here. I wouldn't want Alessa here. Since the drug traffic is set up in the east, Danny is now our number one priority," James reminds me.

"Someone must be helping him hide. It's like he vanished from the face of the earth."

"Did we contact all associates?" James asks.

"All of them. There isn't any trace of Danny Mancuso."

"Feds?"

I shake my head in denial. We have men everywhere, even in the FBI. "No."

James stands up and gets his jacket from the coat rack. "We have a meet with Leggia in an hour."

"Why?"

"I have no idea. You know how it goes - if a meet is requested, I must go. If it's not important, we'll leave immediately. I don't trust Leggia. He's frustrated by Crystal Lake."

I think he's wrathful. "He knows about Fallon. He had someone following her when she was spotted with me."

James turns to me and his hands clench in anger. "He also had Alessa followed this week. Leggia's a jealous, power-hungry idiot. At least his underboss is smarter than him. It's only a matter of time until that Syndicate implodes. Nobody looks after each other. Let's go. We have to be at The Carlton in the city."

I rise from my seat. "I need someone to look after Fallon. As a precaution, let's take Adriano with us to Leggia. Is *Consigliere* coming here or meeting us there?"

"Salvatore is meeting us there. Meet me downstairs in ten." James walks out of the room first.

Damian can stand guard outside, but I don't want him to enter my room. It will scare her to see him again, so my only other option is Camilla, who's ascending the stairs when James heads down. I wait for her at the top. "I need your help. Fallon's in my room. To keep her safe, she's locked in. Long story, I or Adriano will tell you tonight."

Camilla looks appalled.

"Calm down. She's fine, but she needs food today. I need to leave now, and I don't want to send one of the men to her, understand?"

Camilla glances at me uncertainly, obviously hesitant to get involved. "Yes."

"Get savory food, one thing with no carbs, and some chocolate pastries. Take it to my room. Can you do that? I'm entrusting you with her. I don't want to see a scratch on Fallon. *Capito?*" Understood? "Just leave the food in my room. Here's the key."

"*Ricevuto.*" Got it. She takes the key.

"Camilla, I'll explain tonight." I step down the stairs, and Adriano appears from the kitchen eating a sandwich. "Let's go. You're coming with us to meet Leggia," I instruct him.

"Right now?" he asks with his sandwich hanging out of his mouth.

"Yes. Move," I order and head outside. "You have to fill Camilla in on Fallon tonight. Tell her what's needed to calm her down. I just asked Camilla to bring Fallon food today. She'll ask for her help, so talk to Camilla."

"I will. Don't worry about Camilla." Adriano eases my apprehension.

***

Giacomo Leggia ordered an executive hotel room for a meet - which is highly unusual. Meets are short and quick, most of the time in cafés or restaurants of our associates.

We meet Salvatore in the lobby of the Carlton Hotel and go straight to the room. Leggia's underboss, Biagio, welcomes us into the living room seating area, and we're not searched for weapons because none of us will take the risk of using his gun in this hotel - we're on camera and the reception saw us walking in. I'm positive every one of Leggia's men is packing a piece, as are we. Leggia's with two men, flanking on either side of him. Luckily we're with one more person in case of any trouble.

"James, Luca, Salvatore, Adriano," Leggia welcomes in a fake hospitable tone while he stands up.

"Giacomo." James shakes his hand. James and I sit across from him. Adriano and Salvatore stand behind us.

"So, gentlemen, I have an interesting offer for you," Leggia starts.

James and I wait for him to continue.

"You're not curious?" he asks.

"I'm not in the mood to play games," James says calmly. "What do you want, Giacomo?"

Leggia motions for his underboss. "Get the boy."

Biagio disappears into the bedroom.

"Drinks, gentlemen?" Giacomo offers.

"No," all of us decline. Never take drinks at meets. You never know what poison might be added to it.

His underboss comes out holding a blond, surfer-type hacker: Danny Mancuso. James and I avoid eye contact; we never give anything away at these meets. Danny's hands are tied behind him and his mouth is sealed shut with a piece of grey duct tape. His eyes round in horror as he takes notice of us.

"I seem to have found your hacker. Word on the street is that you're quite determined to get him back." Leggia's looking from me to James.

"How long have you had him?" I query in a bland tone.

Giacomo's eyes cut to me. "A few days. As an offer of my friendship, I'd like to propose a deal."

I'm afraid I foresee where this is going, and I'm trying extremely hard to remain calm.

"I have something you want, and you have something I want." Leggia displays a snide smile while he adds, "I know Ms. Fallon Michaels is in your hands. I'll trade you Danny for Fallon." He keeps his eyes on me to check my reaction before moving back to James.

I keep a straight face, masking the pure fury that's scorching through my veins. He's finally using her as leverage.

James asks, "What do you want with the girl?"

Leggia retorts, "What *I* want with the girl is of no importance. I have the guy *you* want."

"What you want with the girl *is* important to me. I'm not into human trafficking, Giacomo. However, I do want Danny, so I'll think about it and will get back to you tomorrow night." James rises and heads out.

Leggia's speechless by James' dismissal of his proposal.

Adriano, Salvatore, and I steadily follow. I look at back at Giacomo before closing the door, and he holds up his drink to me with a derisive sneer.

It was only a matter of time before he would use her against me.

We're quiet as we enter the car. Adriano steps on the gas while I'm silently fuming and having difficulty containing my reaction. I'm losing control over this fucking situation. Fallon's being pulled into my world, yet pulled away from me instead of toward me.

"Do you have Fallon Michaels?" Salvatore starts asking questions first.

"We do," James answers from the back seat. "What is he playing at, Luca?"

"He's trying to create a wedge between us. Leggia thinks I haven't told you about Fallon. He's still one step behind, thinking he can use her as leverage to hurt me - to indirectly hurt you and create a wedge in our Syndicate. He can't take us on as a team. He needs us to fall apart first," I answer tersely without turning my head to face the backseat.

"Yes," James agrees. "How did he know we had her?"

"He must've had her followed last night," I say.

"Somebody fill me in," Salvatore interrupts.

"Fallon is Luca's woman. She's Syndicate protected now," James explains.

"What does Leggia want with Fallon?" Salvatore asks.

"He doesn't want anything with her. He's only using her to create a problem between James and me. He knows I would never allow the trade. Leggia thought James would agree immediately," I retort.

"Adriano, we need to make two stops to pick up money." James shows Adriano the addresses on his phone.

CHAPTER 31

Fallon

All I can do is lie in this bed and go over last night and the last few months with Luca. If I hadn't gone through that alley. If I had just stayed at the venue. If I had listened to my instincts from the start, I wouldn't be in this situation. If I had just called the police with the phone. If, if, if...

Deep down, not even deep down, I knew something was wrong from the start. His vague business trips, the different phones, the priest, his hot and cold demeanor at times. I freaking knew this was not good, but I let my physical attraction to him win over my common sense. Why have I been so reckless? I curl into myself. I couldn't have ever imagined he would be a part of the Mafia. Does he kill people?

I want to believe he won't hurt me, but this is a world I don't know. How does he function as the underboss? What does it mean to work in the underworld? Drugs, human trafficking, murder? Have I been blinded by love for this entire time? He deceived me, but I allowed him to feed me lie after lie and ate it up. His intensity shone through the first time I met him. The darkness shining behind his façade is of a corrupted man, but this corrupted man has a gentle side that I fell in love with. I didn't fall for the man I thought I knew. I fell in love with a façade.

I need to focus and get out of here. I keep repeating those words when my mind wanders to 'what if's.' Denying my tears for now, I angrily wipe my eyes with the back of my hand, grimacing when I rub the bruise under my eye too roughly. I sit up, alarmed, when I hear a key turning in the door.

A tall, young woman with an auburn bob walks in holding a tray of food. She smiles at me shyly as she sets down the tray on the nightstand, and she flinches slightly when she sees the bruise on my face. "Are you okay?" She makes an effort to close the distance between us before she stops her movement.

Another woman is here? Do I take the risk of asking for her help? The risk being she could tell Luca or someone else in this house and create bigger problems for me. Of course I take the risk. "Who are you?" I get up and stand before her so she can clearly see I've been beaten. "You have to help me get out of here."

Shock is all I'm getting in return. "Did one of them hurt you?"

Who are them? Luca and James? The other men who brought me here? "Yes. A blond guy and one with brown hair kidnapped me yesterday."

Her perfectly-shaped brows wrinkle in thought while she eyes me. "What's your name?"

"Fallon."

"Luca's girlfriend?"

Who the hell is this? I thought Luca said nobody could find out I'm with him. More lies from Luca, perhaps? "Yes. Who are you?"

"Camilla. You're here for your own safety." She waves to the tray. "I brought you drinks, a chicken salad, and a croissant."

I don't want any food! "Look at me." I point to my bruise and battered knees. "I'm not here of my own free will. They took me last night and the blond man tried to rape me."

Camilla gasps and shoots me a disbelieving look.

What did Luca say this place was? Headquarters? Is she staff or something? She can't be part of the Syndicate with that reaction. "Are you part of the Syndicate?"

Legitimate confusion marks her reaction. "Syndicate?"

She's apparently not part of the Syndicate. "Listen to me. What do you do here? They kidnapped me; if you don't help me, you'll be an accomplice. I was assaulted last night."

"Adriano would never allow that," she refutes.

Adriano? Why would she mention Adriano? "Are you Adriano's girlfriend?"

A sadness glimmers behind her eyes. There's evidently some history there. "No," she resolutely answers. "I work here. I'm told you're here for your own safety—"

"That's not true! They took me."

"But you are Luca's girlfriend?"

I sigh heavily. "Yes. But look at me. Look at my appearance. You must know something shady is going on here."

Camilla snorts. Maybe she does know more about this Syndicate. "I see that." She turns away from me and palms her head. After a stretch of silence that feels like forever to me because Luca can come through that door at any moment and ruin my chances of persuading Camilla to help me, she edges back to me and whispers, "These are dangerous men. Don't talk too loud; someone's manning the front the door."

I nod my head.

"I work here. There's a small bar downstairs. I've never discovered anyone being held captive here and was only asked to give you your food. This…I don't know what to do. Do Adriano and Luca know what happened last night?"

"Yes, they know," I retort hurriedly.

She steps back and just stares me down. Suddenly, she spins around and is out the door.

When I try to open the door, it's already locked. I slam my hand against it in frustration because I don't think I've gotten through to her. Marching to the night stand, I grab the food tray and fling it against the door in defeat. All I want is to go back to the safety of my own home. Too many confusing thoughts are crowding my mind. Do I trust Luca? I can't take that risk again, but - for now - he might be my only option for getting out.

CHAPTER 32

Luca

As soon as we arrive back at the house that evening, I sprint to the second floor with Adriano to find Camilla behind the bar. She's visibly upset. Not bothering to sit, I immediately ask, "How did it go with Fallon?"

Camilla cuts her eyes from me to Adriano and back. "She's hurt."

"What did she say to you? Did she ask for help?" I'm almost positive that Fallon must've asked for help. Camilla's answer will let me know if Fallon has gotten to her. Camilla knows insignificant matters of our business. She's never been involved in any activity until today, which will reveal a great deal of our Mafia business once Camilla starts connecting the dots.

"No," she counters resolutely.

I signal to Adriano to walk me out, and as he falls into step beside me, I share my thoughts. "There's a very small chance that Fallon did not ask for help, but I can't imagine Fallon not acting on her first instinct to escape. Talk to Camilla."

I continue on to my private room where Damian's outside my room sitting in a chair.

"Did she eat?" I ask.

"No. She had a tantrum, threw all the food around the room. At least it was all wrapped in paper and plastic," he jokes.

I scowl at him.

"I didn't do anything. Camilla asked her if she wanted a drink or anything to eat."

"You can go."

He hands me my room key. Unlocking the door, I see Fallon lying on her stomach on the bed. Her favorite position to sleep is lying on her stomach. I take the chair into the room and place it at the window, facing the bed.

After I check her face, I let my fingertips trail over the slant of her neck and back. The swelling has subsided and seeing that she's lying with her knees touching the bed, the scrapes must hurt her less too. Dancing my fingers over the soft skin down the small of her back, I can't contain myself and bend forward to place a kiss above her behind and rest my forehead on her lush body. Tightly shutting my eyes, I whisper her name in the dark to nobody, "Fallon." And I palm her ass softly. Having her this close and yet so far is conflicting. I'm too fucking conflicted most of the time when it comes to her. Her association with me has changed her life and will affect her future. She offered me love, and I gave her hurt and danger in return.

When she suddenly stirs lightly under my hand and I hear the tiniest, gentlest moan from her lips, all the blood rushes from my brain. As much as I want to fuck her, I know chances she'll slap me are higher. "Fuck," I mutter harshly.

I can't take her home now. She's in more danger at home because Leggia's started the war.

I strip out of my clothes quietly and slide into the chair. My hands rake through my hair to temper my outrage over Leggia's proposal. My new plan with Fallon is full disclosure. I'll fill her in on everything tomorrow. Everything. She has to know how much danger she's in, or else she'll never agree to stay here, but I won't pose it as a question. If she knows she can leave, she will take that option. Leggia's a great threat to us, and I don't know what James will decide regarding the trade.

Fallon's eyes slowly open and they land directly on me while she sits up. I see that she looks much better than this morning - the swelling under her eyes has lessened, but she has a faraway look. "I read once that the first twenty-four hours of being kidnapped are crucial. Most people who aren't found in those first twenty-four hours are never found." She lies back down. "My twenty-four hours are up." Her head falls to the side on the pillow, glaring at me with bleak eyes.

"I'm trying my best to protect you."

"Then explain it to me, Luca. I think you owe me that. All you're doing now is scaring me by leaving me in the dark."

She's desperately trying to find a way out of here. She was lethargic this morning and was angry later this afternoon. Silence is all I can give her now because I have no plan at this moment. The emotional turmoil in her lithe frame is shining through her eyes.

Fallon gets up and removes her shirt and boxer briefs in front of me.

My hand shoots out to touch her soft skin.

She crawls onto my lap and straddles me. Is she going to seduce me in the hopes that I will release her?

I place my hands on the armrests and clutch them tightly because I want to touch her instead.

"You love me, Luca." Not a question but a statement. She rubs herself over my boxers while streaming her nails up my chest, over my shoulders, and down my arms as she rotates her hips and moans quietly.

I'm hardening underneath her and hold in a deep growl while our eyes are steadfastly fixed on each other.

Which one of us will end this game first?

Fallon pries my fingers loose from the chair and places my hands over her rounded breasts. I grip their softness and leave a wet trail with my tongue over one without losing eye contact.

She exposes my already raging hard-on and grinds her wetness all over me.

Fuck. I want to lose myself in her warmth.

I squeeze her breasts hard as I watch her sliding over me. But when I look up, I'm confronted with our situation and bitterly thrown out of my need to fuck her. Her eyes aren't filled with lust; she's staring at me with a calculated look.

What was her intention? Did she even have a plan?

I cup her ass and rise quickly while her arms drape around my neck and fall back on the bed as I push us into the mattress. I widen my legs, forcing her knees apart further and growl while pushing against her. With my elbow on the bed, my left hand rests next to her head, I skim my right hand over her knee, slowly up the inside of her thigh until the tip of my thumb flicks her core. I take her chin between my fingers and thumb, and I tug her head to have her eyes on me. She wants me to fuck her so she can hate me. I capture her lips with mine, prodding my tongue between her parted lips while panting furiously.

Fallon's calculating look has been replaced by anxiety.

I pull back an inch, keeping us face-to-face. "I do love you. I'm risking everything to keep you safe. You just want to validate that all I want is to hurt you. You want a good reason to end this relationship when all is said and done. I'm not like that guy who forced himself on you yesterday."

"You're not? What is he? Isn't he one of your *men*?" she spits.

"He was," I explain.

Her eyes turn to slits.

"Did you think I would allow someone like that in our Syndicate? You know nothing of us. And you don't know me at all if you think I would accept someone forcing himself on a woman, let alone you." I pause. "He's been taking care of."

"What does that mean?"

"He isn't among us anymore," I confess. Appalled and stupefied, she goes still underneath me. I swear I saw a flicker of satisfaction cross her face. She understands that I mean we killed him. "You don't look saddened by that. As long as we only kill bad men, it's fine?"

"He tried to rape me," she cries and stops sharply after her reaction sets in. Fallon didn't deny my question. Softly, she adds, "You killed him?"

Point made. "*You* are the one who will regret it in the morning if we fuck, and *I* won't do that to you."

I get off of Fallon to lie beside her and adjust my boxers. After a few minutes, she turns on her side with her back to me. I move in behind her and let my hand rest on her stomach, pulling her to me - my favorite position. She makes an effort to push me away, but I hold on to her firmly.

I barely sleep for the second night in a row.

CHAPTER 33

Fallon

A ray of sunlight illuminates the room. I've been awake for hours. So has Luca. Tomorrow is Monday. If I'm not at work, people will start to ask questions.

He's right. I wanted him to be forceful so I could hate him. My mind is angry, but my heart still loves him. My body still wants him. I don't hate him. I hate that I felt relieved after hearing that blond guy has been taken care of. I hate that in my confused state I mistakenly thought I could seduce him into letting me go. The sheer fear I felt that first night has been quelled by Luca's presence. There's something much bigger going on. I've known it for weeks, but I didn't listen to my gut instinct.

Luca sits on the edge of the bed, his head resting in his hands. "I'm going to tell you everything. You need to listen and understand what I've been doing and why it's important for you to stay here with me."

I sit up too and clutch the sheet over my naked body.

Luca sighs. "You have to listen to me, okay?"

I don't think I have a choice. "Okay."

Luca swirls his body to me. I'm in the middle of the bed and he's on the edge opposite me. "Danny used to work for me."

My ex-boyfriend? "Danny Mancuso?"

"Yes." Luca swallows heavily.

"For the Syndicate or your company?"

"The Syndicate."

"Danny was our hacker. He betrayed us and has been hiding for months. I have been looking for him ever since. I found out he was hiding in The Loop. A quick search showed me his only connection there was his ex-girlfriend: you."

This revelation has me gaping at him in bewilderment. I know Danny's a hacker. "Wait, you planned to meet me?"

"No, let me finish, then you can ask all your questions," Luca says as he holds up one hand. "I was following you that night into the club. I was not supposed make contact, but you literally made contact with me. I wanted you from the moment I saw you in the club, Fallon." He scoots a little closer.

I'm too shaken to move. He has been lying from the start about everything. A horrible feeling of dread overwhelms me.

"On our first date, I saw that he tried to call you. Your phone rang when we were talking."

I'm searching my mind about our first date. "When did he call? When we were at the restaurant?" My brows furrow in thought.

"No, our first date was the first time I met you in the coffee shop," he explains.

He sees that as our first date? Danny did call me. I never called him back. "So you followed me to the coffee shop as well? It wasn't a coincidence when we met there?"

"Yes, I followed you. I knew your routine. I knew I could find you there in the mornings. After that first time, I knew you would be of no help in finding Danny, but I was attracted to you. I didn't want to walk away when I met you. I fell in love with you, Fallon. However, a hacker betraying us is a serious crime in my world. I needed to keep you safe, and you being linked to me would put you in danger. One of the other bosses has been out to get James and me. He had a guard following me when you were with me. Sometimes I've had someone watching over you to make sure you were safe when I wasn't with you. This other boss, Leggia, has been waiting for the opportunity to use you against me."

I'm silent as my gaze bores into him. As if my life is ending, every piece of information flies through my mind. Because he was looking for Danny, he met me. He's an underboss of a powerful and influential Syndicate - they must be powerful because they're functioning completely under the radar. He sells drugs, kills people, and deliberately kept his criminal life a secret by stacking lie upon lie while letting us grow closer.

What have I gotten myself into by getting involved with this guy?

"At Lake Forest…" He pauses to meet my eyes. "There was a guy following you. It was Leggia's man. He has also been taken care of. The priest - I know you saw me with him. The priest is Leggia's priest. I've been gathering information on him to make Leggia back off."

I was followed and didn't even realize how much danger I was in. And he knew all along I spotted him at the church? All the pieces are starting to fall perfectly into place. "That's why you called that day and showed up at my apartment."

"Yes, I was expecting you to start questioning me about the priest. You didn't ask, though. And I didn't know how to react in that moment. You have been slipping away from me for weeks, Fallon. I've felt the disconnect between us."

"I felt like you were slipping away from me." My accusing glare targeted on him. "But I never had you to begin with."

"That's not true." He waves his hands around. "This doesn't define me. I'm still the Luca you fell in love with."

"How can you say that? Of course this all defines you. Do you even realize how differently you think from other, mundane people? No. Yesterday you just pragmatically confessed you killed another person. All you know is Syndicate life. I'm not used to being around people who kill, for god's sake! I've never been subjected to criminals or any criminal activity. I'm a simple girl who never thought she would become mixed up in this...this mess. You have no idea how it all affects me. You live in a completely different world than I do. People are dispensable in your world of violence. A world outside the law."

A condescending snort escapes him. "The law? The law is also us," he enlightens me. "The Mafia is everywhere. We have people in the police. *You* can't go to the police because the Syndicate will know. You are under Syndicate protection now - as my girlfriend. And what would you accomplish by going to the police? They'll draw up a statement and never look at your case. The guy who assaulted you has been dealt with by me. Don't people go to the police looking for justice, looking to have the accused punished for his crime?"

His logical explanation is disconcerting me because I have no retort.

"Your boss is also connected to us. Alex has been borrowing money from *us* for his charity. He has also embezzled money from said charity. You were already indirectly tied to the Syndicate."

I rest my palm on my forehead. "This has to be some kind of nightmare I'm about to wake up from." The sheet has fallen in a pool around my hips, and I tug it up again.

Luca continues. "If I let you leave now, I don't know how to protect you. One more thing: Leggia has Danny. I was planning on taking you home last night, but Leggia wanted a meeting with us. He had someone watching you Friday, and he knew you were taken by our soldiers. Leggia's determined to break this Syndicate apart because he wants more power, the kind of power and influence James has. He has offered to trade Danny for you."

My eyes snap up and I jump from the bed. Terror has found its way back into my being with that last sentence, and oxygen isn't filling my lungs as I gulp for air.

Luca immediately mirrors my action and closes the distance between us. His hands are on either side of my head. "Look at me, Fallon. Breathe calmly, in and out. Nothing is going to happen. Breathe *dolcezza*." Luca inhales and exhales slowly with me until my gasping subsides.

My panic regresses as time ticks by slowly. I rest my cheek on his chest and pull back instantly because I don't want any of his comfort. "What does he want with me?"

"Nothing, he's only out to rile me up." Luca walks us back and sits me down. I cover my trembling naked body with the sheet when he crouches before me. "James and I will find a way to eliminate Leggia."

Suddenly a thought arises and I shoot up again. "What about my parents? Are they safe?"

He guides me back on the bed by my shoulders to calm me down and resumes his position. "They're fine. Leggia isn't stupid enough to have a civilian lawyer involved in this. That will create too many questions."

This is so much information for me to take in. The situation is an even bigger mess than I ever anticipated. His rival has Danny and wants to trade me for Danny, which would mean I would be a captive of another Mafia boss. The enormity of my dire situation dawns on me. I fell in love with a man I don't know at all. I fell for what I thought he was. I'm in way over my head in a world I never realized existed so close to me, and he brought me into this dangerous world. "You never once said you were sorry." I catch his pained eyes.

"Sorry for what?"

"For bringing me into this."

"Would it have made any difference?"

I avert my gaze. "No."

"For your own safety, you need to stay here a couple more days. Fallon, do you trust me?"

No.

"I don't know. I'm hurt, disappointed. I'm mad at you. This is all too overwhelming and so…so surreal." Currently, my best option is to let Luca believe he has convinced me. Hopefully, Camilla will have to bring me food again today, and I can try to talk to her once more.

Luca rests his head in my lap. "You know what attracted me to you? Your serene appearance. In that club with your loud-mouthed friend jumping around you, you carried yourself with grace and a quietness that was simply stunning."

I avoid touching him. "Stop. I don't want to hear this now."

I'm inclined to believe him.

I'm inclined to distrust him.

Luca raises his head. "What are you thinking?"

"Have you told me everything?"

"Yes, full disclosure. I took a risk here too by telling you. I vouched for you. If you go to the police and anyone in this Syndicate finds out and tells James, you and I and your family could be in far greater danger."

My face contorts as I allow the first tears that have been burning behind my eyes to wet my cheeks. "This is such a…"

"A cluster fuck. I know."

"Am I to stay in this room?" I'll let Luca believe I'll be cooperative.

"No, you can walk around. I'm trusting you not to run. Do know there are guards, Fallon. You can't just walk out the door here."

"I figured that. And after this business with Leggia is over, am I safe to go home? Is my family safe?"

"Yes, but your life will forever be connected to me. I will look after you."

That's what I'm afraid of. "Is that a threat or a promise?"

Luca winces. "Not a threat."

Should I tell him?

If I can walk around, I can find Camilla. "How many people are in this house?"

"Not many. I'll make sure as few people as possible will be here as long as you are. No one will bother you. If you want to leave the room, you can. If you want to stay, I'll bring everything you need here."

"I'm overwhelmed. I don't know what I want." My empty stomach rumbles and clenches.

"You need sustenance, Fallon. You have to eat something."

"Fine," I snap. He's a Mafia underboss who kills and has lied to me from the beginning of our relationship. I don't trust him.

I need to get out of this mess.

CHAPTER 34

Luca

Fallon has fallen back asleep after our talk. I'm skeptical about how to interpret her simple acceptance of the situation. Last night, she was all over the place, I was bracing myself for one hell of a battle with her. There's an elusive undertone in her behavior that I can't discern.

I shower and dress in record time. In the walk-in closet, I remove the fake back of the top compartment next to where my suits are hanging and take my Smith & Wesson out.

I despise myself for bringing her into a world filled with insecurities and lies, but I would do it all over again if given a second chance. There wasn't a moment I considered walking away. I realize now that I never stood a chance of resisting her. Her beauty attracted me. Her innocence countered my ruthlessness. Her body challenged my passion. Her humor addicted me. Her disarming touch fed my love for her. I had forgotten what it was like to live in a world where the Syndicate doesn't exist. And even though I can and will never leave the Syndicate, maybe she can accept it.

In the kitchen, I get yogurt and fruit for Fallon to eat. Adriano's searching the fridge for food.

"Did you talk to Camilla?" I ask him.

He comes around the table and grabs a green apple from the bowl of fruit in the middle. "She was a little upset."

"What did Fallon tell her?"

"I don't know. Camilla was too secretive. She acted distant and just said that Fallon didn't say anything. By the way, she knew of Fallon. Well, not by name but Camilla knew you had a woman." Adriano's inquisitive eyes rest on me.

"Camilla helped me pick out a gift for her a couple of weeks ago."

"Camilla wants to see and talk to her, make sure Fallon's fine. I obliged her, told her it would be okay." Adriano grins ruefully. "I can't deny Camilla anything. You have to help me out here."

"I don't know if it's smart to have them talk. Fallon's erratic right now. First she was fearful, then apathetic, then angry. I was expecting the range of emotions, but this morning she was accepting of the situation. It was peculiar - I told her all of it: Danny, the trade, how we met. To reclaim some trust, I gave her free passage through the house. Now she's sleeping, thankfully. I'm not keen on letting her out of the room in her current state."

"She's confused and scared about accepting her current situation."

I nod absentmindedly. "James and I are going to discuss a course of action on Leggia and Danny. I'll fill you in later." I shift back to Adriano in the doorway. "Check on Fallon. I'm leaving the key inside the room. I don't think she'll venture out, but if she does, follow her every move. And have Camilla buy her some books, romance novels."

"Done," Adriano replies as he takes a bite of his apple.

Fallon's still sound asleep when I enter the room, so I leave the food on the nightstand before I go downstairs to meet James in his office.

Sitting opposite him, I immediately want to know what we're planning. "Do you have a plan yet?"

He's silent before he carefully touches the issue. "Luca, I think we need to trade—"

"No! Trade is not an option for me, James." My tone layers with indignation.

He holds his palm up. *"Calmati. Ascoltami."* Be calm. Listen to me. "The only way to get Leggia to agree to another meet is if we trade Fallon for Danny. We need a meet to take him out. He wasn't expecting me to think about his offer. I only did that for you, Luca. But, son, we have no choice here. He has upped his security since yesterday. Prolonging the inevitable will cause us more trouble. Danny has too much insider information that he can and will share with Leggia in exchange for the right amount of money. Leggia's taking huge risks with this offer. He's fighting with all his power against the fixed hierarchy, and the New York Syndicate and I want him out. He's too big of a risk."

This will be it. She'll never forgive me. She'll never let us have a life together again beyond these walls. She's going to throw a fit when I just regained an ounce of trust back. *"She* will be at risk; I don't like that." I rise before his desk. "I don't know if I can do this, James. And *you* can't do it without Adriano or me. We are your best men. Kill him without having the trade take place."

James remains seated and says in a level voice, "How? He's in public constantly, with security now. He knows I will not target him in public. "She'll be safe."

I don't know how she'll be safe, and that pisses me off. I loosen my tie while grating my teeth. "What's the plan?"

CHAPTER 35

Fallon

I open my eyes after Luca has stepped out again. Feeling deflated and empty, I stare at the unappetizing apple on the nightstand. Even though I'm starving, I'm unable to eat. Every bit of information is flying through me in fast forward. I lie there, unmoving, for hours and hours with nothing but a blur of memories flashing across my eyes.

We live with the choices we make. And all those – sometimes seemingly insignificant – choices affect everyone and everything around us. We love and hurt each other. However, there's always that one person where even the magnitude of the hurt doesn't lessen the intensity of the love. I'm afraid Luca is that person for me. I chose to believe him, and he chose to lie to me. I'm in love with something that never was.

As I'm standing under the hot stream of water under the showerhead, my head is starting to clear. I need to stay focused, and - like yesterday - I remind myself of that throughout my shower. Stay focused and get out of this mess. So far, Luca has tried to comfort me into a false sense of security before telling me some guy wants to trade me. He hasn't hurt me physically, but I can't afford to trust him again.

Dressed in a clean pair of boxers and a t-shirt that was left on the comforter, I sit on the edge of the bed gazing at the door with sweaty hands. I could walk around, find Camilla. But I'm anxious about running into someone. What do I say? Who says I'll be safe? Maybe this is a test Luca set up?

Unexpectedly, the door opens and Camilla has returned. Exhaling a long breath of relief that it's not Luca, I give her a small smile.

Camilla closes the door quietly behind her and joins me on the bed after she sets a book on the dresser. "Hi," she starts hesitantly. "I'm sorry for bolting out of here. I-I didn't know what to do."

But she must be inclined to help, or else she wouldn't be here having this conversation with me. Unlike yesterday, I don't bombard her by desperately begging for help. I'm approaching her calmly today. "I understand." I point to the book and tilt my head to the side to read the title of the spine: *The Summer Garden* by Paullina Simons. The book I'm currently reading - Luca knew that. Does he think this will make me feel better?

"Luca asked if I could bring some romance novels, then ordered me to get that one," she explains with a bemused expression. I don't even understand what's going on in Luca's head, so Camilla must be even more mystified about what's happening now. "Did he hurt you last night, Fallon?"

I could lie and say 'yes' in hopes of convincing her to help me, but the earnest look she's sending me prevents me from lying. "No. Not physically."

"Did he tell you anything? How long until it's safe for you to go?"

"He told me. And it's even more complicated than I initially thought. Camilla, I don't know when it will be safe for me. Apparently I'm some kind of bargaining tool for a trade to another Mafia boss." I reveal what he told me, omitting some details.

Camilla's stunned into silence.

"I don't know what exactly your role is in this house, but I have a feeling you're caught up in this just as unwillingly as I am. Maybe not as deep into this mess as me, but you can't possibly condone all of this?" The woman with kind eyes facing me is my only hope.

Camilla stands up and starts to pace. "Of course I don't condone this." She tucks her hair behind her ears decisively. "I've heard the term 'Syndicate,' but I didn't realize that's what they call themselves. Shit! I don't condone this," she emphasizes with urgency while catching my eyes. "I can't pretend nothing is wrong like Luca and Adriano do. As long as they kept me out of their business, I was fine. However, since they dragged me into this and nobody is apparently telling the truth, I feel obligated to help you. Yesterday was just..." She blows out a tormented puff of air while inching toward the window. "Overwhelming for me.

I haven't slept because I was worried for you. Adriano's refusal to explain and the way he was drilling me last night was weird. I don't know how or if I can help you."

I immediately move to the window to join her. "You must be scared too?"

"I am." She avoids my gaze. "I guess I underestimated the ruthlessness of Adriano and Luca. Of course I realized they were into drugs, but I never heard or saw anything hinting that they're part of some powerful Mafia. I thought I knew Adriano."

I can relate to how she feels. There's a past between her and Adriano. "What is it between you and him?"

She snorts to conceal her hurting heart. "Nothing. Well, nothing for him."

I'm wondering how a beautiful woman like Camilla ended up here. "Camilla, why are you here in this house? How did you meet Adriano and Luca?"

"James and Luca offered me this job after I was fired from a restaurant because of them. I started last year. I overheard drug business only twice; usually these men are tight-lipped."

"How old are you?" I interrupt.

"Twenty-three. You?"

"Twenty-six."

Camilla faces me. "Look, I want to help you, but I have no family. My life has actually been better since I started working for Luca and Adriano. I'm hesitant because as much as I want to help you, I'm left wondering what will happen to me out there."

She nudges her chin to the world outside the window.

"Apparently, they're very powerful from what you've told me."

"I think they're very dominant in the underworld. Camilla, I promise you if you help me, you will not be alone." And I mean that. "I have to find a way to escape."

Camilla doesn't nod or consent, but a ray of hope is starting to shine through the dark. Silence follows as we're probably mirroring the same thought: *how did we end up here?*

"How was *The Phantom*?" Camilla suddenly asks.

"What?"

"*The Phantom of the Opera.* How was it?"

I went to The Phantom matinee with Luca for my birthday weekend in New York. "How do you know that? You seem to know a lot - you knew I was his girlfriend. He told me nobody in the Syndicate knew of us."

"Nobody did - only Adriano and me. I helped him pick out your gift."

"I see." She has a friendly bond with Luca then. Maybe she can fill in some gaps for me. "Do you know Gina?"

As if she tasted something vile, the corners of her mouth tilt down. "Yes, but how do *you* know her?"

"Who's she?"

"One of the strippers here."

"There's a strip club here?" The strip club Gina works for is a club in this house? "You mean the bar you tend?"

"Yes," she confirms.

"Does she still work there? Did Luca sleep with her?" My curiosity wins.

"No, she left out of the blue a couple of weeks ago. And yes, he slept with her. Only once though, as far as I know. She was always all over him. Luca isn't often in that room - not to be entertained by any of the women at least."

I snort and stop my line of questioning because I don't want to know any more. "And Adriano?" Feeling drawn to her like a kindred spirit going through the same waves, I ask about Adriano.

"Adriano is a man whore," she mumbles.

CHAPTER 36

Luca

I jolt awake after my first deep sleep since Friday.

Fallon.

As I roll my head to the side, she comes into my vision, sleeping on her stomach.

What day is it? Monday.

The trade will take place Wednesday night. I sweep the back of my hand over Fallon's spine. Mostly she sleeps. Camilla brought her a book yesterday, and she started reading it last night. She doesn't talk much, but at least she ate.

I rub my hand over my face and check the time on my watch. It's already ten. Leaping out of bed, I shower and dress in a hurry. Fallon's still in the same position snoring softly when I leave the room.

On the second floor, I stroll into my office and retrieve her tiny purse from Friday from my desk drawer. Sitting behind my desk chair, I take out her phone to message her work that she's sick. A message I would've sent earlier this morning had I not overslept. The display tells me that she has received three messages: two from Teagan with nonsense about her dates over the weekend and one from Jason sent this morning around nine.

Babe, you okay? Alex told us you're sick
at home. I'll call later. Feel better soon.

My eyebrows crinkle together in perplexity as I lean back in my chair and re-read the text. There is one missed call from Alex before nine. There hasn't been any contact, but Alex says she's sick when she doesn't show up at work. She could be late. He doesn't know what the reason for her absence is. This is odd. Something is off and I'm not liking the possibility of what this could mean.

With my phone, I call Adriano to meet me in my office immediately. I check the e-mails on Fallon's phone. Nothing out of the ordinary stands out. Mostly work-related communication, some mails from Teagan and her father.

Adriano opens my door and before he can greet me, I fill him in. "I was going to call Fallon in sick at work, and I discover that Alex told her co-worker she wasn't at the office because she felt sick."

"That's weird. Let me see the message."

I hand Fallon's phone over to Adriano, and he wears the same perplexed reaction that I experienced a minute ago. "I need to talk to Fallon."

"I think you do." He throws the phone back to me, and the sympathy reflected in his eyes confirms to me that he suspects Fallon might have been playing us for a fool.

I race upstairs, feeling in every bone of my body that she hasn't been truthful with me. A few times I've noticed a sudden change and distance from Fallon over the last couple of weeks, but I thought it was the result of my demanding work schedule. I've been preoccupied with keeping track of Leggia for weeks. It has put a strain on our relationship, pulling me away from her because I didn't want to lie to her anymore, so avoidance has been my tactic. Only I suck at avoidance when it comes to her. When she called, I wanted to immediately see her. When I would see her, I wanted to immediately bury myself in her. When she would come, and I witnessed her writhing in ecstasy underneath me, I didn't want to leave the comfort and pleasure her presence and body offered me so willingly. When I'm with her, she sucks me into her calm, simple, and happy life.

Only now, I'm dreading that Friday and whatever follows in the next couple of minutes have put a definite end to how we were. I've uprooted her calm and simple life, and before I've even exchanged one word about Jason's message, I sense this will tear us further apart. When it comes to her, I have no control.

Silently, I unlock the door and find Fallon standing by the window, facing the sky.

Dolcezza, cosa sta succedendo nella tua testa? What's going on in your head?

Fallon swings around when I bang the door shut.

I hold her phone up in my hand and dissect her every move.

She approaches and expects me to hand it over. Fallon has always been most beautiful in the mornings. Her long, dark hair flowing over one shoulder and sultry bedroom eyes combined with her wearing my t-shirt have me distracted for a moment about why I came up here.

I extend my hand, holding it up out of her reach. Succeeding at keeping any angry emotions at bay until I've listened to her, I'm silently begging for my instinct to be wrong this once. This time I must not have missed something crucial because of my love for her. "Your colleague messaged you. Seems that dear Alex has come to the conclusion you're sick before you *or* I ever texted him. You could've been late. Why did Alex tell your co-worker you're sick?"

Her eyes widen slightly and her bottom lip twitches just a fraction of a second, betraying her panic. "I- I don't know." She shrugs in a forced blasé manner that isn't convincing.

I round her slowly. She must turn unless she wants to talk to the door. When I pocket the phone, I take a swift step forward and back her against the door, without any of our body parts touching, and lock my icy eyes with hers. "We said full disclosure," I remind her. Trembling to refrain from touching her bare, smooth skin, my accusing glare starts to show. Her sweet smell floats around me but I ignore any distractions. I need answers at this exact moment, and she's the one who has them. I'm sure of it. Pushing the fact that she's the one woman I love to the back of my mind with much difficulty, I wait for her lips to move in the flooding silence of the room. Not a peep out of her. She's withholding something from me. I place my left palm next to her head. "You have one chance to tell me everything." My right arm shoots out to cage her in.

"I don't know what you're talking about," she says quietly and avoids eye contact while her rigid body seems to be battling anger and annoyance and fear.

I'm pushing her buttons, hoping she will lash out with the truth. "One. Chance." I already see her anger bubbling to the forefront. "I can find out any—"

"You don't think I know that?" she cuts me off as our eyes finally connect, ready to battle. Her voice hardens as her temper flares. "You've said that already. That you can find out anything. Your Mafia is everywhere. You don't think I know that!"

What the hell is she talking about?

She stands firmly. "I knew." She releases a bitter laugh, tinged with rancor. "I knew you were part of the Mafia."

I stammer back because of her hostility and declaration.

She knew? She fucking knew?

CHAPTER 37

Fallon

"I knew you were part of the Mafia." Anger that has been building up since Friday starts to rule my mind. "Don't you dare be angry with me for being dishonest." I point my finger at him. "You have been dishonest for months."

He takes me by my shoulders and shakes me roughly, causing my hair to fly across my face. "How the fuck am I supposed to protect you when you lie to me?"

I struggle free from his hold. "I didn't know how to react or act. You have no idea how it was for me to find out!" I blurt. Irritated, yet surprised at my own outbursts, I finger my hair back angrily.

He steps forward and crowds me. "Lower your voice," he fumingly demands. With a clenched jaw, he backs me up against the door again. His hands slap against it, blocking me in. Luca's entire body is trembling in fury while he quietly speaks. "Have I done nothing to help you?" His fingers mesh in my hair and pull my head back, forcing me to look at him. "I've watched over you every fucking second since you've been here. I've been going through every scenario possible to protect *you*."

My newfound anger dissipates as quickly as it came on. "Luca, you're hurting me," I breathe.

He lets go of my hair. "I don't want to hurt you," he mutters in a broken voice.

Luca increases the distance between us, like he can't stand to be close to me. "What do you mean you knew? How long?"

"A few weeks." I wring my hands together in unease.

"Alex?"

Luca is going to flip if I divulge everything now.

What if he doesn't help me anymore?

"Answer me!" he barks.

My body shivers because of the tremor in his voice. "Yes, he told me."

"When?"

"Last time we had lunch at the deli, he saw us together," I hurriedly explain.

Luca faces the window and clutches his hair. "Keep talking. I'm not going to ask you every damn question. Tell me what happened after you went back to work. I can't protect you if I don't know everything. You're smart enough to figure that out."

His insult stings and adds another jolt of anxiety to my already disordered state. I reveal everything. "Alex saw us sitting together in the deli. After returning to the floor, he called me into his office - I thought for more workload. Inside his office, he mentioned you immediately. He asked me, and I quote, 'If I knew with whom I was getting involved by dating the likes of Luca DeMiliano.' He thought I was working for you. When he caught my surprised expression calling you a Mafia man, he

302

realized I didn't know. He plotted a way to use me. Alex has been threatening my life since then. My fear began that day. He threatened not only me but also my parents if I didn't get him incriminating information on you within a month. Something he could blackmail you with." Too confused to think clearly, I kept that information to myself. I didn't believe Alex, yet I didn't trust Luca enough to confide in him. Deep down, I just didn't want to believe Alex. Accepting the truth also meant accepting how I've been purposely ignoring warning signs because I fell in love. I could've never guessed Luca lives an entirely different life in the underworld. Until Luca explained everything to me yesterday, I didn't understand the enormity of the danger I'm in. Luca's distance helped me to keep my secret. As the days progressed and Alex kept his distance too – only twice verbally inquiring if I had information - I became increasingly confused and was foolishly thinking I could maybe end things with Luca to have Alex back off. In the back of my mind, I knew I was in trouble. I let the days slip by, evading and prolonging the inevitable, and it took me two weeks to decide to confide in Luca. After finding the 'make a marriage' message on Luca's phone, I Googled it and landed on various sites explaining that it's Mafia slang. This was my confirmation that Luca was part of some Mafia. However, between Luca and Alex, Luca then was the lesser of two evils that I hoped could help me. I never believed he was married, but I had to think quickly when he caught me with the phone, so I led him to believe my lie. Later

that night, I decided to tell Luca about Alex. I couldn't handle
the fear Alex instilled in me anymore. It was a risk I was willing
to take, but I acted too late because that night I was taken by
Luca's men. Everything happened so fast and I, again, didn't
know who to trust.

Luca's hands clench powerfully. "Did he hurt you?"

"Not physically; only with his threats."

"Why didn't you tell me before?" Luca doesn't spare me a
glance, keeping his fuming focus trained ahead.

"I haven't trusted anyone since that day. My fear shut me up.
Alex told me that he would find out immediately if I told you. I
had no idea what kind of Mafia you and Alex were in. I didn't
even know if he was telling the truth. I was scared, Luca."

"Why didn't you tell me yesterday?"

I have been withdrawn from Luca since the day Alex called
me into his office with the news that tilted my world on its axis.
Alex preyed on my panic. The angst he instilled in me robbed
me from making smart decisions. Tears drip from my eyelashes.
"Luca." I move toward him by the window. "I haven't been
thinking clearly. I'm not sure—"

"Were you going to tell Alex what you learned here? You
have absolutely no evidence. I think he meant incriminating
information in the form of tangible evidence. Are you working
with him?" Luca demands in a hostile tone.

"No, no," I deny with a shaking head. That thought hasn't
crossed my mind. I hesitantly touch his back.

Luca crosses the room to get away from me.

"I was going to tell you today. After the weekend and everything that happened, I do trust you a little again, Luca. I finally felt that you could help me with Alex, but I wanted to know for sure to trust you before I got myself into more trouble." Luca needs to believe I do trust him. If he's angry with me, he might change his behavior. I do fear him slightly because anger makes people irrational. And these people are members of a Syndicate who murder others.

"Why is he telling people you're sick?" Luca's voice is soft and controlled, yet he's unsuccessful at hiding his growing impatience with me.

How am I supposed to know that?

"Maybe he doesn't want anyone to ask questions, and he must know that my disappearance could be connected to you? Maybe he thinks I'm retrieving his information?"

"Are you sure you're being honest?" Luca's eyes narrow, hardening the lines in his face.

"Yes," I answer resolutely. When Luca opens the door to leave, I go into panic mode. "Wait. Where are you going, Luca?" The urge to know his next move explodes inside me.

Resentment and doubt cloud his eyes as he scans the length of me before closing the door.

I dash forward in alarm when he locks it and smash my fists against the door while I scream for him. "Luca, Luca!"

I should've confided in him. He loves me, and he would've helped me. Why didn't I confide in him when I had the chance? As I peer down at the floor, a few tears land on my bare feet and I irritably dash them away. Will he still help me? I'm back to being locked in. Is he going to trade me? Luca loves me, but I know all too well how love can be ruined by disloyalty. One message from Alex, and the tables have turned. He knows everything I've been holding back, except for my plan with Camilla. Do I know everything he lied about? He said full disclosure, but a man as conniving as he apparently is must have held something back. I'm no match for the shrewdness of men like Alex and Luca.

What will Luca do now?

CHAPTER 38

Luca

I storm back into my office antagonized by conflicting feelings. Her confession is sending me down a spiral of raging emotions that are on the verge of blowing up.

Adriano twists his hand up in question. "Not good news?"

I lean forward with my palms on my desk. "Alex has some balls. He's been threatening her for three weeks and disclosed that I'm part of the Syndicate to her."

Adriano copies my stance. "She knew?"

"This never leaves this room. *Chiaro*?" Understood?

Adriano confirms I can trust him with an instant consent.

I vehemently rub my hand over my lips. "She's been lying for weeks too. He wanted intel from her."

"Is she working with him?" Adriano inquires, aghast.

"No." But my judgment isn't the best when it comes to her. I believed Fallon was easy to read. I piece back all our interactions from the last weeks. Fallon was distant and quiet, more so than usual. She was pulling away from me, but I wouldn't let her.

Fuck!

I slam my fist on the table. I was aware of her overreaction on Friday and distinctly got the impression she was acting. No, she can't be working with him. Fallon's not that good an actor. With a sharp breath, I drop down into my seat. "This mess keeps on getting bigger. I can't trust her, and that enrages the hell out of me."

"Is everything out in the open now?"

"Yes. No. Not positive. I'm not positive of anything anymore when it comes to her."

Adriano starts to recap. "Alex threatened her. With what?"

"Only words. Her parents, the usual bullshit when you want to intimidate someone." Could it be I've underestimated Leggia? "Alex doesn't have the nerve to threaten a woman he believes is dating me. You know how skittish Alex is when we pay him a visit. What if someone put him up to it? Someone like Leggia? Leggia did the background check on Fallon the second he found out she was connected to me. His intel must've notified him that she works for Alex. And Leggia knows Alex is our associate."

Adriano nods, following my line of thinking.

I continue connecting the dots out loud. "What if Leggia contacted Alex and is pulling all the strings from different angles? Leggia instructed Alex to terrorize Fallon to break us apart."

Adriano interjects, "But how would Leggia know Fallon wouldn't just come clean to you?"

Good point. "Risk he was willing to take?" I offer as explanation.

"Possible."

"Now Leggia has two operations set in motion to break me loose from James' Syndicate. And both involve Fallon - the trade for Danny and the fact she was being disloyal. I think this is playing out even better than Leggia had planned. Frank kidnapping Fallon gave Leggia the upper hand." I take Fallon's phone out of my pocket to see if any new messages have been sent to her. Nothing.

"Motherfucker is smarter than we gave him credit for. Where's Fallon now?"

"In my room, locked in."

Adriano's brows crease. "You're probably scaring her. What's our next move?"

The need to protect her overwhelms me. I vouched for Fallon, and although my scenario about Alex and Leggia is pure conjecture, all the pieces are falling together. Her distance, her contradictive behavior - she wanted to believe I wasn't part of the Mafia - her odd reaction Friday, why she wanted to avoid seeing Alex Friday night and went in search of the back entrance. "Alex is out. We proceed as planned with one small addition. Where is the meet Wednesday?"

Disapproval sculpts Adriano's face. "Parish of the Blessed, Father Eli's church."

Of course Leggia is taking precautions and chose a public place like his church, but he doesn't know that Father Eli is already on my radar and this I can use to my advantage. "That's good. We can use Father Eli. Where are we meeting Biagio tomorrow tonight?"

"Warehouse." Adriano stands to leave. "Luca, what are you doing with Fallon?"

I need to calm down before I speak to her again, so I toss my room key to Adriano, and he catches it with one hand easily. "Let Camilla help her today. I can't see or talk to her now. Let's take care of our business." I have three days to clean up this cluster fuck, and James must not find out about Fallon's disloyalty. Since I vouched for her, it will not go well for her or me if James was to know so I'm determined to fix this mess.

Without going back up to Fallon, I leave the house and her behind to handle our business. She used to be the only thing in the world that could calm me, but with one five-minute conversation, did she manage to rip out my heart and slice it into tiny pieces.

This is how betrayal feels.

This is what *I* did to *her*, but far worse by lying all those months.

This is retribution. And it hurts like a motherfucker.

Redemption is not meant for men like me. Only a constant stream of retribution is what lies in my future.

And if she was to ever function in the Syndicate, she would be eaten alive.

CHAPTER 39

Fallon

After hours of distress polluting my mind, the door opens and I breathe a sigh of relief when Camilla appears. "What happened?"

Frantically, I tell her bits and pieces, enough for her to realize I'm still the one held captive here. Luca hasn't been honest, but I get locked up for lying. "He was furious and left, locked the door," I emphasize. "Camilla, I just hit rock bottom. Even though I don't trust Luca, I still felt his undeniable devotion to me. The last couple of days have been bearable because of him, yet I'm here because of him." I swallow back an avalanche of mixed feelings. Fear of the unknown. Guilt for lying. Panic over what to do. And still, still a layer of misguided love for Luca envelops it all. I shake it off quickly. Resolve slowly finds its way through my jumbled thoughts. I've probably destroyed his trust and lost his devotion now. I'm not the innocent party here anymore since I lied to him; I saw that much in his eyes. "I need to leave as soon as possible. What if Luca comes back just as furious? I don't know what he'll do in this state." There's no more time for me to gradually convince Camilla to help me. I need the help right now, so I pound her with questions, hoping we can figure out a way for me to escape. "Where are we exactly?"

The bed dips as Camilla sits beside me. "Melrose."

That's close to Lake Forest.

"In the middle of nowhere though. We're at the far edge of the suburbs," she mentions, solemn. "Shit, I've never seen him this pissed off."

It's not a good sign if Luca doesn't return to this room because he's the kind of guy who needs to cool off and then comes back to fight. If he doesn't come back, then he's still brooding. And I really need to avoid a brooding Luca now. "There has got to be a way out," I implore.

Camilla continues. "I don't know. I have to be downstairs again. I'll be back as soon as I come up with something."

***

She didn't come back the entire day. Neither did Luca. My first night alone and I feel just as scared as I did on Friday. Luca's out of reach, and I'm petrified of what the consequences of not divulging Alex's blackmail will be for me.

CHAPTER 40

Luca

Drenched in sweat, I sit up straight in bed as my eyes adjust to the sunlight streaming in.

Tuesday.

My head jerks to my left just when my hand shoots out to the side to touch her. She's not beside me.

Fallon.

I take in the unfamiliar room, one of the rooms of the strip club. I haven't seen Fallon since her revelation. Adriano and I came back late to the house. Camilla informed me she was crying up in the room. My anger prevailed over my affection, and I couldn't be the one to console her.

Rubbing my eyes, I desperately want to be with her, but I need to concentrate. Only two more days. I don't think about anything beyond those days. Gathering my clothes, I tuck my legs in my grey pants. I don't bother to unbutton my dress shirt and pull it over my head, then drive my hands through my ruffled hair. From the bedside table, I retrieve my silver watch and clasp it around my wrist. It's almost ten thirty a.m.

Leaving the room, I glance left and right and am welcomed by complete silence. I get a bottle of water and down it while sitting on the half-round couch in the middle of the room and let my head fall back on the couch. How am I going to handle Fallon? Will she even cooperate with the trade? She can't be trusted. While I've been patient with her because I do feel responsible for this mess, she's been holding out. If only she had told me about Alex, so much could've been prevented. She broke down my walls with her innocent nature. I would've done anything to be with her when this was over, but we're slipping further and further away from each other with each passing day. Maybe we were just two people meant to journey together shortly and redirect the way. Only instead of redirecting the way, giving it a nudge in the right direction, we clashed and imploded. Maybe, it's time for me to let her go, but that thought is cutting brutally through my chest.

The front door of the room opens with a low creak. I slowly lift my head, and in walks Skye in her short jeans skirt and white see-through tank top. She smiles as her eyes land on me. Skye has the same brown hair as Fallon, only Fallon's hair is thicker and shinier.

"Good morning, Luca." Skye invites herself to sit right next to me.

"Morning." My leg brushes hers and a blush colors her cheeks.

"Rough night?"

"Yeah." Leaning forward with my elbows on my knees, I attempt to escape her penetrating eyes.

Skye places her hands on my shoulders and starts to massage the knots out. "I can help you relax, Luca," she suggests.

I tense on instinct, but relax as her fingers work their magic. Skye stands and pushes me back with her palms on my chest, her cleavage at eye level. My eyes travel upward, and meet her hungry look, and a plan quickly forms in my head - a plan that could backfire on me. What if we use Skye for the trade instead of Fallon?

Skye's making it so easy.

Palming her bare thigh, I allow her to touch me. As my fingers contact her skin, Fallon's exquisite caramel brown eyes emerge behind my eyelids - her eyes disapproving of using another innocent woman. I'm starting to get sick and tired of myself. Of my need for her validation. Of her constantly dancing in the back of my mind while she has been lying to me too.

Skye actually moans from that slight contact, and her fingers travel to the nape of my neck as her mouth inclines to mine.

When her breath blows across my cheek, I say, "I have a favor to ask you, Skye."

"Anything for you, Luca," she answers in a husky voice.

I meet her desirous gaze. "I need…" When she pouts her lips, I shrink back slightly because I can't do this. I don't need to bring another person into this.

A sharp intake of breath steers my attention to the door. My eyes zero in on Fallon blocking the doorway, shocked and repulsed. She's still wearing the same t-shirt as yesterday, underneath peaks a pair of my black boxer briefs.

What the fuck is she doing here? Why is she roaming the house?

My hand instantly leaves Skye's bare leg while I lock eyes with Fallon. She spins and sprints back into the hall while Skye's oblivious to it all.

"I'll be right back." Removing her hands quickly from my neck, I bolt out of the room after Fallon.

"Luca," Skye whines, but I ignore her.

Fallon's heading toward the first staircase.

From the other end of the hall, Camilla advances on her.

"Fallon!" Camilla screams.

I increase my speed. Fallon grabs the banister with her left hand to turn and start her descent, but I push her against that banister before she can take the first step down and circle her waist with one arm.

"Get off me." She's trying to elbow me, so I hold her firmly.

"Calm the fuck down." I fleetingly glance around to make sure nobody is witnessing this. The door I exited is still closed. I swivel us around, my intention to quickly climb the stairs to the third floor. Capturing her arms underneath mine as both my arms encircle her, I shake Fallon to disorient her and continue toward the stairs.

Her legs are flailing, kicking wildly at the air. "Calm down." I whisper yell in her ear. "If you don't calm the fuck down, so help me…"

"Fuck you," she spits.

Camilla blocks my path up the stairs. "Luca, it was my fault, don't hurt her—"

"I'm not going to hurt her. Go to Skye and ensure she's not following me. Now!" My patience is wearing thin. "Give me the key to my room." I open my palm, arms still around Fallon who's determined not to hold still.

Camilla places it firmly in my hand and steps back. Looking from Fallon to me with an uncertain glare, Camilla hesitates for a second, and then runs off.

Fallon's still struggling in my hold, so I tighten my arms and lift her off the floor, racing up to my room as fast as I can.

She coughs as I plant us against the door of my private room, her body flat against it. The key almost falls when I try to unlock it while restraining her. When I get the door open, we fall into the room, me on top of her. I scoot her up and kick the door closed with my foot. Then I pick her up and throw her on the bed.

Our heavy breathing fills the silence as we scowl at each other. Food's scattered on the floor beside the drawers from where she flew out of the room when Camilla brought her breakfast.

"What were you planning to do when you got out of the house, Fallon?"

She scurries back on the bed as I advance on her.

"I went to look for you. You left me yesterday. I didn't know if you were coming back. I didn't know if... I don't know if you're still helping me." Her tears soak her cheeks as they fall in trails down her face. "Why didn't you come back?"

"I'm trying to help you." With both my hands, I grasp my hair in desperation from wanting to give her some sort of comfort, yet my anger about yesterday prevents me from doing so. "I- I." I sigh deeply. "You have to trust me, Fallon. I needed time to figure things out. I *am* helping you. Everything I do nowadays is to help *you*."

"Who is she?" she asks in a small voice. I can see the resentment building up in her again. Even through her worry, her jealousy succeeds to be heard.

"Nobody of importance."

"Were you with her last night? How is kissing another woman helping me?"

"How was lying to me helping us?" I counter furiously. I have been working nonstop to get us out of this mess, and she's not comprehending the danger of this fucking situation.

Fallon wipes her tears with the back of her hand and stands on the other side of the bed. "I wanted to tell you. I made a mistake in omitting it. I get that, but put yourself in my shoes. This is all new and petrifying territory for me. And you locking me in again… I didn't sleep at all last night. Despite all I've found out - and I've discovered a hell of a lot more than you - I still ache for you to make me feel safe." She draws in a deep breath. Her anger is getting the best of her too. "But do *you* still need *me*? Was she worth it? Did it make you feel better to kiss another woman while the woman you supposedly love is stuck in this room because of *you*? Make no mistake, I wouldn't be in this situation if I'd never met you."

Her admission is true. Fallon knows exactly how to rile me up. Seeing her torn between spewing her guts and latching onto me for security is a cold reminder of how my world is already staining her beautiful spirit.

"I just want out, Luca," she cries. "I need to know, otherwise it will destroy me even more. Who is she?" Fallon adds in a calm tone.

Her struggle cuts through me. "You misinterpreted a situation. I was not with her, and I didn't kiss her. Give me a little credit. You have got to trust me to end this nightmare for you."

She stalks toward me.

I take a step forward because I don't want her close to the door because she's volatile, and I'm losing my grip on her.

"Trust you?" Her tone reeks of contempt for me. "You were about to kiss her. How can I misinterpret that?"

"Because sometimes the end justifies the means, Fallon," I retort.

"What does that mean, Luca?"

I choose to remain silent.

"Are you going to trade me for Danny?"

My weariness, combined with her attitude, is grating on my nerves. "Yes." A second before she caught me with Skye I decided to follow James' plan, our initial plan.

Confounded, she gasps at me. "What?"

I rub my forefinger and thumb over my eyelids. "I told you to trust me. I'm just repeating myself, and you are only managing to anger me." I take a step back.

She's lost in thought for a couple of minutes, putting together the pieces of what will happen. "No, Luca." Fallon clutches her hair in disbelief and inches closer to me. "Your need to protect me, how long did that last? What am I now? Just a pawn in the Syndicate's sick little games? Just a woman you fucked?"

Her source of irritation - jealousy coupled with fear and resentment – is creating foolish thoughts in her head. "You're making no sense. You're not *just a woman I fucked*," I throw back indignantly. "You are the woman—"

Her trembling finger is pointed at my chest. "Don't you dare say it. I hate you. I hate this. What kind of life is this?"

She will always be the only woman I ever loved. I use her words. "Make no mistake, whether you're with me or not, our love will go on," I promise her. She's going to lose it - I can tell by how eerily slowly she spoke of her hate for me, and I need to leave before I break too. As I head for the door, she follows me immediately. "Fallon, stay back," I demand and clench my jaw without facing her while I push her back and open the door quickly to step out.

She steps forward and throws her arm into the small door opening.

"Goddammit!" I yell. "Be careful." I open the door marginally in an effort to nudge her arm back without hurting her.

Fallon's putting all her body weight in the opening, scratching her arm open, and starts to scream. "No. Luca!" She doesn't look at me while she's uncontrollably trying to push herself through the opening.

I have to close this door before someone comes up and walks in on me not being in control of her. "I don't want to hurt you, Fallon. Remove your arm," I almost beg her. She won't back down, and even though I can easily overpower her, I don't want to frighten her more. However, my annoyance is rising, so I shove her violently back into the room.

She falls on her behind and darts back up, but I've closed the door. She bangs on the door with all her power and all her anger is voiced in her fists hitting the door. "I hate you so much for doing this to me!" she yells at me repeatedly.

My forehead rests on the door while she curses at me, and my hand constricts on the door handle until my knuckles turn white. I want to open it. I want to comfort her. Hold her in my arms, to make her feel safe in my embrace, but I can't - not now.

I stand there for over an hour until she calms down. My throat is dry from holding in my raging emotions so I don't break down alongside her.

The banging lessens after she has exhausted herself, and I hear her sliding down the other side of the door, hitting the floor with a loud thump. She's quietly crying. In a broken voice - a voice that terrifies me because maybe she has given up - she utters, "I'm scared. L-look what you did to me. Why...why...why me?"

She can't give up because I'm afraid she'll hurt herself if she loses hope. The brokenness in her voice is pinching my battered heart. My palm rests on the door as I clutch my throbbing temple with my other hand and let out a heavy breath in a futile attempt to force out the agony coursing through me.

I answer without letting her hear. *"Perché ti amo."* Because I love you.

***

Back downstairs, I slam the door shut to get Camilla and Skye's attention. Camilla takes this as her cue to start explaining, but I shush her by holding up my palm and face Skye. "Skye, can you wait in the last room?" I nod toward the adjacent private room, and she leaves eagerly. Turning back to Camilla, I ask in a worn-out tone, "What happened upstairs?"

"She ambushed me when I brought her breakfast. She was asking where you were. I had no idea so I told her that. She was pacing and suddenly pushed me aside, tray and all, and ran out of the room. Is she okay?"

"Yes. She'll leave the day after tomorrow. I'm trying here, Camilla."

She peruses me with scornful eyes.

"Nobody can know about her little incident," I sternly tell her.

Camilla's guilty face gives her away. "I already told Adriano. He's on his way."

"Nobody else, okay?"

She nods in acceptance.

Adriano comes barging in, standing possessively next to Camilla. "Are we all fine here?"

"Yes," Camilla offers and breaks a small smile.

Adriano softens immediately and presses his lips to hers. "Fallon's lost it?"

"I can clean up the room," Camilla offers.

I hand her the key. This situation is spiraling entirely out of my control, intensifying my anger, because I'm not used to working this way. "Only to clean, then you leave immediately. Do not talk to her." She nods and leaves hurriedly. "I slept here last night." I point to the room Skye's in. "Fallon didn't take that well. She saw me almost kissing Skye."

Adriano makes a disgusted face. "Why did you kiss *her*?"

"I didn't kiss her. I thought we could use her," I confess. "I was 'massaging' her into being more pliable. The plan was never to kiss her. I was seducing her a little."

"Use?" he questions.

"Never mind. It was a fleeting thought." Adriano and I have a busy day ahead. We have to be in The Loop at noon to sign off on new investment plans, and we have to drop off some cash to several associates. Tonight we're meeting Leggia's underboss, Biagio, in private. It's imperative that I get Biagio in our corner before the trade takes place tomorrow.

Adriano and I get in my car. Every day, I need to change plans, do damage control, keep myself and Fallon in control. I'm exhausted. Drained. Her wariness and distrust is draining our love. Her constant need to fight me is infuriating.

We're drowning quickly.

CHAPTER 41

Fallon

"Why me?" I whisper, sitting on the floor with my back to the door. I kick a piece of fallen fruit away with my foot. My eyes are swollen from worrying the entire night. Not for one second did I drift away into the comfort of my dreams. Away from the harsh reality that the man I was building a life with is going to trade me to some corrupt Mafia boss.

Hearing the fast approaching footsteps outside, I scoot forward when the door is unlocked.

Camilla hunches before me on the floor beside the bed and asks me in a worried voice, "Are you okay? Luca and Adriano are pissed. They just gave me the key and stormed out."

"No," I cry quietly while looking up into her concerned eyes. Being locked up will cause you to make hasty decisions. Spur of the moment confusion. This morning I told Camilla in my agitated state that I should just dash out of here. She desperately tried to convince me otherwise, but she also realized Luca's absence could have horrific consequences for me. Quickly, I told her that I needed to at least give it a try to escape now. My growing alarm propelled me forward, out of that room, and she followed me because I had no idea which way to go.

He's going to trade you now. You're causing him more problems every day.

"Fallon?" Camilla asks and puts her arms around me, silently allowing me to let my tears drop on her shoulder.

"It was definitely not a good sign when he didn't come back. He's so mad at me." I pull back to catch her eyes. "He's going to trade me," I mutter, still not believing it myself.

"What?" she questions, unable to imagine Luca making that choice.

"I asked him if he was going to trade me for Danny. He said 'yes.' Period."

"Shit," Camilla comments and starts to gather the food littered on the floor. "I'm not supposed to talk to you. They'll be gone all day today, I think."

Time is up for me. "Camilla, can you think of any way for me to escape? Please?" I plead.

She bites her lip softly. "I'm picked up and driven back home."

"Are you here every day?"

She helps me from the floor and together we sit on the comforter. "No, four times a week. I also sleep here sometimes when there's nobody to drive me home. There's a guard at the front door and men walk around the house constantly. In the early mornings and late at night, it's most quiet around here. Most activity takes place in the afternoon and dinnertime. The back entrance is usually open and you can easily round the house to the front entrance. If you had a key for one of the cars, you'd have your getaway," she muses. "But getting your hands on a key won't be easy." She looks at me disappointed. "These guys pocket everything and keep it close." A hint of fear brims inside her sad eyes. "You can't do anything while being locked in here." She palms her forehead and rubs it excessively before catching my gaze. "The only way out is with my help. But they will know I've helped you, Fallon. I'll have to steal a key from one of the guys."

"I kind of need you. I need you to drive us out of here as fast as you can. You know the roads here." I can't allow her to help me and then live with myself if anything happened to her. "If you help me escape, you can't stay here. There's no way that will end well," I warn Camilla.

"I know." She sighs and leans sideways on her arm heavily with her hand flat on the bed. "I'm leaving with you, Fallon. These people are too dangerous. If they can trade you this callously, what will they do to me when Luca and Adriano turn on me?"

"We have to act quickly."

Silence again.

I blink back gathering moisture behind my eyelids and look at Camilla. "You have got to find a car key as soon as you step out of this room. Come back when you have one."

"I'm scared," she softly says and meets my eyes.

I cover her hand on the bed with mine. "So am I."

***

Tedious minutes turn into hours that belong to the past now. All the while I sit on the bed, waiting and waiting. Once Camilla came in to check on me and brought me food and water. Feeling weak from dehydration and lack of nutrition, I force down the water and swallow back a few bites of the tomato sandwich to fill my empty stomach. I need my strength replenished to stand a chance of escaping. Adriano and Luca are confirmed to be away today, but we don't know until how late and it's already almost evening. The waiting game continues.

CHAPTER 42

Luca

That night, Adriano and I pay Alex a visit at his apartment. We drive through the streets of Chicago, alongside the river back to The Loop, watching all the skyscrapers fly by.

"You have everything?" I ask Adriano in the passenger seat.

He holds up a tiny plastic bag filled with white residue.

Parking the car blocks away from Alex's condo, we walk back and use the rear entrance of the glass high-rise. "Where are the cameras?"

He points to our upper left. Adriano scouted the place this morning. "There's a blind corner. Follow me."

Adriano leads the way into the apartment complex while dodging the cameras. It's almost midnight and dead quiet in the building. We have to take the stairs to the fifteenth floor to evade the reception area by the elevators. His apartment is the first door to the right.

Adriano hands me a pair of plastic gloves, and I block the peephole with one hand before knocking softly. Footsteps approach on the other side of the door and it opens immediately.

I push open the door quickly, and Alex stammers back. "What the—"

Turning him around by his arm in one swift action, I cover my hand over his mouth.

Adriano steps in and closes the door quietly. "Alex, how are you?" Adriano greets.

I twist Alex's arm behind his back as he struggles in my hold while I shove him forward into his living room. Throwing Alex on his black suede recliner, I pull out my gun from the back of my pants. "Tell me, did you think I wouldn't find out how you threatened Fallon?"

Alex rises immediately with wide eyes and jumps off the back of the recliner to be met with Adriano's handgun pointed in his face. "Sit. Down," Adriano commands.

He holds up his hands in surrender and stays rooted. "Listen. This has become... I-It's out of hand," he stutters nervously.

Adriano motions with his silencer. "Go sit."

Alex's eyes switch from me to Adriano in slow motion, and he takes one step sideward to bolt to his front door, but Adriano blocks his path and overpowers him. He pushes Alex face down on the recliner with the end of his barrel on his neck.

"Be careful. I don't want any marks or bruises on him." That's not in line with our plan.

"You going to sit, Alex? I brought your favorite opiate," Adriano taunts Alex.

I motion for Adriano to back off a little while Alex catches his breath, and Adriano pulls him up again. "Last time. Sit down."

"Alex, if it's out of hand, then let's talk. Maybe we can make an arrangement." I slide onto the glass coffee table in front of Alex and tuck my handgun back in my pants. "I think we need a drink."

Alex's eyes narrow, and he doesn't twitch a muscle.

"Calm down, Alex. Do you really think a woman would mean that much to me? I wanted to alert you. Mission accomplished. Now let's talk this out. We need your charity and you need us." I raise my eyebrows. "Where's your liquor?"

Alex keeps glancing between me and Adriano before finally answering without a stutter, "Bar. Next to the kitchen." His eyes follow Adriano when he steps into the kitchen.

Adriano can prepare our drinks - Alex's will be spiked with heroine. I snap my fingers to get his attention. "Alex. I want to have a talk."

"That was Leggia's doing. I had no say in it, Luca," he confesses immediately

"What was Leggia's or your plan?"

"I had no plan. I'm getting your money though." He inhales deeply and slowly continues. "Leggia cut off my drug supply. I couldn't get anything anywhere. I needed my fix." Spoken like a true junkie.

Adriano hands Alex a drink, and Alex downs it one motion. Adriano retreats to get another one.

"What did he want you to do?" I ask.

Alex stares at the view outside. "Scare her. He never gave details but told me to wait until I saw you with her and then make it seem like I wanted information from her, information about you."

"What did he offer you in return?"

"My fix and paying off my debt to you. I was never going to hurt her. Leggia was pressuring me into badgering Fallon. He kind of hates you."

"You could've talked to us and avoided all of this, Alex," I lie.

"Could I have? I was screwed either way. I know how you guys work. Leggia was supposed to protect me. Looks like I bet on the wrong horse." He sighs heavily and coughs like an old man after finishing his second drink from Adriano. "Is she with you? Leggia told me to call her in sick. She hasn't been at work in days."

I was right. Leggia *is* just using everyone he can to cause problems between James and me. Alex, Fallon, Danny; they're all collateral damage to him. Alex did bet on the wrong person and will now pay with his life. For a long time, I watch Alex. Hating to be the one to end it, but my rage hits me in full force when I imagine Fallon's fear over what Leggia set in motion with Alex's help.

Adriano hands me a drink too, and I take a small sip when he faces Alex. "I need a fix. You want one too?" Adriano asks and places a tablespoon, syringe, and a belt – from Alex's bedroom - on the table.

"I didn't know you guys used your own drugs?" Alex inquires, surprised.

"We don't," we both say in unison as I jump up beside the top of the lounger and hold down Alex while Adriano tightens the belt around Alex's right arm.

"No..." Alex struggles uselessly.

Adriano presses his knee on Alex's thigh, and he grunts in pain, but I smother his cries with my gloved hand. He then lights the lighter under the spoon filled with a lethal amount of heroin. Adriano fills the syringe and taps his vein. He injects it into his arm and, within seconds, the heroin rushes into Alex's veins, relaxing him again. Mingling with the alcoholic drink that was already filled with his drug, he's unconscious quickly. Adriano sets up the scene - the syringe thrown on the table and the belt half undone around Alex's arm - after he pockets the plastic bag he brought in. "Should we wait for him to stop breathing?"

When taking too much heroin, a person falls asleep and his respiratory system will shut down. Essentially Alex's body will forget to breathe. Adriano injected a lethal amount. With the heroin spiked in his drink and this strong injection, he won't last long. He'll never live through the night.

"No, we can go." Carefully, I open the door to make sure that the hall is clear. I lead Adriano back down and out into the warm summer night air to find my way back to what will be my last night with Fallon.

For a man who never gives second chances, I can't stop putting her welfare above all else. For her, I'm breaking rule after rule. I'm taking too many chances. Everything I do is for her, for Fallon. She was the woman I never knew I was searching for. She gave me what I didn't know I'd lost. She gave me a sense of calm with just her presence and touch. She let me just be.

What are your reading, dolcezza?" I ask with a perked brow, smiling down at her head in my lap on the couch. Content to have a quiet night at her house. I love it when she reads and I can stroke hair while her head rests in my lap. My legs are stretched, feet on the coffee table. Relaxed. While pointing the remote at the TV, I glanced at her reader and read a few racy lines with questionable content.

She looks up with a roguish, innocent expression. "Depends on what you read."

Slowly, I put the remote down and place her reader on the table – the reader needs to be handled with the utmost care or else she'll have a fit – and stare down at her full pink lips as my large hand searches for bare skin to touch under the hem of her shirt. Her warm skin always manages to inflame my need for her. Skimming my hand down, I push her sweatpants slightly off her hip, exposing more smooth flesh. Gripping her hip, I pull out from under her and lie on top with my knee nudging her legs apart. Her back bows and I take the opportunity to forcefully slide my palm inside her panties. She groans when I mold her soft flesh and trace my middle finger over her entrance as I grind into her. "Is that what you want?" I growl and my mouth turns up as I lock eyes with her. "You want me to call you a dirty little sl—"

"No," she warns and returns a lust-filled smile. Her soft moans have me pushing my full mast hard-on against her warm center. "Just fuck me," she breathes in that sultry voice of hers. "I love it when you talk semi-dirty to me." I grin down at her. Only she can make me feel aroused as hell, happy, and peaceful simultaneously.

Her lovely face breaks into a smile that conveys her happiness when I graze my lips over hers and dip my tongue between them, kissing her ever so softly. The hurried groping and grinding shifts to a slow motion as I taste her love and lust for me. Craving to give her this gentle side of me, I taste every inch of her mouth. She melts in my arms while I stroke the curve of her hip, up and down in lazy trails. I pull back to see her eyelids flutter open with a look of adoration that locks her in my heart forever. She has dug her way into my cold soul, warming it with the pleasure of her body and the comfort of her mind. Her being gave my restless soul a home.

"Ti amo." I cover her lips again. This time ravenous to be inside her right now, my home. Rising from the couch, I pick Fallon up by her waist and throw her over my shoulder. She

shrieks in surprise and delight as I swat her round ass sticking in my face and hurry us to the bedroom.

Instead of ravaging her, I took my time that night. Peeling the thin layer of fabric off her luscious body, I kiss and lick every surface of satin skin until her moans fill my ears. As I lie on top, pushing inside her, I palm her face in my hand and watch her as if I'm afraid she'll disappear, my eyes memorizing the shape of her full lips when she climbs to release.

It was one of the few times I made love to Fallon. I wish I would've done it more often.

336

CHAPTER 43

Fallon

The night's sky is pitch black, illuminated by a million stars. It's impossible for me to determine what time it is, but it's definitely late. I wring my hands together in unease as someone fumbles with the key. I'm silently praying it's Camilla, and not Luca returning to his room. If it's Luca, I'm stuck here for another night. And another night of worrying when the trade will take place, or what could happen to me until then, is too much for me to handle.

The door opens and tension instantly recedes when I'm greeted by Camilla. "I've got a key," she announces hesitantly, yet surprised that she did it, and holds up the car device.

I'm instantly on alert and take the few steps toward her. "How? Is Luca still gone?"

"Yes, they're both away. I had to go really far to get Damian's car keys. He's passed out. There's one guard at the front door. We can only slip into the car when he's on his break; the car is parked in the driveway."

"You thought of everything," I muse aloud.

"Well, they were wrong thinking I'm some delicate flower. Let's hurry." She gives me a once over quickly and stops at my bare feet. "Shoes?"

"I don't have any," I confess. Wearing only Luca's t-shirt and boxers, I urge her to start moving. "Come on." The same trepidation I felt this morning when I dashed out of here is swimming to the surface. I follow Camilla, who's leading the way at a quick pace, through the dark hall.

"Almost everybody is gone," she murmurs.

At the top of the staircase, the beating of my heart is accelerating from the adrenaline starting to rush through me. We race down and have to turn the corner to enter the hall leading to the first staircase.

Camilla peeks around the corner and back to me. Unease creeps across her expression. "We have to go the middle of this hall and sprint downstairs. At the last step, turn left, then go straight ahead to the back door in the kitchen, which is unlocked. You have got to trail close behind me, okay?"

I nod my head up and down hurriedly as we catch each other's worried eyes. This is our window. The urgency to act now and fast is pressing since Luca or someone else could walk in this house at any moment.

Camilla nods too and checks the hall one more time. "Go." And she races ahead of me.

The paintings hanging on the walls pass me by in a blur while my feet stick to the wooden floor on this warm summer night. To decrease the amount of noise my feet are creating, I run on my tiptoes. One wrong move and I can break my foot, but we're almost at the staircase.

As soon as Camilla can peek over the banister to make sure the foyer is empty downstairs, she slows down to turn and gestures to me that we're still safe.

I follow her down the flight of stairs at lightning speed. More artificial lights are lighting this stairwell and foyer, causing me to feel extra exposed. On the last step, I place my left hand on the banister to take a sharp U-turn toward the kitchen, but I slip away, landing hard on my flat palm and bare knee on the marble tiles. The wound on my knee starts to bleed instantly and burns in pain. Unfortunately, I couldn't stifle my soft cry when I fell. My head whips around to see if anyone is coming into the foyer, and I push back up just as quickly as I fell. Stumbling while I rise, I sprint straight ahead to the kitchen.

Camilla's holding the door open and waves me to her frantically. "Hurry," she whisper yells right before I race through it and slouch forward with my palms on my upper thighs to catch my breath in the middle of the dark kitchen. Our heavy and erratic breathing cuts through the silence of the darkness.

Camilla lets the door fall closed silently and moves toward the back exit in this massive state-of-the-art kitchen. She pushes her shoulder into the door and it barely opens, so I push with all my weight as well. The door is ridiculously heavy to open, and I grunt as my shoulder hits the cold surface of it. The outside air flows into my lungs, and for the first time in four days, I feel the natural caress of the cooling summer wind on my cheeks. Shuddering from nervousness, I suck in the night air to calm my nerves.

We're outside!

Now we have to get to the car. We grimace at each other when the door creaks loudly as we close it, and the porch light flicks on, detecting movement. Camilla dashes to the right side of the house and rounds the planted hedges leading to the front. Jumping after her, I step off the porch onto the soft grass and hunch down next to Camilla. We wait until the light flicks off. For a moment my entire vision goes black as it tries to adjust to the dark. Not a sound but the blowing of the wind passes my ears.

Camilla motions forward with her hand, and we inch toward the driveway. She looks around the corner and pulls her head back immediately. "Guard is still standing at the front entrance," she mutters. "He's going to take a break and move inside the house soon. Wait."

I look past her to the rounded driveway and spot three cars parked on our side. "Which car?"

She turns the car device that she's been clutching in her hand and checks the logo. "A BMW."

But as the device hangs off the key chain, it clinks in the stillness of the night and the guard's head whips to me.

I rear back instantly and Camilla clutches the device again. Our eyes widen in horror, and I mouth, "Guard heard." I don't dare to look again, afraid my eyes will meet his.

Camilla grabs my hand and drags me a few feet back, pointing to the hedge under a rounded window with closed curtains. She makes her way through the hedge, thick with leaves, and disappears.

The dry earth creeps between my toes when I follow Camilla. Branches scrape and cut open the bare skin on my arms and legs, but I grit my teeth and wedge myself against her, hunched down into a tiny open space against the wall, hiding behind the hedge.

Dark. Soundless.

My heart is pounding in my chest so loudly that I'm afraid it can be heard in the deafening silence.

Camilla loses her balance and clutches my thigh, forcing me to plant my fingers in front of me to keep us unmoving and quiet. It's difficult to remain still above the thunder of my heartbeat.

A blur of light comes into our line of vision through the thick leaves. Footsteps approach. The light shines through the leaves, coming closer and closer to exposing Camilla and me. The light is an inch away from my hand planted in front of me, but I'm afraid to move and cause a noise. The worst thing is that the second before you're discovered feels like hours.

Oh my god, please don't let him see me.

A split second before I would've been exposed, another sound coming from the driveway distracts the guard. His directed aim of light recedes quickly and a deep breath rushes out of me. I've been adamantly forcing myself to keep some semblance of rational thought, even through my constant trail of fear. I'm holding my breath again while we stay rooted until we can't hear the guard's steps anymore.

We crawl out of the hedge, keeping low. We deny ourselves any time to think to avoid having our fear take control of our actions. Camilla checks the front and swivels around. "He's gone. We have to go now." She hits the button on the device to unlock the car. The first black BMW clicks open while Camilla's already started toward it.

The gravel cuts painfully into the skin of my feet. Opening the car door, Camilla gets in and starts the engine. Checking the front entrance – still no guard or movement, I close the door and fall into the passenger seat. "Go!"

Steering left and out of the driveway, the house shrinks in the rearview mirror and disappears as she steps on the gas when we hit a main road.

"Oh shit," Camilla voices my thoughts. Full of tension, she's driving the car anxiously through this deserted place.

My chest is rising and falling heavily. "How long until we reach the first gas station?"

"Twenty, twenty-five minutes." She wipes the glistening sweat from her forehead.

"What are we going to do? Call the police? Go straight to The Loop. Home? According to Luca, the Syndicate is also part of the police force. I have no idea if that's true or not."

Camilla bites her lip. "I don't know." She catches my eyes briefly with a lost look similar to mine.

"Let's just get out of here first and—" My gaze travels forward, and in the far distance, I see headlights approaching. My spine stiffens in alarm.

"Fuck," Camilla mutters when she spots them too.

"Turn off the lights," I order and try to buckle my belt with trembling hands, missing.

"What?"

"Cut the lights!" I scream while desperately trying to buckle the seat belt. "The other car won't see us."

"Shit. Okay." She checks the dashboard on her right and turns them off. "Fuck, I can barely see anything!" And automatically she steps on the brake, and the vehicle slows down.

The other headlights are turned off as well, kicking my unease into even higher gear. "Keep hitting the gas, don't go too slow." I'm bumped out of my seat from left to right when Camilla drives off the road and then steers us back on the right track.

"The other car should pass us soon." Camilla's gripping the steering wheel with deadly force. "I have to slow down, I can't see shit."

And just then the other car blazes past us, making us both yell in fear of a collision.

Camilla checks her mirror quickly. "Their lights are still off."

"Turn on your lights and step on the gas. It's someone from the Syndicate, or else they wouldn't have cut their lights too." Sweat trickles down the side of my face. We're so close. Do not break down now. Help Camilla stay calm. "Our best chance is to just step on it and reach a populated area as soon as possible."

Camilla nods hesitantly, eyes glued to the road.

Suddenly we're engulfed in light from behind. My head swings around, and I'm blinded by the bright white lights of a car now following us.

"What do I do?" Camilla shrieks. "Who is it?"

The car is gaining speed on us quickly and moves in beside us with an absolutely furious Adriano motioning like a rabid dog for us to pull over.

Camilla's trying to control this car going over a hundred miles an hour. "What do we do?" she shrieks again.

I grip the door handle to brace myself when I see Luca pulling his steering wheel to the right. "Brake. NOW!"

She hits the brake too late, and Luca hits the side of our car, causing us to jerk to the left. Camilla and I both scream as she's desperately trying to avoid being forced off the road.

I'm jolted sideways and to the front and my temple collapses against the window with a loud bang. A burning pain shoots through the side of my head while Luca's Maserati speeds on forward. The tires screech on the asphalt as the BMW comes to a full stop and the seatbelt pushes me back into the seat when I'm thrown forward. Our breathing is irregular and we sink back into our seats.

"You okay?" Camilla asks, with eyes closed, in a regretful tone.

Almost. We we're so close to get away and my hope is crushed instantly. "Yes." I rub my aching head.

The Maserati returns and stops sideways, blocking our car, and both men jump out and flank us in a few determined strides that glow with their fury.

Camilla hurriedly locks the door in response, clearly concerned about the men's deadly demeanor too. "Shit!" she whispers and turns her head to me just as Adriano stands before her window with a menacing look. "What are we going to do? I've never seen them this mad." Her breathing still mirrors my heavy sighs. Everything happened so quickly, we almost got away.

Adriano roughly pulls the door handle. "Open it, Cam," he orders in a dangerously low voice.

I've been ignoring Luca, who's silently burning holes into the back of my head while I'm facing Camilla. We just dug ourselves a little deeper in this mess. I cover one hand over the other in my lap to restrain the trembling. "We need to go with them. The longer we wait, the madder they'll get."

Luca taps on my window once with his knuckles.

Stoic, I keep my sight on Camilla.

Luca finally speaks in a level voice. "Fallon, open this door or I'll smash in the window and drag you back by your hair."

Tears are brimming behind my eyes, and I want to give Camilla a hug or something because she wears the same desolate expression as me, but I don't want Adriano and Luca to witness our interaction.

Camilla pushes the button and the doors fly open immediately. We're both yanked out of the vehicle. Adriano inspects Camilla and asks if she's hurt.

Luca's fingers curl painfully around my biceps. The wind blows pass us and cools the layer of sweat covering my body. A shiver runs through me, and I jerk away from Luca's touch when he tries to check my head injury.

While I can taste his fury, concern is also perceptible in his dark eyes. "Injuries?" he asks in that same level voice.

I shake my head. Wondering what to say to salvage this situation but nothing comes to mind. I softly say, "Luca."

"Don't," he warns and looks up into my eyes. His nostrils flare in an attempt to keep control over his spiraling emotions. This is Luca almost losing control. He keeps spitting fire into my amber irises when he barks orders to Adriano, "Drive the beamer home. I'm taking Fallon, you take Camilla. Restrain her. We meet in my room." Luca tugs me with him by my upper arm to the trunk of the Maserati.

No, am I going in the trunk?

Popping it open, he searches it and keeps his grip firmly on me beside him. A stack of tie-wraps appear. "Put your hands behind your back," he demands.

"What? No, don't tie me," I protest.

Luca grips both my underarms and pulls them back, holding both wrists captive with one hand easily while I uselessly attempt to break free. My wrists are being tied with one black tie-wrap. Luca pulls the wrap tight and hisses in my ear, "Don't say a word. You're pushing my limits with you."

His warm, unsteady breath fans my cheek when I crane my neck to see Camilla being heaved into the back seat by Adriano. The same is done to me.

Adriano and Luca step on the gas with urgency. The drive back is excruciatingly silent as the Maserati speeds back to that damn house. Not once does Luca catch my eyes in the rearview mirror. His sight is frozen on the road. His silence is scaring me most. Luca parks the car in the driveway. He cuts the engine and stares ahead for several minutes, his labored breathing constantly increasing my anxiety.

Adriano pulls in behind us, hiding the damaged part of the BMW from the guard's view, and jumps out of the car to the front guard. Camilla and I aren't seen behind the tinted windows of the back seat. Adriano and the guard disappear into the house and Adriano returns alone, striding toward Camilla.

Luca tries to wrench me out of the BMW but stops sharply when he notices my bare feet. Didn't he see my lack of shoes earlier? He stands up straight. I shiver uncontrollably when, out of the blue, his fist comes down on the roof with furious power, and I can hear an anguished 'fuck' being muttered.

Adriano and Camilla are already inside the house.

Luca clutches my arm and pulls me out with heavy force. "Get out and move."

His directive tone discourages me from fighting, and I comply promptly. With Luca at my back, we're back in the room I despise within minutes.

Camilla's sitting on the foot of the bed, face hanging down, as Adriano stares unbelievingly at her from the window. Camilla and I lock eyes ever so briefly after Luca shoves me to sit next to her.

Adriano hands Luca a pair of scissors that he uses to cut the ties, freeing my hands. I rub the skin on my wrists softly. No marks.

"How the hell did you get out of the house and in possession of Damian's car keys?" Luca seethes with his arms across his chest towering over us, still avoiding eye contact with me.

Damian? Another name I need to remember. My eyes roll sideways to Camilla whose lips are quivering as bad as mine.

"I stole them from Damian," Camilla answers quietly.

"How?" Adriano bellows at her and joins Luca standing in front of us.

Her shoulders hunch forward. "I spiked his drink," she confesses.

Adriano's hands wave around, and Camilla and I rear back on impulse. He braces them behind his neck. "What the fuck? Where is he?"

"Passed out in one of the private rooms," Camilla says.

The second Luca's stare is fixed on me, I feel the hairs along my nape stand on end in distress. Through my eyelashes, I meet his terrifyingly dark and bleak eyes. He stares at me without blinking or moving a muscle.

Adriano continues. "Private room? Did you fuck him?" he demands to know angrily.

"No." Camilla shifts closer to me. "We... kissed..."

The storm brewing inside Adriano erupts at Camilla's confession. "Are you fucking kidding me?" he roars and starts pacing back and forth.

I gawk at her too. She has some balls to seduce him. While Camilla was obviously scared too when we attempted to escape, she was also tough and determined. Now she's acting like a delicate, shy victim. The noticeable difference in her personality has me frowning in thought. Immediately, I try to disguise my surprised expression, but Luca – who has been watching me with careful, perceptive eyes - has caught it.

Luca motions for Adriano to calm down and they move to the door, whispering back and forth until Adriano turns and tugs

Camilla up and out the door so quickly, she doesn't even get the chance to look back at me.

Alone with Luca, his quiet rage suffocates the air in the room. I've never encountered him with this level of intense anger.

Luca closes the door with his head bent down and his left palm planted against it. I can clearly hear him inhaling deeply, and then he smashes his fisted right hand through the wall.

My body tenses up, seeing him unleash his anger on the wall.

And another punch before he swivels around and fumes, "Why can't you just fucking listen for once!"

Another shock jolts me, due to the level of his voice, and a lump fills my throat.

"Everything, I have done to keep *you* safe. All you had to do was listen to me until I could safely bring you home. Because of you, I'm constantly worrying about fucking damage control. And did you think beyond escaping?" His words drenched in fury. "Without any shoes?" He grits his teeth and edges toward me. "You have no clue who you could've met, or what could happen without anything to protect yourself!"

On instinct I scoot back on the bed as Luca's control completely shatters before my eyes.

He clutches his hair and kneels in front of me, pulling me roughly back to the edge of the bed with his hands behind my knees.

With widened eyes, I keep still when he buries his head in my neck and pulls me to him while my arms hang limply to avoid returning his suffocating embrace. My eyes fall closed as his lips move against my collar bone.

"I'm so fucking angry at you. Yet…yet I can't retaliate the only way I know how. I don't even want to. I want to go back." Luca's rests his forehead on my shoulder. "So conflicted…" His voice chokes as he looks up into my wary eyes.

Where is he going with this?

Out of nowhere he cups the back of my head and kisses me with bruising force. In a quick move, he drives me back on the bed with his entire rigid body and surprises me by cuffing one wrist to the bed and stands back up just as quickly. Back to the status of Friday night - I'm cuffed, and Luca and I glare at each other.

The days have been slow, except for this morning and the last hour where so much has happened. My brain still hasn't caught up. From being taken Friday night and thrust into an underworld where Luca works, to constantly being on edge about what's to come, I'm weak. But I'm not confused enough to forget the most important thing. "When is the trade?"

Luca cocks his head to the side and shifts his hair back. When I don't think he'll answer me, he speaks in a voice I don't recognize. "Tomorrow, midnight."

I fought my best to escape. For nothing. When I close my eyes, the last shred of hope leaves my body with a tormented cry.

"I'm not trading you, Fallon," Luca divulges suddenly.

My eyes snap open in astonishment. "What?"

Luca rubs his fingers over his forehead. "I know you're confused, but you have to cooperate for one day." He sighs tiredly. "You constantly trying to escape is making this more difficult. I get you don't trust me, but for now, stop being clueless and open your eyes. See and feel how much I'm sacrificing for you. I thought you were smarter than this." He shakes his head in disappointment. "Yes, we're taking you to the trade. However, I'm not trading *you*. We need you so that we can end this. You'll be safe and after you've cooperated with us, you can return home, to your life."

I stare at him with thinning eyes. It can't be this easy. "What will happen at the trade?"

"We'll capture Leggia and Danny."

"Then I'm free to go?"

"Yes. But you'll be tied to this 'crime' and can't inform the police without facing charges yourself," he relays without any emotion.

There's the catch. "Blackmail?"

"Insurance. I think we both lost all trust in each other," he retorts in a cold voice. And with that he strides to the bathroom.

My head is pounding, so I'm glad when Luca returns with a glass of water in one hand and a towel and first aid kit in the other. He cleans my feet gently with the wet towel and hands me a Tylenol with the glass of water. "There's a bruise forming."

352

Luca hunches beside the bed and caresses my temple. "Does it hurt?" he asks harshly and releases a pained sigh.

I shake my head, and the tears that have been brimming behind my eyes find their way out.

Luca rubs my tears away with his thumb and cups my face. "Please just do as you're told for one day. I've been protecting you from day one. I will still protect you, even if I'm so fucking angry at you. I'm also angry at myself." He shuts his eyes tightly for a brief second. "I didn't want any of this."

I know he didn't want any of this, or plan this for that matter. But this mess was caused by him.

By him allowing me to fall for him.

By him lying to me.

By him scaring me.

And yes, he has taken care of me in his own way while I've been occupied with failing to escape. My muddled feelings still tell me to distrust him, but the exhaustion of tonight is weighing my fighting spirit down. Maybe for this one day I should trust him? I'm cuffed anyway so I can't do anything else but wait. "What kind of life is this, Luca?" I ask sadly.

"Not a life for you, Fallon." He combs my hair back with his fingers, and then stands to leave me alone.

Having no choice anymore but to follow his instructions for one day, I resign myself to my fate. I'm too exhausted to fight. Working against Luca is pointless; he's too powerful. My failed escape attempts and the unbearable wait until the trade doesn't alleviate the tension from my body at all.

Sleeping with a cuffed wrist is impossible.

CHAPTER 44

Luca

I storm into my office where Adriano is already seated with his elbows on the desk, head resting in his hands. Shrugging off my suit jacket, I undo an extra button in agitation after I drop into my chair. I'm torn as I rake my hands through my hair twice, keeping them clasped behind my head. I'm torn between wanting to kill her for being stupid and wanting to whisk her away to safety forever, away from all this. I'm still furious at her for leaving and putting herself in that kind of danger, and I hate that I had to cuff her. She's being led by her fear instead of logic. When I cleaned her feet and saw her empty eyes, I wanted to comfort her despite my anger. I held back and it took everything in me to leave.

The reality remains that I'm the one who took the risk by falling for a non-Syndicate-related woman. I have not only fallen for her, I'm obsessed with her. Consumed by her. I'm hers. Period. But she can't be mine.

She would be eaten alive.

I need to accept that she can and will never accept to live in my world. I need to accept that I can never trust her again, and she will never trust me again.

Not a life for you, Fallon.

"Damian is indeed passed out in the private room. He'll just think he drank too much," Adriano says when he leans back slowly, worn out from this long night too.

I never would've predicted these two women would collaborate.

"I texted Damian that I took his car and had a slight accident. The car will go to the garage tomorrow. Camilla's in the private room. I'm sleeping there with her to keep an eye on her." He shakes his head and rests his elbows on the armrests.

"She has to go," I tell him. He knows she can't work for us anymore.

"I know. We're not hurting her." He gives me a pointed look.

"No. Fire her, make sure she's bound into silence. I don't care how." They did manage to escape quietly. At least I can call it a night since Adriano took care of every loose end. Nobody witnessed them escaping. "Get some sleep."

Adriano heads out first to join Camilla.

As I stroll through the deserted house, I battle with myself to sleep in the private room and not run up those stairs to Fallon. Eventually - after minutes of standing lost in the hall - I step into the lonely private room with nothing but regret and resentment to keep me busy through the night. The depth of my conflicting emotions concerning Fallon follows me deep into the night, triggering constant insomnia.

CHAPTER 45

Luca

Tonight, the trade will be at The Parish of the Blessed.
Around six this morning, I went into my room to check on
Fallon. I adjusted her sleeping body after releasing the cuffs, and
I left her food and drinks, along with a note that I'd be back
tonight.

James, Adriano, Salvatore, and I meet up in James' office
that evening to discuss our plan.

"Fallon's on board?" James asks from behind his desk.

The rest of us are seated across from him. I take a sip of my
coffee. "She is. And *I* will protect her constantly. She's the first
to leave if anything, *anything*, goes wrong."

Adriano suggests, "I think Damian should come too. He can
scope out the perimeter while we're inside the church. Leggia
will have men outside too."

My overwhelming anxiety is quieted slightly by Adriano's
offer. I tap my fingers on my thigh. I can't afford to be distracted
by Fallon's presence. This is my only chance to end this quickly.
Only for her am I able to put my anger aside and focus.

James grants the request. "Fine. Father Eli has been
instructed as well?"

"Father Eli will help anyone who pays him enough. But as back-up, I have photo evidence of his unsavory proclivities," I state blandly.

"Biagio is informed?" Salvatore inquires.

Adriano and I talked to Leggia's underboss, Biagio, Tuesday night. We etched reasonable doubt with Biagio, and now he'll work with us to eliminate Leggia. The underboss has to be the one to search us for guns tonight and allow us to keep our piece. Biagio's far smarter than Leggia and not as power hungry. He's a family man who doesn't want the war Leggia's inciting. "Yes, he agreed on the course of action when we spoke Tuesday night."

"Then let's end this fast." James puts on his beige jacket.

"Get Damian. I'm getting Fallon," I order Adriano while leaning forward as I conceal my handgun in the ankle holster and slip my pants over it.

Trudging back upstairs, I find Fallon's already waiting on the bed in a dark green summer dress Adriano got from Camilla.

"Are you ready?" I ask her. I'm not, but this must happen. She lifts her eyes. "No."

Closing the distance, I kneel before her. "You have to listen to me, Fallon. Stay with me at all times." Last night, the thought crossed my mind that she might want to help Danny. Fallon's volatile behavior makes it difficult to predict her next move. She appears to have calmed down since we caught them last night.

However, I'm keeping my eye on her every second because she can turn on us the moment her fear overrules her mind.

Needing to end this fast, I clasp her hand in mine and we walk out of the house.

Damian drives out first, via another route, to the church.

Salvatore takes the driver's seat, next to James. I slide in the back middle, next to Adriano and then Fallon moves in beside me.

"Ms. Michaels," Salvatore and James greet.

"Hi," she says in a weak voice, not daring to look at them. She's also evading Adriano's eyes.

Due to the heat, I left my jacket at the house and just wear my white-collared shirt sans tie. I roll up the sleeves and see Fallon's hands trembling uncontrollably in her lap while she stares out the window. This time, my love triumphs my anger, and I can't resist comforting Fallon by resting my arm behind her and hugging her to my chest while kissing her hair.

Tensing up, she hides her face in my chest without making a sound.

"It will end today, *dolcezza*," I whisper.

Only these few more hours, then Fallon can go back to her life. The last obstacle to ensure her safety and end a Mafia war before it has a chance to ignite. Fallon's only been informed of her role. She's to stay behind me and remain quiet. If anything goes wrong, she's to follow my instructions. Silence consumes the vehicle during the entire ride because we can't talk any business with Fallon present.

The Chicago skyline sparkles against the night sky when we enter The Loop. We're right on time, and Salvatore parks the car in front of the church. The street is deserted this time of night except for a pedestrian walking his dog.

As James and Salvatore exit the vehicle, I tilt Fallon's head up and rehash the plans with her. "Don't say a word, even if someone addresses you. And stay close to me *at all times*."

She nods with an uncertain glow behind her eyes.

"Tell me with words, Fallon." I need to hear her voice.

"Yes," comes out in a small tone.

Salvatore opens the car door, signaling that it's showtime. James leads the way through the massive church doors to the vestibule. The historical cruciform architecture of this place is similar to the church I used to attend with my parents. We pass the aisle down the middle, heading toward the elevated altar in the center end, which is surrounded by devotional statues and lit candles. The massive black organ pipes behind the sanctuary are visibly running up the walls. Every inch of the dome is decorated with Renaissance paintings of angels.

Fallon's pressed behind my back, following me with unstable steps.

Biagio and his *Capo* are waiting to search us in front of the altar.

James and I spread our arms in front of the two men. Salvatore is the only one not packing. Adriano, James, and I have our guns holstered, as discussed with Biagio Tuesday night.

Biagio nervously searches James, which concerns me. James keeps his stare on him the entire time. James and I tower over this short Italian man. Biagio's *Capo* stands back while his boss takes his time to inspect all of us. I tug Fallon more behind me as my unease over Biagio's anxious expression grows. Restless prickles stroke down the back of my neck.

"The girl." Biagio motions Fallon over to him.

What the fuck? We never discussed the girl being searched. My arm shoots out behind me to calm Fallon who tensed up instantly at Biagio's request. "Nobody touches the girl," I hiss through clenched teeth.

Biagio drops it immediately.

I'm the last to be searched and step forward as Adriano moves beside Fallon. Biagio and I lock eyes. Is he betraying us? He's dripping with anxiety.

Biagio puts my arms up, and his hand meanders over my clothes. Padding down to my legs, he looks up when his hand comes in contact with my ankle holster. Sweat is glistening on his upper lip.

I bend my head to display a warning glare in case he's considering fucking me over.

He swallows heavily. "Clear." Biagio rises to whisper, "Danny is in the adjacent bathroom. Leggia has a Glock in his shoulder strap. Eli hasn't ratted on us. Leggia ordered me to strip search the girl to piss you off." He gives me an apologetic look. "You calm?"

I nod once for him to continue and immediately step back to feel Fallon's warm breath on my back again.

Biagio moves toward the sacristy - the chamber where Eli prepares for mass in the back of the church - and lets us through the door.

Leggia welcomes us with a smug smile. "I was wondering how long it would take for you to come to your senses, Calderone."

Biagio stands by the door behind us with another *Capo* as the other one joins Leggia. Leggia came very well prepared with his entire fucking army. A guy holds guard in front of the bathroom where Danny is to my right. That guy is not a high-ranking soldier of his Syndicate – which confirms how stupid Leggia is. Breaking the most essential rule of how to keep yourself out of the eye of law enforcement. Only the first soldiers can come to meets. *Capi*, underbosses, and bosses do not go out in public with random soldiers. Only with their first soldier; a soldier without a criminal record, like Damian. This way the high-ranking officers are never connected to any criminals.

"Leggia." Nobody can aggravate James in public. Leggia's condescending remarks don't bother him a bit.

"Welcome, Ms. Michaels." Leggia peruses Fallon. "You're quite the sight for sore eyes." Leggia's taunt is directed at me.

She shivers but doesn't make a sound, and I block her from his view entirely. He's stalling. I take a step back and Salvatore and Adriano mirror my action. We need to be ready to retrieve our weapon. Adriano has an extra weapon for Salvatore if needed.

"Leggia continues. Tsk tsk, why so protective, Luca? You want Danny, right?"

"Where is the boy?" James demands to know, growing impatient with this farce. Leggia is such a theatrical yet ignorant man.

Leggia is seemingly uncomfortable. I anticipated for him to act on his own plan of action, just like us, but we have Biagio and at least one *Capo* in our pocket. He's breaking out in a sweat because his plan is about to set off, or because he knows my plan will fail. I'm still not convinced by Biagio's odd behavior.

Commotion behind me has me hurriedly reaching down for my gun on instinct and aiming at Leggia. I shouldn't have acted so suddenly because the *Capo* behind me grabbed Fallon as I bent down for my piece.

James cocks his gun at the soldier to his right in one easy move.

Leggia jumps out of his seat with a vicious scowl and takes out his piece too.

Everyone has their gun out now.

Leggia's aim on James.

Biagio's end of the barrel on me.

Mine on Leggia.

James targets the soldier in front of the bathroom because he realizes that this soldier can't escape whatsoever - he has seen our faces.

Adriano targets the *Capo* next to Leggia.

Salvatore's unarmed.

Fallon takes in the scene with her mouth half open, and tears coat her cheeks in revulsion and complete terror. Her eyes follow my controlled aim on Leggia while she's being hauled back against the *Capo's* chest with the barrel at her temple.

The room that was starting to spin in all the commotion instantly freezes on Fallon. My aim switches in a split second to the soldier threatening Fallon with his weapon.

Fallon gulps in panic of the movement.

Biagio's finally proven himself worthy when he works with me instantly and finds a new mark in Leggia.

"What the fuck, Biagio?" Leggia screams and fires his gun - still aimed at me - as realization of the betrayal of his underboss sets in.

I duck and turn, frenziedly trying to find an open shot on the *Capo*, who's now hiding behind Fallon. My ear feels like it's burning when a slice of flesh is grazed off by the bullet almost hitting me, and the sound of the fire arms is muted. Fallon stoops down and to the side, giving me an opportunity to shoot. I blast my gun, hitting the *Capo* in his shoulder – he's obviously not the one in our corner. He sways on his feet from the push of the bullet inside his flesh, and I take another shot, this one fatal to the head. Then I sprint to Fallon and push her down, throwing myself on top of her, shielding her with my entire body.

Her arms cover her head, and she screams from the impact of hitting the floor on her knees and stomach.

James is much quicker than the soldier blocking the bathroom door and shoots him in the heart before he has a chance to properly cock his gun. The soldier sags down and hits the floor right in front of Fallon and me.

She screams louder when she sees the dead body collapsing in front of her with a crimson halo surrounding the upper chest.

Placing my arm over Fallon's head, I say, "Don't look. Stay down, Fallon."

Salvatore and Adriano jump behind a bookcase.

Leggia dives behind the desk when he realizes his own men are betraying him and empties three bullets into his own *Capo*.

James dodges a shot from Leggia and dips down in front of the desk.

Fallon and I elude the bullets, and I rush her to hide beside a dresser against the wall, folding my body over hers as we're crouched down.

James motions for me to keep launching bullets at the top of the desk, above Leggia's hiding place. He rounds the corner and stands up. "Drop it."

I hear a weapon being dropped on the floor and see it slide out via the side when James kicks it away. Leggia rises from the desk with his hands above his head.

My vision blurs slightly and I feel a warm fluid trickling down my shoulder and onto Fallon's back. I keep her head down because I don't want her to see what James will do next. An incessant ringing has started in my ear, but I ignore the pain on the side of my head.

Leggia tries to provoke James. "Do you see your underboss protecting the woman and not you?"

James just smiles. "Dear Giacomo, always a step behind."

My smartest move was to disclose my relationship with Fallon to James. He's been standing behind me and helping me all the way.

Biagio lowers his gun.

"You work for Calderone now? The moment he doesn't need you, they will kill you," are the last words of Leggia to Biagio.

James shoots his bullet into Leggia's chest. "All of this could've been avoided if you were a tad smarter, Giacomo." Leggia drops down on his back and James kills him with another bullet that penetrates his heart.

Fallon convulses in shock and I see her peering from behind her fingers, witnessing the killing.

"I'm getting her out of here," I say to James with wide eyes and a swift nod to the bathroom, hinting that I don't want her to see Danny. With all the commotion of the last couple of minutes,

I'm sure helping Danny is the last thing on her mind, but I need her away from here now.

"Go. We'll handle this," James answers.

I straighten up and take her with me, out of the sacristy. As soon as the door closes, I round Fallon and stand before her.

She gasps in horror. "You're bleeding." Her hand moves to my ear.

"The bullet only grazed my ear, Fallon." I evade her touch and check the length of her, letting out the breath I've been holding when I verify that she's not hit.

"Come." I take her hand in mine and run down the aisle with Fallon trailing behind me.

Damian's just driving by and stops.

"Any witnesses?" I ask.

"Nobody has walked by. We're clear." Damian then spots my blood. "You okay?"

"Yes. James is handling Biagio and the clean-up." I can't mention Danny because I'm truly glad Fallon has forgotten about him during the entire chaos inside the sacristy.

"Need me to stay here or go inside?" Damian inquires, looking from me to Fallon.

Fallon's hiding behind my back, gripping my shirt. Damian's the one that took her and this is the first time they've seen each other again. I put my weapon away in my pants and rake a hand through my hair. "Go. Clean up the mess. James will give you orders."

Damian hurries inside.

I help Fallon slide into the passenger's seat of the vehicle we arrived in - Salvatore handed me the key before entering the church. When I pull the safety belt over her and click it in place, she speaks in a panic-stricken tone. "Danny. What about Danny? Where is he?"

I'm only focused on one thing; getting her home. Danny will be taken care of by James. After everything she witnessed tonight, I can't lay that on top of it too. She will struggle to process everything she's seen tonight. I can't look her in the eye. "I don't know," I lie and head to the driver's seat. Putting it in drive, we leave this nightmare behind and I'm finally taking her home.

Her erratic breaths slow down as she stares ahead, unmoving.

With our decisions, we choose our path in life. My decision to let my guard down and start up a relationship with Fallon based on a lie led us to this point. It led to the deaths of Vasquez, Frank, and Alex. It led to endangering her in the worst ways possible. The one thing I wanted to avoid detonated in my face.

I park the car in front of her condo. We stay seated, frozen in time.

From the glove compartment, I recover her mini purse with the smartphone and keys.
"Your things."

She takes the purse and opens the car door.

I jump out of the car and follow Fallon inside her apartment. Closing her front door silently, I keep my eye on her.

Will she freak out? Or send me away?

Fallon steps into her living room. "It seems like forever since I've been here," she mentions idly and sits on the edge of the couch.

Almost a week ago, she was taken by Damian and Frank. The dried blood on my ear and the left side of my head is starting to pull at my skin, making me grimace.

"Are you going to the hospital?" she hisses with tears waiting to burst out of her eyes.

"No." I'll have it stitched back at the house if the doctor is there, or I'll just have it bandaged and wait until morning. My hearing is impaired from Leggia's first shot. I'm holding my concern and receding fury on a tight leash, guessing she's going to lose it any moment now.

She breaks down when she sees darkening bloodstains on her shoulder strap; my blood. Her hollow, silent gasp has me inching toward her the instant she slides down to the floor, and I bend down to pick her up.

"No!" she cries into her palms. "Don't touch me." She sweeps her tears away determinedly. "What happened to Danny?"

"I don't—"

"Do *not* lie to me. Please tell me if he's dead or not. The trade was about him. *You* wanted him. Where was he?" She looks up at me with swollen eyes.

I heave out a ragged breath. "In the bathroom. James has him now."

She realizes that's Danny's death sentence. "I saw you kill a man. I saw James kill two other men," she whimpers. "*This* is your life? Killing people?"

"No. This is a part of it."

"Am I safe now?" she demands and leans back against the back of the couch.

I'm hesitant to answer. If I confirm, will she throw me out because she thinks she doesn't need me anymore? But I'm desperate to relieve the fear she has been living with this past week. And it's time to end this. "Yes."

"What now, Luca?" She looks up again through wet lashes. After everything she's been through, she's still the most beautiful woman to me.

Not having all the answers, I ask her the one question that has been plaguing me. "Do you regret meeting me?"

"Don't you dare turn this around! You are a criminal," she emphasizes each word with bitterness.

I feel like she's sucker punched me in the face, so I keep my lips sealed. She needs to vent. The emptiness that's spreading a hole in my heart overpowers any anger I had toward her escape attempts.

370

Fallon continues without looking at me. "I can't answer that because of course – right now – I regret it. What the hell do you expect of me? Don't you think I know that we would never have a normal life? Would I have to lie to everyone around me? Would I have to walk around with guards? Would I always have to worry if you will come home alive? What kind of life is that? I need to protect myself before you drag me into more of your Mafia mess. I can't do this, Luca. It will change me. That life will suck the life out of me."

She belonged to the Luca I've created for her. The Luca without the Syndicate. And that Luca does not exist. Luca and the Syndicate will forever be one.

I kneel in front of her, realizing I need to come to terms with the fact that it's impossible to keep her safe. Tonight, anything could've happened to her. She was a challenge that reeled me in and became too much. "I can't change my past, Fallon."

She hugs her legs to her chest. "You should go."

"I don't want to leave you here on the floor," I plead.

"Go," she repeats and buries her head in her knees, already blocking me out.

The emptiness is about to swallow me up. There's an invisible bond that ties Fallon and me together, from now on, for always.

Turning away, I refuse to look back and softly close the door on us.

Once I'm back in the car, I punch the steering wheel repeatedly, until the skin on my already-bruised knuckles tears, in an effort to let out my agony.

It takes only a few minutes before her bedroom lights are turned on. Then I ride back to the house alone. She won't be in my private room waiting for me.

***

James and Adriano are quietly talking in the living room. I address James, "Is the doctor here?"

"He will be within minutes. I called him for your injury." James motions toward my ear.

"Good. I think I need stitches." The side of my head feels like it's on fire. "Did you clean up?"

James replies, "Damian and another soldier are cleaning up. Eli will not talk, I reminded him of what will happen when he does." We won't end his life, but we will expose the pictures of him entertaining young boys and let him live with a life of scandal. For him, that is far worse than death. "Biagio will inform his Syndicate. I do believe we have an ally in him. Danny was taken care of in the sacristy."

When the doctor arrives, he immediately stitches the skin behind my ear. It will heal properly and my hearing should return to normal within the next couple of hours. The doctor's out the door in twenty minutes.

"I'm going home," I announce and rub my neck.

"What's wrong, Luca? How's Fallon?" James inquires.

"I took her home." As far as James knows, she has cooperated the entire week. I discussed with him that I'm binding her into silence as a precaution – which was needed.

"Son, one day you'll find a woman who can accept this life."

"I've already found plenty of women who could accept this life. The only one I want just can't."

"Why don't you stay here tonight?" James suggests.

"I can't stay in that room without her," I admit and exit the house.

CHAPTER 46

Fallon

Assembling my thoughts is impossible. When the door closes, I jump off the ground and lock it and recheck the lock. It feels surreal being back in my own home. On shaky legs, I reach my bedroom.

Danny's probably dead. He was right there in the bathroom. I could've helped him. I saw men die. Blood splattering. Lurching forward to my bathroom, I heave painfully into the toilet when I smell the vile stench of gunpowder and spilled blood - a too lifelike memory.

I stand before my mirror and remove my sandals and dress. I'm greeted by a pale Fallon with dark circles under my eyes, scratches, and yellow and purple bruises all over my body. Every inch of my body is sore, as if I'm black and blue all over, inside and out. Under that layer of soreness, I feel nothing. Nothing because right now, I can't cope with everything that's happened. No longer able to bear the sight of myself, I step into the shower. Under the hot stream, my tears mingle with the water as if they never fell from my eyes.

I cry because I've seen too many people die. I cry because I don't know where Camilla is - I don't even have a last name to find her. I cry for the life I will never have with Luca. I cry for the life I longed to build with him. But mostly, I cry to let out all the tension and fear of the past few days.

I down two painkillers before going to bed - after checking the front door lock one more time.

For a couple of hours, I'm sound asleep from exhaustion. But after that, as fast as I fall asleep, I wake up again. Sitting straight up in bed, my eyes fly open and I'm comforted by the surroundings of my own familiar room.

As I lie back, I still feel depleted. I miss him. I hate him. I'm lost. In the end, he did help me. All I want is for everything to be over, so I'm not going to the police. Maybe he was telling the truth. If I go to the police, I'll bring more trouble my way.

People say time heals all wounds. Does it? I don't believe time heals wounds. Time makes us forget. New memories push back the old ones until our mind is forced to forget what we desperately long to hold on to. The bad memories always manage to stick to the forefront while the good ones vanish from our remembrance. Only, with us, the bad far outweighs the good. The bad almost got me killed.

I get out of bed to retrieve my phone from my clutch in the living room. As I sit on the couch and go through it, I'm surprised that I don't have too many missed calls and messages. I frown when I see Luca has texted Jason, my mother, and Teagan that I have been sick at home. He took care of everything to explain my disappearance.

I call my mother and assure her that I'm all better. She, of course, immediately notices something is wrong, so I tell her Luca and I broke up. I'll call Teagan tonight. I also briefly speak to Jason, who apparently visited my apartment Tuesday, so I tell him I was too sick to answer the door, probably didn't hear the buzzer - he doesn't question me.

I chew my fingernail wondering what to do about Alex while I walk back to bed. I wanted to let my loved ones know I'm fine, and now I just want to crawl back into bed. Devoid, except for the rumbled thoughts constantly racing through my mind, sadness overtakes me. I hope for sleep to overtake me instead because I feel absolutely hollow.

Thankfully it does, and all I do is lie in bed all day Thursday and Friday.

Friday night, I wake again to call Teagan, and I even manage to lie to my best friend about the past week.

Saturday morning I'm awakened by a call from Jason. "Hi," I mumble.

"Oh my god, Alex died of an overdose."

I'm wide awake instantly. "What?" I sit up in bed and glance at the phone to check the time: ten.

"Alex is dead. Cleaning lady found his body in his apartment. Alex Gentry suspected to have died of a drug overdose," he reads a line from an article.

The Syndicate.

Luca has something to do with this. Flustered, I say, "Can I look up the article and call you later? I'm... I'm shocked."

"Yes, of course. I'll e-mail you the link. Call me later."

I read the article on my phone and palm my forehead. Part of me is going to be sick. Did he die because I told Luca about his blackmail? But what would've happened to me if he had lived? What do I feel? Maybe a hint of a sick kind of gratitude?

This means it's over. I cover my mouth with my hand, unable to grasp the reality that this has been life since a week ago. I don't get much time to contemplate because the doorbell rings - the doorbell of my front door, not the entrance downstairs.

I immediately jump out of bed and tiptoe toward it. Nervous shivers run down my spine when I stand before the door.

A knock shocks me backward.

"Miss Fallon Michaels?" a male voice asks. "This is Chicago PD."

Police? Why?

"Can I see some ID?" I retort and check the peephole as two young men ID themselves. I open the door and stand in the doorway.

"Good morning, miss. We would like to ask you some questions. Can we come in?"

"No." After what I've been through, I don't trust anybody. "What's this about?"

"It's regarding Alex Gentry."

I arch my brow. "I just found out he died."

"I'm sorry for your loss, miss. It appears to be a drug overdose, but in the security box in his apartment, the following note was found:

If anything happens to me, contact Fallon Michaels.

My blood drops ten degrees after reading the note. "I'm just an employee of his," I say softly, not knowing how to react.

"We would like to talk to you, Miss Michaels."

"Now is not a good time." I need time to think about what this means. "I need a moment to process the fact that my boss died," I state curtly.

The police officers at least look regretful. "Miss, please call me for an appointment at the precinct on Monday."

"I will." I grab the card and close the door, expelling the breath I've been holding.

Why the hell would he leave that note? Did Alex leave that note or did the Syndicate? Am I being framed by the Syndicate?

This means it isn't over. This is just the beginning.

The story of Luca and Fallon will continue in *For Luca, Chicago Syndicate #2*

COMING FALL 2014

Acknowledgements

It's been an exciting journey to have this book released, and I couldn't have done it without the man in my life. Thank you to Ritez for taking care of everything while I read and write – and I read and write a lot. Thank you for always pushing me. Thank you for choosing to be with me, *lief.*

Thank you to Renee for your editing acuity. A huge thanks for going through this manuscript until the middle of the night. Next one, I won't send so late – I promise. Seriously, I promise. Not a Luca kind of promise, but a real promise.

Thank you to the beta-readers – FeiFei, Jen (another skank) and Christine – for your honest and critical input, which was very much appreciated.

Thank you to Christine for your never-ending and enthusiastic help. To you, I promise that I will not forget the difference between a 'release day blitz package' and 'blog tour promo post.' Okay, so I'll probably ask you all the same questions as I did when I released this book, but bear with me, I'm giving you fair notice, skank!

Camilla, grazie per il vostro aiuto entusiasta nella traduzione italiana.

A big thank you to all the ARC reviewers, bloggers, and Street Team who helped to promote *For Fallon*. I had such a pleasant time working with you all! Thanks for taking the time for Luca and Fallon.

Thank you to *you* for reading Luca and Fallon's story.

Proof

Made in the USA
Charleston, SC
13 August 2014